The Kingdom
and
the Song

Text copyright © 2016

John Sanderson Duncan

Acknowledgements

Hearty thanks to my father. I don't know how I would have managed without his tireless encouragement and correction over the years taken to write this book.

Thanks also to Rachel Starr Thomson for her very fine editing work.

Prologue

J. R. R. Tolkien claimed that fantasy would never lose its charm because people long for another world – one in which love does not die and people live happily ever after. This story is fiction, not fantasy, but it reflects that great longing to see love and loyalty take on all the forces of a wicked world and win. A few brave souls refused to accept that the cold steel of evil swords was the last word in the universe. They clung to the hope of the ancient stories. They heard and sang the song – a melody which no king or army had ever managed to snuff out.

The song does not tolerate being sung from a distance. Those who sing it find themselves taken up by it – and thrown into the midst of a battle far greater than themselves …

Some would call this a kids' book. I would rather say that it's a book for kids aged from 12 to 99 years old. May you enjoy reading it as much as I enjoyed writing it,

John Duncan

Hemmingen, Germany

May 26, 2016

Table of Contents

PART I

Table of Contents

PART 2

CHAPTER 1

The Arrival

A lot is said about the old days, a long time ago, when our weary old earth was still young and fresh. They say, for example, that in those days the rainbows came right down to the earth and gave shelter from the rain, and that chestnuts and walnuts grew to the size of your fist, which was good news for farmers and hard work for squirrels. The sun was much friendlier, and the rain didn't beat down as cold and hard as it does now. There are also many stories from that time—of great heroes, of giants and dwarfs, and of ordinary folks like you and me.

The story I will tell you now is my favorite. It is the story of a simple country boy who turned the world upside down.

It all started on a warm summer morning in a village deep in the forest. The air was still cool and moist from the night before, and the sun in the cloudless sky no longer lit just the tops of the great trees but was rising and casting its rays further and further down. The birds were already singing and chirping with great excitement, and it seemed that the forest and all its inhabitants were celebrating the coming of another glorious summer day. All, that is, except for two.

Two boys came trudging out of the village with baskets in their hands and frustration written all over their faces. The lad on the right was eleven years old and tall for his age; he walked in even, steady strides with a kind of unhurried dignity. His clothes were the simple trousers and shirt of a village boy, but they were neatly tucked in and buttoned up. His dark, wavy hair was well kept and combed to the side. Despite his look of serenity, his deep brown eyes constantly watched the path before him and the thick forest around it.

His companion, a freckle-faced, red-haired boy of ten, was bouncing his way up the path, swinging his basket around as though he were using it to fight off an imaginary dragon. Anger simmered and sparked in his green eyes.

"We could've got out of this, you know! Mama wants us to pick mushrooms and you don't even argue? It's going to rain! We might get lost! We don't know the way! We don't even know what mushrooms to pick! We could pick the wrong ones and get poisoned and all die! My sore foot is playing up again. But oh no! Travis the goody-goody has to say yes!"

He paused to change his voice and imitate his brother. "'No problem, Mama dear, Brody and I will go! You know me, Mister Wonder-Boy. Oh, Mama, if you take off your shoes I'll be glad to kiss your toes! Aren't I just wonderful!'"

"It's probably another quarter-mile now," said the older boy calmly, running his fingers through his dark brown hair and not even looking at his brother.

"Don't you get it? We could be fishing right now!"

"We can go fishing after we get back."

"When we get back? Are you crazy? Do you know how long it'll take us?"

"The fish bite better in the evening."

"And so do the mosquitoes! The day is already over! This is girls' work!" Brody paused and said with all the seriousness he could muster, "This is not what I was put on earth to do!"

Travis couldn't fight back a smile. This was a line he had heard many times from his father, and now his little brother had added it to his already large rhetorical collection.

Travis didn't make any attempt to defend himself. Brody just wanted to lure him into an argument for the fun of it. No, this time Travis was not going to play along. He had naively hoped for a quiet walk to the mushroom patch, but then again, this pestering wasn't all that bad. Nobody could make him laugh like his little brother.

Brody was a wild and crazy, snotty-nosed rascal, always with some crazy new idea, always pushing the limits. When he was at home, the place came alive. Travis didn't tell him so, but he had volunteered them for mushroom duty to get Brody out of their mother's hair for a while, especially after yesterday's disaster. Brody had decided to make a chariot out of his wagon and have their thirty chickens pull it. With great care and a lot of string, he had tied all thirty to the front of the wagon; when they failed to pull it he attached the pig; when this still was not enough, he tied on the dog as well. Everything seemed to be shaping up well until the first crack of the whip on the pig's behind. The pig and the dog went wild, all of the chickens promptly panicked, and the sky was blackened by chickens frantically flying to the end of their string.

The commotion brought villagers from every direction, and it was only after some time that they managed to calm things down. There were feathers everywhere, except of course on the chickens. Their father, the village chief, said it would be at least two weeks before they would see the next egg.

That was yesterday, and today, by ignoring his young brother's outbursts, Travis managed to calm Brody down—or at least to move him on to a quieter topic. His brother's voice drifted up from the path behind him, where Brody was jumping from rock to rock and generally making no great effort to keep up.

"Dad never had to do this as a kid! Mom doesn't care that this is girl's work. Next thing she'll have us wearing dresses, but of course you won't mind doing that, will you, Wonder-Boy? 'Do I look better in pink or green, Mommy dear?'"

Travis paused and turned to look at his brother, whose basket was hanging from his elbow as he leaped along the path in fits and starts. "You really don't want to live to see tomorrow, do you?" said Travis, who was slowly reaching the wide limit of his patience.

"Oh, I like how you said that," said Brody. "'You really don't want to see tomorrow, do you?' If you want to scare me, you have to speak a bit lower. I mean, you are *such* a wimp, you've got to work hard to cover it up. Try again! Blast me like a bear, and maybe you'll come across like a chipmunk!"

And so it continued. Brody had forgotten his frustration with his mother, and everything was fine again. The world was a very simple thing for him: birds sing, fish swim, and Brody annoys his brother. Travis pretended to have endless patience, but the truth was its end was always just around the corner, and nothing was more fun for Brody than finding it!

On they went up the path, across the occasional creek, joking around, teasing, provoking and threatening, but mostly laughing. Brody was actually very good for Travis, who had carried a quiet burden ever since his father, Dorn, became village chief after their grandfather's tragic death. Brody's bubbling laughter and crazy ideas were just what Travis needed when life felt dark and serious.

They arrived at the edge of the valley where the mushrooms grew. A spooky thicket of cedar trees crowded a damp, mossy forest floor. This was where the mushrooms grew best. Down they went into the cool hollow and started picking. Brody pranced around looking for the best of the mushrooms, talking much and picking little. Travis smiled to himself and worked hard filling his basket, one mushroom after another.

For whatever reason, Brody grew more serious and started saying less and picking more. Slowly but surely, the boys became uneasy. It was the kind of feeling you get when something's not right, but you don't know what's wrong. It's not something you've seen or heard. It's just something in the air—but it's' there. It's most definitely there.

"I don't like this place!" said Brody suddenly.

"Me neither," replied Travis. "Let's just get these mushrooms picked and get out of here!"

An unusual cold settled into the valley, and its stillness was broken by a distant, howling wind.

"Is it just me, or is this place getting darker?" asked Brody.

"I don't know!" replied Travis, but he also had the feeling that the thicket was darkening. He frowned down at the nearly full basket under his hands. "How much more do you need?"

"Maybe half a basket," replied Brody.

Travis found himself working faster and more nervously, as though something inside him was getting more and more frantic. It *was* getting darker. He could no longer see the freckled pattern on the tops of the mushrooms. Their dull grey outline grew ever vaguer beside the moss.

The wailing of the wind was getting closer, and in its strange, repeated gusts it was like someone calling out in the woods.

"My fingers are freezing!" said Brody.

"Hey, Brody, let's get out of here," said Travis tensely. "Something's happening." He looked over his shoulder and could just barely seeing Brody in the growing darkness.

"Yeah," said Brody, "it's like . . ."

CRASH!

While he was still speaking, a mighty lightning bolt struck with a crash.

The next thing they knew, the boys were lying facedown in the moss. Rain pelted down through the forest as though the whole heavens had opened at once.

"Travis, you there?" came Brody's cry through the darkness and rain.

Travis shook his head, slowly stumbling to his feet. "Yeah, I'm here. Let's get out of here!"

"The road to the mill is just over there!" shouted Brody over the roaring wind.

"Okay!" Travis shouted back. He grabbed his basket and took off, following the blurred outline of Brody through the pelting rain and wind.

Off they went toward the road as fast as their legs could carry them. Amid the chaos, Travis could just see Brody a few paces in front of him. The trees were shaking so vigorously that they were striking each other at the tops, and the cracks of breaking and splintering branches could be heard from all sides. Again and again bolts of lightning blasted overhead, filling the forest with a blazing, blinding light and leaving behind a darkness much blacker than before. It was as if the whole forest had come alive, with trees and vines swaying violently in all directions and branches and even trees falling where you would least expect them.

The boys stumbled on through the soaking underbrush, scrambling over the broken branches that now littered the forest floor.

"It's up ahead!" shouted Brody. Travis squinted but could only faintly make out the road before them. Brody struggled through the last of the underbrush and staggered out onto the road.

Exactly what happened next was hard to recall. It seemed as though Brody ran full speed into something as solid as a tree and bounced off it like a rubber ball. Suddenly he was on his back, had dropped his basket, and was screaming in terror, "Travis! Travis!"

Travis ran onto the path, jumped over his brother's head, and stood ready to fight the large figure towering over his brother. As Travis gazed through the darkness he could slowly make out the form. It was not a bear, not a monster, but a strange man. A great flash of lightning lit up the sky and showed the boys exactly what they were up against. He was clearly a man, and a tall, muscular man at that, unlike anyone the boys had ever seen.

In an instant he snatched the boys up, holding them around the waist as a shepherd would pick up two sheep, one in each hand to carry them to safety. Travis and Brody struggled to get free, but it was hopeless against his great strength. They dangled helplessly from his arms as he carried them to a small hill. He then sat them both down. Too afraid to move, they watched as he took the pack off his back and sat down between them. With one stroke, he pulled his massive cloak up and over his shoulders, wrapping it around himself and the boys and holding it down tightly. It was like a tent, and despite the storm raging outside, they felt warmer and protected from the rain and wind.

Travis was trembling uncontrollably. A thousand images of those fiendish monsters—tall, red-skinned savages—described around the late-night fire by his schoolmates had come alive and were screaming in his ears.

Among their cries he heard a familiar voice. "Travis! Travis, listen!" It was Brody. "Don't worry! I don't think he wants to hurt us. Just sit!"

Travis took a few deep breaths, and indeed things suddenly seemed much better. Shepherds wrapped themselves up in their cloaks when caught in unexpected storms; this . . . brute must be a shepherd. His thick woolen cloak smelled of sheep. In the occasional flashes of lightning, Travis could see an outline of Brody and of the man. His legs were thick and muscular, his arms solid. Thick, wavy hair framed a strong, clean-shaven face.

The wind continued to roar and the rain pelted down, but Travis felt protected by this strange man and his wonderful cloak. Brody was quiet and strangely calm. The man's calm breathing and slow, steady heartbeat soothed Travis's fears. It was like lying in bed beside their dad when they were small.

No one said anything. Even roaring with all its strength, the storm did not upset the peace of this man, and the three sat without speaking while the storm raged around them. The forest people have a proverb: "Patience outlives every storm," and indeed this was true. Slowly the winds died down, and the fierceness of the rain followed.

With a mighty heave, the man threw his cloak back over his shoulders, and the warm, brilliant sun shone in all its glory from a clear blue sky. The boys leapt to their feet and turned around slowly. Their protector had taken a deep breath and now just sat there with his eyes closed, soaking up the warmth with pleasure. The birds were singing with startling vigor, and were it not for the fact that everything was soaking wet and broken branches were lying everywhere, you would barely have believed that a storm had struck.

The man stretched his great arms, rose to his feet, and put his pack on his back. He was unusually tall and had broad shoulders, a deep chest, and a surprisingly slender waist. His legs were muscular and thick as pillars. There was also something noble about his broad cheeks and leathery, sunburnt complexion. His thick, wavy hair, which was black but bleached red by the sun had obviously never seen a comb. It hung down to his grey woolen cloak. All of his clothes seemed to be made of a kind of woven wool, held together here and there by straps of leather and large bone buttons

The stranger put his hands on his hips and bent down curiously to get a better look at Travis and Brody. His large blue eyes shone with life and the curiosity of a small child. Travis didn't move. His eyes were fixed on the great man who, seeing the baskets and soaked mushrooms scattered everywhere, bent down, picked up a basket, and started filling it with mushrooms.

They stared at him in wonder. Ignoring their stares, the man picked up the other basket and handed it to Travis, who, as if awaking suddenly from a dream, started filling it—but kept a close eye on the man.

Soon the baskets were full again, and the man handed his to the boys. A warm, amused smile grew ear-to-ear and revealing strangely pointed teeth, as he looked into their eyes. Travis wondered what he could be thinking.

There was no chance to ask. The man turned abruptly and walked down the river path toward the village.

As he was disappearing around a corner, Travis suddenly saw the pack on the man's back move as though by magic. It widened and narrowed like someone stretching after a snooze.

He closed his eyes and shook his head and looked again, but the strange man had suddenly vanished.

"Did you see that?" he asked.

"See what?" answered Brody.

"Nothing," Travis muttered.

"Who on earth was that?" asked Brody, obviously still shaken from the encounter.

"I don't know, but he's walking toward the village."

"We've got to run ahead and warn them!"" said Brody excitedly.

"He's not dangerous; he just looks scary."

"But they don't know that."

"Yes, you're right," said Travis. He paused to think. "He'll take a while if he takes the path beside the river. If we run over oak ridge, we'll get to the mill well before he does."

Brody nodded, and off they raced through the forest leaving, as boys do, their baskets behind them. The only thing on their minds was getting to the mill before the great man.

CHAPTER 2

A Surprise for Bud

The path over the oak ridge usually only took about ten minutes, but the slippery mud and broken branches everywhere made the passage much more difficult. After about twice that time, the two boys came stumbling out of the forest into the clearing where the mill stood. They were covered in mud from head to toe.

In the distance they could see the miller, a small, slender man with grey hair and a thick grey moustache, named Bud. He was walking around his vegetable garden, inspecting the damage from the storm. His beanpoles and tomatoes had all been knocked flat, as had his sunflowers.

Their hearts leapt for joy when they saw Bud. He and his wife, Clara, had become very close to the boys over the years. Who better to see at a time like this.

"Bud! Bud! There's a man coming!" blurted Brody as he raced toward Bud's house.

Bud, who was trying to stand the tomato stakes up again, looked up as the lads staggered out of the forest, huffing and puffing.

"He's really big, . . . and I ran into him . . . and Travis jumped between us . . . and he didn't do us any harm. He sheltered us from the storm," said Brody, taking great gasps of air.

"Yeah, he took us and held us under his cloak," blurted Travis between gasps and pants.

"You wouldn't believe how strong he is! Like a horse!"

"And he's walking this way!" said Travis excitedly.

"Now hold on," said Bud, looking a little confused. "You came out of the forest and met a big man?"

"Yeah!" said Brody. "Wearing a woolen cloak."

"He's a big man, walking down the river path," said Travis more slowly and calmly. As he caught his breath, he told Bud all that had happened and described the man.

Bud just listened with increasing thoughtfulness as Travis spoke (and Brody interrupted) and rubbed his hand in his thick moustache as he always did when thinking about something.

Finally he lowered his hand. "What was he wearing exactly?"

"Kind of loose wool clothes, tied with leather," said Travis.

"What color?" asked Bud.

Travis tried to remember—in the rain it had been hard to see much. "Uh, no color—just raw wool."

"Did he say anything?"

Bud's questions seemed to be leading somewhere, but Travis couldn't think where. "Nothing. Nothing at all."

"Did he smile?"

That was the most surprising question of all. "Yeah, this big ear-to-ear smile, with big pointy teeth."

"Did he have sort of red, leathery skin?"

"Yeah, yeah! That's him!" said Brody. "Do you know him, Bud?" Travis was too surprised for words.

Bud didn't answer. He just stared to the ground in thought, rubbing his moustache. "A mountain man," he muttered.

"A mountain what?"

"A man," said Bud, looking up at the boys with grave anxious eyes. "Just like us. They live high up in the upper valleys and tablelands. They keep sheep and yaks and live in tents."

"Are these people friendly, Bud?" asked Brody.

"To us, yes."

Travis looked closely at Bud. If this were true, then why was Bud so uneasy?

"We'll tell the people what happened, Bud—so they know he's friendly," said Travis.

"Oh, no! Don't tell a soul! Not a soul, I tell you!" Bud grabbed Travis's shoulder and looking deep into his eyes. "We can't let anyone find out that a mountain man was anywhere near here! Especially not the soldiers!"

"What do they care?" asked Brody.

"Oh, they care. That's for sure! What was he doing? Where was he going?"

Travis struggled for words. Bud's sudden seriousness had caught him by surprise. "We don't know! We didn't talk to him!"

Bud straightened up and frowned deeply. "Boys, go home! Go straight home and don't talk to anyone on the way. Promise me that you'll tell no one except your father. Will you promise me that?"

"Bud, what's the big deal?"

Travis didn't think Bud's expression could get any more serious, but it did. The miller lowered his voice even though there was no one to overhear.

"The king has ordered that any mountain men found in the forest are to be killed immediately, and not just mountain men, but also anyone who has anything to do with them. That includes children, just like you two, and believe you me, he will show no mercy. You two get home right now, and tell *only* your father."

Bud's tone sent a shiver down Travis's spine. Bud was known for his cheerful spirit and good humor; the boys had never heard him sound as serious as this before.

"You said he was coming this way?" asked Bud.

"Yeah," answered Brody, "he was coming down the river road."

The miller nodded. "I'm going to try to find him."

"You want to catch him?"

"Of course not!" gasped Bud. "I want to *hide* him. Either he's lost his way, or he's on some important mission. Anyway, you two! Off you go! And remember, not a word to . . ."

But the boys were not listening. They were both staring at something behind him. Bud turned around to see the mountain man come around the bend and approach them with great, cheerful strides.

Before they knew it the mountain man was there, and Bud found himself face-to-face with him, as though staring into the face of a legend. The miller's slight figure looked almost childish before this bear of a man.

The mountain man fixed his gaze on Bud alone, with an intensity that seemed to shut out the rest of the world. Bud stared up into his eyes without uttering a word. There was no fear, no threat, no challenge, but a great, serious silence as each searched the eyes of the other.

Slowly but surely, a grin appeared on the face of the mountain man, until his whole face seemed to glow with a deep satisfaction. Bud also was beaming with joy. Travis, who was unable to take his eyes off the two men, wondered if Bud's joy was that of seeing an old friend or of suddenly making a new one.

It was clear that the mountain man had learned what he wanted to know, and he suddenly pulled his leather pack off his back and handed it to Bud. As Bud held it, the mountain man pulled aside the wool cloth that had covered the contents of the bag.

And there it was. A small child, maybe a year old, with a round, freckled face, a few tufts of curly blond hair, and big blue eyes that looked at the three strangers with great curiosity. Travis's jaw just about dropped out of his head. The child looked at Bud and gave him a playful smile, seeming to sense the joy and celebration of the moment.

The mountain man placed the bag and the boy firmly in Bud's hands. He stared again into Bud's eyes as if to hand over a great responsibility and administer a solemn oath. Bud nodded, as if to say "I will."

Suddenly the mountain man turned around, and as quickly and silently as a deer, he returned to the path and was gone. Travis felt dizzy—he'd been so busy watching all of this that he had forgotten to breathe. Brody and Bud seemed to be in a similar kind of shock, and as they looked around, all three realized that they were not alone. A few people from the village had come, probably to buy flour.

Nobody said anything, but the fearful looks on their faces showed what they were thinking. They all hurriedly disappeared as though nothing had happened—as though nothing had happened at all.

CHAPTER 3

The Meeting

Brody rolled about in bed that night. He just could not sleep. It had been such a crazy day.

After Bud's encounter with the mountain man, the boys had gone home and told their father all that had happened. Dorn listened with great interest, but the look of worry that clouded his face was one Brody knew only too well. He missed the lighthearted, joyful father he had known in earlier years. Since the sudden death of Dorn's father and his becoming chief, his joy and laughter were gone.

As news of Bud's visitor had spread, several people came to talk with Dorn. They all spoke in hushed, serious tones in the dining room, and the boys found themselves banished to the kitchen by their mother. It was one of those "Well, you boys have had a big day. Off to bed early now!" nights where Mom "bossed" the boys to bed, as Brody always said.

The visitors had gone, but Brody still lay awake, thinking about the events of the day. He knew this story was not over yet. Indeed, it had only just begun. Thinking, rolling, listening in the silence. The light of the moon had moved a long way across the room. It had to be very late.

Then suddenly he heard a familiar sound. It was the latch of the front door.

Jumping down from his bunk, Brody looked through the window. His father was going out the door. Two burly figures waited for him at the gate. These could only be Hoss and Willow—brothers, the sons of Aaron the blacksmith and the informal bodyguard of the chief and the elders.

The three men disappeared silently down the path that led out of the village and to the mill. Brody ran to Travis on the lower bunk and shook him.

"Travis! Travis! Get up. Dad has just left with Hoss and Willow. They're going somewhere."

Travis was on his feet in a flash. They got dressed as quickly as they could and snuck out the door behind the men, going out as quietly as possible.

The three men walked silently out of the village and stopped at the butcher's smokehouse outside the village. The boys followed on from a distance, staying off the path so as not to be seen.

In the moonlight, they saw three other figures join the first group. They couldn't see for sure, but Brody guessed it must be Georg the tanner, Harst the shepherd, and Aaron the blacksmith. They were the three village elders who made up the village council along with Dorn.

After exchanging a few words, the men all returned to the path and continued out of the village toward the mill.

"They're not carrying any torches!" Brody whispered.

"No, of course not! It's a secret!" replied Travis.

The boys followed at a distance, trying to make as little noise as possible. Soon enough the party had arrived at Bud's house, and Dorn knocked quietly on the door. It opened, and Dorn and the elders went inside, leaving Hoss and Willow outside to keep watch.

A faint light appeared in the house. It must have been only one or two candles, thought Brody, and then all of the shutters were closed. It was dark.

The boys came as close as they could and looked around the clearing; the mill was now fully lit by the moon.

"What are we going to do now?" asked Brody in frustration.

"I've got an idea," said Travis. "Come!"

Travis went first, along the edge of the clearing. "Get about three stones, as big as this," he said, showing Brody a stone. When each of the boys had three or four stones in his hand, Travis crept close to a chestnut tree that grew beside the house.

"Now, what we want to do is throw these stones over into the water beside the mill wheel, and when Hoss and Willow go over there, we'll climb up on the roof. We'll have to be really fast."

"Okay," whispered Brody excitedly. The idea was perfect!

"One, two three!" whispered Travis, and the boys threw the stones quickly one after the other. It sounded like someone running through the water. In an instant Hoss and Willow were there with swords drawn, speaking hastily to each other and searching around the reeds for the intruder.

Like cats, the boys were up the tree and onto the roof in no time. At some distance from each other, they lay flat on the thatched roof and climbed ever so gently toward the center. They could barely hear what was going on below, so they both slowly but surely pulled bundles of thatched grass apart to make a gap through which they could hear.

Their father's voice came through the gaps loud and clear.

"You can't keep that child, Bud!" he said with no small emotion. The conversation had already become heated. "You will put the whole village in jeopardy! It's bad enough if the king hears that a mountain man was here, but if it seems that we had any dealings with him, he could wipe out the whole village. Remember what happened to Aiberg and Reelhouse!"

The boys heard Bud's voice: "They were different, Dorn. They were trading with the mountain people."

"You can't keep that child!"

"We *must* keep that child! The Lord of the Forest has just entrusted him to us. Can't you see that?"

"No, I can't see that!" retorted Dorn.

"Have you all forgotten? The mountain people are our brothers! We are the freemen of the forest! We have no king except the Lord of the Forest. You are our chief. You all are our elders! This is what you stand for. Now is the time to show your colors!"

"Bud, you've got to understand," said Harst the shepherd, his voice rising coolly to where the boys lay. "We have been entrusted with wives and children. We have to think of that."

"Of course. And that's why the Lord of the Forest promises to step in for those do right:

> *"He is there, and strengthens those*
>
> *"Who dare to take a stand.*
>
> *"It is his will, yes his delight*
>
> *"To stand at their right hand.*

"We sang that together as kids! All of us did! Come on, man! Now's the time to live it out!"

Brody's heart stirred at Bud's impassioned tone, but it was their own father's voice that cut him off. "Now hold on," said Dorn earnestly. "These are two totally different things. We don't know for sure that it was the *Lord of the Forest* who entrusted this child to you."

"You don't know because you don't *want* to know!" said Bud angrily.

"May I remind you to talk to the chief in a manner worthy of his office!" said Georg the tanner.

"I am begging the chief to *act* in a manner worthy of his office!" answered Bud with disgust.

"Darling, please!" This was the gentle voice of Clara, Bud's wife.

Then there was silence, a rather heavy silence.

"Bud may well be right," said Aaron the blacksmith.

"You must be mad!" blurted the tanner. "Are you willing to risk the whole village for one man's crazy idea that some child has been entrusted to him by the Lord of the Forest? That child must go, and immediately!"

"Where, then?" asked the blacksmith.

"To the kingdom. Handed over to be taken as a subject."

"What?" blurted the blacksmith. "You are going to hand a child over to slave traders?"

"It's our only choice," continued the tanner, "because . . ."

"Hey, you may as well make some money on that, man!" shouted the blacksmith in outraged sarcasm. "Sell him! No one gives slaves away!"

"Nobody wants to, Aaron!" growled the tanner.

"You give that child to the kingdom, and he'll live a horrific life in the mines until he dies a horrific death. You may as well cash in on the deal. Then you can buy something nice for the wife and children who are entrusted to you."

"I'm warning you . . ." snarled the tanner angrily.

"Stop it! Both of you stop it!" This was not the first time Dorn had needed to calm things down between the Georg and Aaron. "There *must* be a solution."

Again there was silence. Brody looked over at Travis. Even in the moonlight, Travis's expression could not be mistaken. He was desperately perplexed. Brody was just as confused. How could his father even consider sending the child away? There must be something the boys didn't know or understand. It could be that their father was ready to give a child away just because of fear. When Brody saw the tortured look on Travis's face, he moved over a little closer and squeezed his brother's hand. He understood.

"I can think of two possibilities," said Harst the shepherd deliberately. "If the child cannot go to the kingdom, then it should either go back to the mountain people or to the Badlands. Association with the mountain people is no real option. That leaves only the Badlands. Life there will be difficult, but at least the child will be free."

There was, once again, silence, as if to say that this idea was not too bad. Suddenly Bud's voice could be heard again.

"Well, then. Clara and I and the child shall leave together for the Badlands."

"You just have to take it there," said Harst.

"We'll do nothing of the sort. We will raise that child in the Badlands."

"You're not going to leave the village!" said Dorn, obviously affected by the thought.

"We most certainly will. The Lord has given us a responsibility, and we will take care of it. How you handle your responsibilities is your own problem, and we shall leave you to sort that out with the Lord yourselves. I expected more from you, I really did."

Brody felt suddenly so desolate, so sad. He pulled closer and closer to Travis as he always did when life got to be too much for him. Travis's face was strained with grief and disappointment. Brody thought his brother might explode with it.

Below, the voices got louder again, and accusation upon accusation flew across the room as the whole discussion slid into chaos.

This all ended as Dorn pounded on the table and stood up.

"Listen to the solemn word of the village chief!"

This was a formula that demanded total silence and obedience. Brody and Travis looked at each other sadly. Why wouldn't their father use his power for the good?

Dorn continued: "Bud and Clara and the child are to leave for the Badlands before sunrise. We shall never see them again. No word of this shall be spoken in the village. Indeed, anyone outside the council and bodyguard, including family members, who learns of this will also be banished to the Badlands. This word is final! The chief of the village has spoken!"

The men and Clara all answered in unison, as the ceremony dictated, "The chief of the village has spoken."

It was at this point that Brody pulled as close to Travis as he could. Now, what they hadn't thought about was the fact that the roof could bear them when they were apart, but as they came closer and closer together, their combined weight grew too heavy. Suddenly, with a great crash, the roof caved in, and the two boys fell to the floor below. The candle blew out, and the whole room was filled with dust and grass.

Clara quickly lit another candle, and the boys looked up at a circle of men with drawn swords, ready to attack. Brody tried to smile weakly up at them, but the air had been knocked out of his lungs, and his whole body hurt.

Dorn's eyes were as wide as saucers. "Boys," he said, but he could say no more.

"Well, boys," said Bud solemnly, "you are now hereby banished from the village. The chief of the village has spoken. You better get yourselves ready. We are all leaving immediately for the Badlands."

Travis got up and stared his father in the face. Only just managing to control his emotion he said, "Okay, Bud. We'll get ready." Brody's heart broke for his brother, who usually seemed so confident. He now seemed confused—so terribly confused, and Brody just didn't know what to say.

The words sank like an arrow in Dorn's heart. He seemed unable to remain standing, and he fell into his chair and sat for a minute with his elbows on the table and his head in his hands.

That was a terrible, heartbreaking moment. No one could deny that. But as it turned out, that moment changed everything.

The village was told that the council had met and decided the child could remain with Bud and Clara at the mill. No one was allowed to speak of where the child had come from, and that was that.

As it turned out, the king's soldiers had not heard about the mountain man. The secret was safe. The child did indeed have

the chance to grow up without trouble or fear in the mill beside
the river.

CHAPTER 4

A Day Fishing

A couple of days passed from that moment when all of life turned upside down. Not much was said in the boys' house. Dorn did not scold them for spying on their meeting. He felt he was in an impossible situation, as helpless as a bird in a trap and ashamed because of it. The daily chores were done with care, but laughter was nowhere to be found. In the evenings, Travis fell exhausted into bed only to lie awake for hours plagued by fears and worries. Brody too was unusually quiet and sober. None of this escaped their mother's eye, and on the third day she sent the boys off fishing, knowing that it often did them good.

It was midmorning by the time they arrived at the river. A grassy patch beside the mill had become their favorite fishing spot, not because the fishing there was better than elsewhere, but because Bud and Clara were there, and the boys had come to treasure them enormously.

Travis stopped abruptly just before reaching the water. He stared at the familiar sight of underbrush on the far side, coming right down to the water's edge, casting dancing shadows in the swirling, flowing water. *The river!* he thought. *What are we . . .? Oh, yes! We're fishing!* His mind had gone through the scene on the roof a hundred times. It seemed that whatever he was doing, he found his mind going through the conversation again and again.

The river. Yes! The quiet of his thoughts was broken by a familiar voice.

"Should we sit in the sun or in the shadows?" said Brody, keen to get started.

"I, um, uh . . . Here, take a worm," said Travis vaguely.

"Thanks," said Brody, taking a worm from the bag.

After a long pause, Brody's voice interrupted again. "Where?"

"Where what?"

"Where should we sit?"

"Um, uh . . . I don't know. Uh, did I give you a worm?"

"Yes, just now! This very second! Hey, what is wrong with you?"

"Huh? There's nothing wrong with me," said Travis. "Where should we sit?"

"I just asked you that!" said Brody in frustration.

Travis nodded unhappily. "Yeah, okay, uh . . . Let's sit there."

He led the way to a flat, grassy area near a bend in the river, and they put their things down.

"Yesterday you said I could try out your rod. Can I have it now?"

"Just a minute," said Travis, looking through their things in the tall grass. "Um, where's the bread basket?"

"We decided not to bring it! Or rather, YOU decided not to bring it! Can't you remember?"

"Oh, yeah. That's right." Travis looked around the riverbank uneasily, not quite sure what he wanted to do next.

"Well, yes or no?" came Brody's voice again.

"Yes or no what?"

"CAN I BORROW YOUR FISHING ROD OR NOT? Travis, what has got into you? You're being totally weird."

"No, I'm not!" And then after a pause, "Did I give you a worm?"

"Yes! And I asked you if I could borrow your rod!"

"Okay. You can borrow it. Calm down!" said Travis.

"Me? You're the one who's acting weird! What is with you today? We decide to go fishing, and you get the basket to collect eggs. Then you give me all the fishing stuff and tell me to wait.”

“I had to look for something.”

“Yeah, you dork! You spent ages looking for the hat that was on your head all the time!”

“I didn’t know you were waiting!” said Travis aggressively.

“You *told* me to wait!”

“Do I rub it in your face when you do stupid things?” said Travis, handing Brody his rod.

“Don’t be a weirdo and I won’t call you one!”

“Now listen to me! That’s enough lip from you!” said Travis angrily. “You can thank me for lending you my rod!”

“Thanks, Weirdo!” said Brody sarcastically.

“Give me my rod!” exploded Travis. He grabbed at the rod in Brody’s hand and tried to yank it away, but Brody would not let go.

“You said I could use it!”

“Give it to me right now!”

The boys went rolling into the grass in a wild struggle for the fishing rod. Both of them had two hands on the rod, and although Brody was weaker, he fought as though his life depended on it. Travis slowly managed to pull the rod closer and closer to himself and peeled Brody’s fingers off one after the other while Brody screamed as though Travis was hurting him. The battle was almost won when, with a mighty crack, the fishing rod broke in two.

“You broke it!” Travis shouted.

“I didn’t!” said Brody, suddenly horrified.

Travis clenched his fists in fury. “I’m going to—”

Before he could continue, a hand fell upon his shoulder.

"The way you two are shouting, you'll scare all the fish away," said Bud's familiar calm voice.

"He broke my fishing pole!" shouted Travis bitterly.

"He said I could use it!" responded Brody, who was bursting with anger and sorrow.

"Well, it just so happens that I myself need to make a new fishing rod," said Bud cheerfully. "So you know what I suggest? I'll get three knives, and we can go over to the willow over there and cut down three branches. In no time we'll all have new fishing rods. And you know what?"

"What?" said Brody, who was fighting back tears but hoping for the best.

"Clara's just put a cake in the oven. She saw you two out the window and figured she'd better feed you."

This was exactly "the best" that Brody had been hoping for. Clara had often prepared them cake and biscuits over the last few years, and many an afternoon ended in them all sitting around the table talking and eating. Both boys found the miller's house a taste of heaven on earth, and a very welcome change to their own tension-filled home.

Soon enough all three were sitting in the long soft grass beside the river, new fishing poles in their hands and the warm sun shining on their backs.

"So, Travis," said Bud suddenly, "what are you thinking about?"

"He's been totally weird all day!" said Brody.

Travis said nothing to defend himself. He looked past his fishing rod into the softly flowing water before him.

"Dad wanted to give that baby to the king, didn't he?"

"He didn't want to," said Bud earnestly.

"He was going to do it," said Travis, whose lips began to tremble.

"We don't know what he would have done," replied Bud quietly.

"But how could he do such a thing?" asked Travis, only just controlling his anger.

"He didn't. Nothing happened. Everything's going to be okay."

"How could he . . ." continued Travis, but he got too choked up to speak further.

There was a long pause as Bud reflected. Slowly, the miller said, "Remember when Aaron's horse, Bella, got stuck in the bog?"

"That was so funny!" laughed Brody.

"Maybe *you* found it funny!" said Travis.

"Yeah, especially when the rope broke and Hoss went flying into the mud! I laughed myself silly!" Brody's whole face lit up at the thought.

Bud fought off a grin, trying not to let Brody get him off track. "But remember, we needed the whole village to get that horse out of the mud. Now, that is a mighty horse."

"Yeah, so?" said Brody.

"So even mighty horses get stuck sometimes," replied Bud.

Travis had well understood what Bud was trying to say right from the beginning, but it didn't help. His father's actions had cast a shadow over his soul, and nothing could get through it.

He didn't really mean to, but suddenly he found himself voicing his deepest fear. "If he had to, would he give *us* to the king?"

"Oh, Travis! No!" said Bud, startled. His eyes filled with pity. "Travis, I'd die a thousand deaths in the battlefield for your father. He is a good man—never doubt that."

Travis remained silent.

"Your father, Dorn, is a sword made of the finest steel, but that steel has been put into the fire. After it is pulled out and cooled, the steel is even harder than before, but while it's in the fire, even the toughest steel is soft and weak."

"But when will he come out of the fire?" asked Travis flatly.

"I don't know. All I know is that the flames are raging hotly, and he's taking some terrible blows from the blacksmith's hammer."

"You're not angry with him? He tried to banish you!"

Bud looked sad but not angry. "I know what it's like to be in the fire. He's under a lot of pressure. He's got the whole village to care for, and there are more soldiers about these days."

"You think they'll make our village like Reelhouse?" asked Brody excitedly.

"Who told you about Reelhouse?"

"Arny!"

"Arny?" blurted Bud hotly, angry at the old toothless farmer who had more time than sense.

"Arny tells us everything you're not supposed to tell kids," said Brody triumphantly. "Did the soldiers really kill everyone?"

Bud sighed. "If there were survivors, we don't know about them."

"And they burned the village to the ground?"

"They did."

"And Dad's worried that they'll do the same thing here?"

"Yes."

"And you're not worried?" asked Travis, turning and gazing solemnly into Bud's eyes.

"No," said Bud. "I don't believe they will come here."

"Why not?"

There was a long pause and absolute silence, and then Bud said, "Because the Lord is with us."

Once again, nobody spoke for a long time. Travis looked down to the swirls and eddies of the river and breathed deeply. He already felt much better, even though no question had really been answered and no problems solved.

"Bud, why do the king's soldiers hate the mountain people?" he asked.

This time, Bud smiled. "If you want to know that, you'll have to go back to the beginning of time. Shall I tell you the story?"

"Yes!" said both boys together.

The miller nodded. He laid aside his fishing rod and stretched out his arms while he thought of how to begin. The boys waited eagerly.

"Well, the very first thing to know is that when the world was young, it was full of music. The whole world resounded from a song. There were many singers, and many tunes, and many songs, but all of these songs made up one song. Do you know what I mean?"

"Uh, no!" said Brody.

Bud smiled again. "Those days were magical. There was something in the air. You could feel it in the mist. The whole forest rang out with it . . . *people sang.* They sang while they worked, while they walked, while they prepared supper, and while they cleaned their boots. And they didn't just sing; they sang *along.* The melody was already there, always in the background, and the wind made the trees sway to its rhythm. The song filled the forest like a thick fog. It was under every leaf on the forest floor, it was settled in the moss, and at the same time it was soaring with the eagle high up in the sky. The forest was filled with the melody. Little children danced to it, and old men bathed in its warmth."

"And now it's gone!" said Travis coldly, staring directly in front of himself. He did not want to listen to this. Far from cheering him up, it make his own darkness blacker.

"Some say it never was. Others wonder if they hear it now and again," said Bud.

There was a long pause; nobody said anything. "I know a few people who still bathe in its warmth," said Bud.

"Like ol' Donger?" asked Brody.

"Yeah! Exactly! Like ol' Donger Bee!" answered Bud, delighted. He poked Brody in the chest, pleased that he understood.

"There is something special about Donger," said Travis suddenly, surprising even himself. He usually chose his words very carefully.

"Donger's one of those people who's got the song deep in his bones," said Bud.

"Have you ever heard this song?" asked Brody.

"I have. Sure I have. My dad used to sing it. He was the happiest man in the world!"

"Happier than you, Bud?" asked Travis with great seriousness.

"Oh, I don't know," said Bud, rather taken aback.

"When do you hear this song, Bud?" asked Brody.

"It comes and goes. Sometimes I'm lying in bed beside Clara and she's breathing ever so softly, and I hear it. I often hear it in the still of the morning when the sun is just breaking over the trees. Sometimes I hear it among the birds, and sometimes the birds drown it out. You can't start it, but you can chase it away."

"How do you chase it away?" asked Brody.

"Oh, when I worry and get all worked up about things."

"You?" blurted Travis. "You never get worked up, Bud!"

He laughed. "Well, I used to. I suppose the song has calmed me down."

"Have we chased the song out of the forest, Bud?" asked Travis. "We villagers, I mean."

"In many ways we have. But don't forget, the song is stronger than the world itself. Anyway, getting back to the story, the song was very much louder in those early days than now. Everyone was a singer, and some special ones were minstrels. They used to travel around and teach people new songs. They would also heal people and animals. Sometimes they would travel and sometimes they would stay put, depending on where the song led them. There were many minstrels, but probably the greatest was the last one, a man named Tarv."

Bud paused. "Did your Dad ever tell you about Tarv or Narvan, boys?"

"Yeah, but I didn't really get what he was talking about," said Travis.

"Me neither," said Brody.

"Okay. Well then, sit back and make yourselves comfortable. I'll tell you their story . . ."

CHAPTER 5

The Song and the City

Travis loved Bud's stories. He decided that as he listened, he would fix his eyes on the sun dancing on the rippling, swirling water, in the same way that he loved looking into the fire when hearing a story. It was only now that he realized what an absolutely magical summer day it was. "The story of Tarv and Narvan goes like this," Bud began. "Tarv was a minstrel who lived in a valley beside a river, and he made many wonderful poems and sang many songs. People loved to hear him sing and play on ancient instruments which we don't have anymore."

"He's the guy who sang the storm to sleep and whose voice echoed off the moon!" said Brody excitedly, remembering words he had heard somewhere.

"Well, we don't know about that," continued Bud. "We don't know much at all about what happened back then, but a few things are clear. We do know that he helped a lot of people and that he wrote a great number of songs, which spread like wildfire to every corner of the forest. He always claimed that his songs were from the Lord of the Forest, whom he loved dearly.

"You know that song you sing before every meal?" said Bud, interrupting his own story. He raised his airy voice and sang,

> *"I am because he is*
>
> *"I have because he gives*
>
> *"I can because he loves*
>
> *"I hope because he lives.*

"Tarv wrote that, and many more."

"Granny told us that when Tarv was a boy he got up early to hear the birds sing, and when he became a man the birds got up to hear him sing!" said Travis with a smile.

"Yeah, that's right!" said Brody. "And he sang his milk into cream."

Bud slapped his knees and guffawed. "My goodness! The stories you boys have heard! You have to be very careful with these kinds of stories! Let me tell you the few things we really know about him. This is my favorite song of his."

Bud sat up straight, and staring at a great oak across the river, filled his lungs and sang a hauntingly beautiful melody. He had a warm, whispery voice that seemed to fill the air.

You dug the well, and tilled the land,

You shaped the tools you took in hand

You sowed your crop and you did toil

To gain a harvest from that soil

And through it all you did not know

That from all this, YOU too would grow

And be my greatest work of art

My love, my joy, my very heart

And stone for stone you cleared the ground

You built the house and fenced it round

You made the walls thick to keep

The cold outside in winter's deep

In all of this you did not see

That I was working, it was me

To make the greatest work of all

That secret work inside your soul

And when your fearful heart is tossed

And all your dreams seem to be lost

As waves that throw and crush you sore

Drive you so deep you rise no more

Know that the work piece is held fast

Sure and in the master's hand

Until that final cut is made

And perfect it shall stand.

When the last note died away, Bud smiled and continued, "Now, he had one child, a son, who was called Narvan. Narvan was a very gifted musician and learned much from his father. They were forest farmers, like all of us, and as the story goes, they lived in a small house with a grass roof. Lots of people came to see him. They brought the sick and the downcast, and sometimes people came just to sing on summer nights. They came in hundreds and sometimes thousands and sat in the meadows surrounding Tarv's house. They sang and sang until the stars came out, and then of course it was too dark to walk home in the forest, so they sang until sunrise, and on the strength of a happy heart they walked home in the morning. Those were magical times, I tell you—magical, wonderful times!"

"And then . . .?" asked Brody with eyes fixed on Bud. He had lost all interest in his fishing rod, which was now lying in the mud.

Bud dropped his voice to a whisper. "And then Tarv died very suddenly. Nobody knows for sure why, but there are suspicions of poisonous mushrooms, and there are as many theories as snowflakes on the mountains. Well, word spread quickly, and a great multitude came to attend his burial. And it was then that many people heard the voice of his son, for the very first time."

Bud stopped for a moment and looked into the sky as though he was revisiting a memory.

"Narvan had a voice like no other. On the day of the burial he sang,

"They say the Lord defines my way

And says what I shall be

There is but one who has a say

And that is only me

My way is in my hands alone

I choose what I shall be

My choice, my life, my plans, my home

I choose my destiny.

"Now this was new," said Bud glumly. "It was new indeed, unlike anything ever sung before. Tarv would have been horrified. Narvan sang about everyone having a dream in his or her own heart, and that it was for them to find their own way— for each one to make his own life and become someone."

"But that's okay, isn't it?" asked Travis noticing Bud's unhappiness with Narvan.

"It sounds good, but wait and see," said Bud. "Over time many people would go at regular times to hear Narvan sing, and he developed a great following. Then at one meeting, late at night around a great fire, the decision was made that they would all leave the forest and go to the flatland beside the great river and build a city. No one had ever thought of leaving the forest before, and the idea of living in a city was absolutely unheard of. But that's what they did—a huge mass of people. They settled beside the river . . . and they did the unthinkable. They chopped down the forest there, and in its place they made a great city surrounded by what they called farms. They cleared field after field."

"But we have fields," said Travis, a little confused.

"We do, for sure. But we borrow small fields from the forest, and we give them back after three years. This was different. This was the building of great machines that pulled out massive trees, pulling their roots right out of the ground. This was taking land *forever*.

"Now, when this happened everyone could clearly see what was going on. It was treason. It was the breaking of the holy law of the Lord of the Forest, and it brought a great reaction. Talk flew around like you cannot imagine! There were a thousand stories of wonderful miracles and terrible catastrophes, and the whole earth was filled with confusion.

"Very quickly, though, accounts of the beauty of the city, of the fruitfulness of the fields, and of health and joy and music and dreams coming true, were spoken of more and more. And the city sent messengers to invite people to come, and so it was that a great many people left the simple and humble life of the forest and went to the city to make a life for themselves.

"Only very few were left in the forest. The city grew and became very great. Its people built a large building where their rulers would live, and after many years when that building was finished, the king—for Narvan had now become king—invited all the people of the whole earth to attend a great feast to celebrate its opening. The people of the forest sent no reply, neither yes nor no. But they did not attend, knowing that the whole city had been built in rebellion against the Lord of the Forest."

Bud stopped and shook his head. His eyes flared with intensity as he looked back at the boys. "This is where the mountain people come in. The mountain people, being more courageous than we of the forest, sent a flat message of refusal. They could not honor that which dishonored their Lord, and they said just that.

"Of course Narvan the king was furious, and all his people with him, and they raised up an army to destroy the mountain people. A huge army left to climb to the high plains to destroy them. On the third day, as they were climbing a mountain, they were caught in a mighty thunderstorm, with lightning, hail, and wind. It killed many and sent the whole multitude into panic. They ran in every direction, and the few that survived returned to the city.

"Ever since that time, the kings of the "kingdom", as it has come to be called, have hated the mountain people. They don't like us much either, but they *hate* the mountain people. If a mountain man is found in the kingdom, he is killed automatically, no questions asked. Even after that, in the old days, the mountain people often came down to us and visited us and traded with us in the forest."

"But what about the soldiers?" asked Travis.

"There were no soldiers in the forest then!"

"No soldiers?" blurted Brody.

We had hundreds of years when they didn't dare enter," said Bud with a sorry tone. "In those days faith was still strong, and the song could be heard all through the forest. The king and his soldiers feared the song, and they stayed away."

"Do they still fear the song, Bud?" asked Travis, never taking his eyes away from the surface of the water.

"They do," said Bud sadly, "but it's much quieter now."

"And the soldiers hate the mountain people more than us," said Brody, who had picked up his fishing rod and was trying to get all the pieces together in his mind.

"The soldiers kill the mountain people on the spot. No questions asked. That is why we almost never see them. Those who have dealings with them may be put in prison or also killed."

"How do you know all this, Bud?" asked Travis.

"All the older people know these things, but they don't speak about them much. My father loved the old stories, and he told me them time and time again. Did I ever tell you boys about him?"

"No," said Brody.

"He escaped from the kingdom."

"Escaped?" asked Brody.

"That's right. He grew up there but really hated the place."

"He hated it?" asked Travis, taking his eyes from the water and looking over at Bud. "But Narvan the king invited everyone to come and see how wonderful it was."

"Yes, he did. But something went profoundly wrong," said Bud with a sigh.

"Like what?" asked Travis.

"I can only tell you what my father told me. He said that people in the kingdom are born as nothing, and they all think they have to become something. Everyone has to prove himself. They want to become stronger, or richer, or more famous than their neighbors, so they step all over each other—cheating and slandering and misusing each other."

"Can't you become someone without pulling someone else down?" asked Travis.

"Well, you should be able to, but for some reason, it doesn't work that well. Father told me that the people of the kingdom are unsure in the very depths of their hearts. They don't really know who they are. If they can somehow make other people like them or respect them, then maybe they can like or respect themselves."

"But is that so bad?" asked Brody.

Bud snorted "At the end of the day, you get a whole bunch of people trying to 'become someone.' The stronger ones use their strength to make themselves stronger and to push down the weaker ones. Those with money use their money to get more money and increase the difference between the rich and the poor. They use money to get power and then more power. Soon you have a few people with a lot of power and very many with little."

"Why do the poor people let the rich do that?" asked Travis. "We would never stand for it."

"The people of the kingdom are not people of the forest. They think very differently than we do. They are afraid of the powerful people, and at the same time, they hope to be like them. Father also told me that most of the poor find others who are even poorer, and they act in the same way as the rich, holding themselves up above those others."

"And what about the really poor?" asked Brody.

"Dad said they were the people who most broke his heart. He could not stand to live in the city anymore and watch them suffer because of the actions of others."

"So he just said good-bye and left?" said Brody quizzically.

"Oh no! You are not allowed to say that you want to leave. The soldiers of the city will kill you if they know that you are running away; they will chase you on horses and with dogs. Father was a clever fellow, and he made a plan. He was working alone in a certain mine, waiting for the other workers to come, and he started a fire in the mine and caused it to collapse. Everyone thought he had been killed and buried in the mine, but in fact he was sitting up on top of a large pine tree nearby. As there were no soldiers or dogs looking for him, he came down and traveled night after night until he got out of the kingdom."

"It took a couple of nights?" asked Travis.

"Yes. There are a lot of towns and villages around the great city, and it takes several nights of walking to get out of the kingdom completely. Not really knowing where to go, he went up to the high plains and lived with the mountain people for a year. Then later, he turned up in a village a long way from here. The people welcomed him. No one asked where he was from, but they all knew."

Then there was quiet. Travis fixed his gaze again on the river, pondering all he had heard, and Brody made himself busy tearing off long pieces of grass and weaving them around his fingers. Bud just sat, looking vaguely at the oak, hoping the boys had understood.

"Let's just be thankful the soldiers didn't hear about our mountain man!" said Bud, trying to end on a happy note.

"I don't like those soldiers. They always look at us as if we're—" started Travis.

"Stupid," finished Brody.

"Well, that's what they think. They think we are primitive, backward peasants, but did you know that you can't drink from their river anymore? They all get their water from wells. And almost all of the fish are dead. And in the middle of the city there is sometimes so much smoke you can hardly see the sun."

"And *we're* the idiots!" said Travis with a smile.

"That's what they say," said Bud, giving Travis an approving slap on the back.

Once again there was a long pause. Travis felt happier than he had for a long time.

"They sound pretty stupid to me!" said Brody suddenly, as though he had just realized something.

"Tell me, Bud," said Travis with a mischievous grin, "did they ever tie chickens to a wagon?"

"You shut up right now!" growled Brody.

Bud shook his head and laughed.

Travis, meanwhile, felt as though he were back to normal. He had heard so much over the years, so many bits and pieces of history, but nobody had ever put them together for him. Now the whole world made more sense. The world might not be happy, but at least he could understand it.

All their eyes fixed on the river with its peaceful swirls and gentle ripples as the threesome mulled over the story and soaked up the sun. Suddenly, a voice was heard behind them. It was Clara, singing as she hung the washing up. Her voice was soft and light but nonetheless strong, and she hit every note with great certainty. She sang an old song of Tarv's, with a haunting, fascinating melody.

Bud joined in, singing bass in a quiet, mellow tone. The boys dreamily kept their gaze on the rippling surface of the water, letting the magical beauty of the song wash over them. Their minds drifted and wandered, and slowly they began to doze.

In his mind's eye, Travis saw meadows dotted with trees around Tarv's house. The sun had already set, and only an outline of the trees could be seen on the hilly horizon. A few wispy clouds, high in the sky, shone bright red in the light of the setting sun. Multitudes of people had gathered there, dressed in simple village clothing. They sang what seemed to be many parts and yet with one voice. There were women with small children in their arms and young boys and girls on the banks dangling their feet in the river. There were fathers sitting on the grass with children on their knees. There were older men and women sitting on blankets and leaning back on trees or stones. There were young lovers sitting side by side, sharing a blanket, and there were dogs of all shapes and sizes, curled up asleep beside their masters. The people sang; how they sang! It was as if all creation was lifting up its voice in a single celebration of all that was beautiful and wonderful. Without any conductor, choirmaster, or organization, and yet with perfect order, their voices rose and united into one.

By the time Clara had finished her song, both boys were sound asleep, so Bud and Clara left them for a while. Bud woke them up late in the afternoon, and after sitting down to cake and root tea, the boys made their way home.

CHAPTER 6

Rawley

In the years that followed, the rough, unfriendly soldiers of the kingdom were seen more and more in the forest, and in ever greater numbers. They ran "patrols" and became more daring by the year. In earlier years they had hurried through the forest as quickly as possible so as not to arouse interest, but now they acted as if they owned the place, taking long breaks beside village wells and leaving their rubbish behind them. Dorn feared that a confrontation would lead to violence and that the first drop of blood would throw the forest into a savage war—a war the forest people would likely lose.

Dorn's dark clouds of fear gathered over the whole village and settled in like a chilling winter fog. There were bright spots, though. Bud and Clara's child grew and prospered as growing boys should, becoming what Clara called their "little sunbeam" who drove the clouds away. They named the child Todd after an uncle of Clara's who, in her view, had the same twinkle in his eye and the same enormous interest in the world around him.

A great deal could be told of Todd's growing up. He was a curious little lad with an active mind and an equally active body. Clara and Bud found themselves constantly running after the tot, who always wanted to pick everything up and examine it, be it a snail, a snake, or anything else. There were also endless questions around the dinner table. One evening he was especially occupied with the sun:

"The midsummer sun always sets at 9:30, but how does it know what time it is? And is it like Dad, who sometimes gets behind and has to catch up? And who wakes the sun up in the morning so that it never comes late? And when I throw a ball up, and it falls to the ground, it bounces, but why doesn't the sun ever bounce when it falls to the ground? It sets in the western sky but rises in the east. Who carries it over to the east every night? Or are there many suns, and every day a new one flies across the sky? And if it flies then where are the wings? And . . ."

Needless to say, even though his parents loved him dearly, they often breathed a sigh of relief when he fell asleep for the evening

Our story picks up again when Todd was twelve or thirteen. He had become not just the apple of his parents' eyes but a favorite throughout the village. His best buddies were Travis and Brody, who were now strapping lads of twenty and twenty-one who both towered over their father.

A cool autumn day was ending, and Bud and Todd were on their way home after their last delivery of flour. The birds were making short, darting flights before going to their special roosting places. The sun was beginning to fade, and their mules looked forward to being home and in their stalls.

Nature was preparing for her time of rest and quietness. Not Todd, though.

"Hey, Dad! Let me show you a new trick!" said Todd. He wasn't surprised to hear a deep sigh from Bud, who cast a weary glance over at his son.

Todd pulled up his knees until he was kneeling on the back of his mule. Then he stretched his whole body out along the neck of the mule till he reached its ears. "Look! I can steer her with her ears!" The admiring grin that grew on Bud's face filled Todd with joy. Indeed, he made the mule walk a few circles, steering it by its ears.

"Well, I'll be!" said Bud with a smile. "If I tried that she would dump me on the ground in no time! How do you do it?"

"Well, I asked her beforehand," said Todd in a matter-of-fact way, all the while struggling to keep his balance on the neck of a circling mule, "and she said okay."

"As easy as that?" asked Bud.

"As easy as that. Mules aren't like people. They don't get angry."

"Yes . . ." said Bud, who had wanted to say something more but was struck by Todd's words.

On they went again, side by side, without a word. All was quiet except the swirling evening breeze, a few birds here and there, and the rustle of feet and hooves through the dry leaves. It was a scene Todd had seen a hundred times, and yet it never lost its flavor. After a while he slid back down to Daisy's back and gave her a big hug around the neck.

"Why are they all angry?" asked Todd out of the blue, surprising himself with his own question.

"Who?"

"Well, I don't know. Everyone!"

"Angry?"

"Yes, they're all angry."

"It's true. Yes," said Bud, rubbing his moustache as he always did when he was deep in thought.

"Is it the money?"

"What money?"

"The money Dorn gave the soldiers."

"You heard about that?"

"Brody told me."

"Hmmm," said Bud. Todd knew the disturbed look on his face all too well. "I don't know. I really don't."

"Do you hate the soldiers, Dad?"

"No! I don't hate them. I hate what they do."

"But everyone hates them."

"No, they don't. Not everyone!"

"Okay, most people. I guess the singers don't."

"You can't hate and sing the song at the same time," said Bud, as though talking to himself. "People hate and are angry when they feel helpless. They are feeling kind of desperate."

"Are you feeling desperate, Dad?"

"I'm doing my best not to."

Todd looked down the road. With such talks it was much easier for both just to look down the road than to look at each other. A hawk had perched high on a branch over the road and was bathing in the evening sun. The tossing to and fro of the branch by the breeze did not seem to bother it. The wisps of cloud overhead had almost all turned orange, a sign that it was high time to get home.

"Hey, Dad. Do you think that—" But his question was interrupted by a startling sight as they rounded a curve in the road. A familiar bent old man was almost staggering along the road.

"Rawley!" shouted Bud in astonishment, and dropping the reins of his mule, he ran and grabbed the old man by the shoulder. "Are you all right?"

The old man gazed into Bud's eyes with a puzzled look, and said, "Bud. Bud, is that you?"

"It's me! It's me all right," said Bud. "What on earth are you doing out here so late?"

"Out here? . . . So late?" The old man stared around in a bewilderment that sent a shiver down Todd's back. There was a childlike lostness on the face of this man that Todd did not like at all.

"Where's Sonny?" asked Bud, looking around for the old man's son.

"Sonny? Yes, Sonny! I sent him home." Rawley seemed somehow to come to himself again. "Yes, that's right. I sent him home. You see, Bud, we were almost home, and I realized that we had left a lamb behind."

"And Sonny let you go back into the forest alone at this hour?" muttered Bud angrily.

"Don't be angry, Bud!" said Rawley in a faint, trembling voice. "I forced him to go on, because otherwise his mother would worry."

"You look just terrible!" said Bud.

Todd had to strain to hear the words of the shaking old man. "I couldn't find the lamb in the meadow, and I looked and looked. I had forgotten to take water, and somehow I just got slower and slower, and then I was walking around not knowing where I was."

"Todd, can you?" called Bud, never taking his eyes from Rawley.

Like a flash, Todd was off his mule with his waterskin in his hand.

"Here," said Todd, holding the skin up to Rawley and grasping his shoulder.

The old man took the waterskin in his quivering hands, and as soon as Bud had untied the opening, he drank with delight. In his trembling, he spilled about half of it down his beard and onto his dirty jacket. Todd was amazed to find Rawley's shoulder cold and wet, as though he was sweating while shivering with the cold. Something was very, very wrong.

When Rawley finished, Todd took the skin from his trembling hand. Rawley took a couple of deep, slow breaths and looked deeply into Todd's eyes, almost as if he had seen something there and was searching them for more.

"Thank you," he said, and as Todd looked into his searching eyes, he could not help but feel a surge of affection for this dear old man.

"Ma-ah-ah," came the bleating of a lamb. All eyes looked down to a very young lamb pressing itself close to the back of Rawley's legs.

"So you're the troublemaker, are you?" said Bud with a broad smile. He seemed very relieved that Rawley was feeling better.

"We had better put your master on a mule and get him home before dark."

"He's a dear little thing, isn't he?" said Rawley, stooping over and picking the lamb up with a great grunt.

"He is!" said Todd, running his hand through the lamb's soft wool. It seemed content in Rawley's arms despite getting shaken around.

"I'll get my mule ready, and we'll—" began Bud when a trumpet blast nearby interrupted him.

"A patrol!" shouted Bud curtly. "Everyone off to the side. I'll get the mules!"

True enough. Everyone suddenly heard the clatter of hoofbeats.

Bud looked over at Todd and shouted, "You stay with Rawley!"

Todd said nothing but looked over to Rawley, who was standing at the edge of the road caressing his nervous little lamb, and that disturbing, confused look returned to his face. Bud strong-armed the mules away to the other side of the road. The hoofbeats grew louder and louder from just around the curve, and the trumpeter blew another warning blast as they grew thunderously loud.

With a start, the terrified little lamb leapt out of Rawley's arms and ran across the road.

"No!" cried Rawley. He lunged forward to grab the lamb, staggering clumsily into the road. Todd tried to catch him, but the cloth of Rawley's jacket slipped through his hand, and suddenly the old man was stumbling into the middle of the road just as the horses burst around the corner.

He disappeared with a shriek amongst the horses as a patrol of about fifteen men rounded the curve in great haste. It was all dust and cries, voices and confusion before the lead soldier shouted and the trumpeter blew again. The soldiers stopped and took a circular formation. Todd gasped as he saw Rawley's body curled up on the ground among them. Before he knew it he had rushed between two horses and was kneeling at

Rawley's side. Somewhere in the back of his mind he heard Bud's voice shouting, "No!" but that all seemed like a dream.

Todd gasped as he saw Rawley lying there with his face in the dirt. His mouth was wide open, and his tongue hung out the side on the dirt. He was breathing with great difficulty, and there was blood everywhere. One soldier dropped down suddenly from his horse. He was tall and broad shouldered, and unusually fat for a soldier. The furious scowl on his chubby face made Todd want to run and hide.

Todd shuddered as the soldier picked Rawley up by the collar and screamed in his ear.

"You stupid old fool! Look at my boot! Look at this boot!" He jerked Rawley's head over to where it dangled just over his right boot. The top of the boot was torn. "What do you have to say, peasant? You tore my boot!" Rawley hung there limp, with bits of dirt falling out if his mouth at every jolt and jerk that came from the soldier. The soldier screamed into his ear, "WHAT DO YOU HAVE TO SAY?"

Todd stared in amazement, down on his knees in the middle of the group. He was terrified and unable to move. His heart told him to help, to do something, but what could he do?

The motionless body gave no reply.

"If you're going to kill the rat, Maldon, then hurry up and do it now," said the rider in the lead. "We have to be in camp before dark."

"Hey, Maldon! Do the neck trick! I want to hear it break from here!" another soldier shouted.

"We always do the neck trick. Use your spear, Maldon! We haven't done that in a while."

Todd couldn't believe his ears. A sick, dreadful feeling came over him. These men around him seemed less and less human and more and more demonic.

"At least wake the old fool up. It's no fun killing someone when he is unconscious!" shouted a wicked voice with a twisted, ugly laugh. This was followed by lots of laughs and jeers, each more villainous than the one before. Maldon was loving the tumult and what seemed to Todd to be a wild celebration of everything that was evil.

Another voice, dripping with disdain, broke through the cackle and shut everyone up: "Would you children hurry up? We have to get back before dark!"

There was silence. A thunderous silence, bursting with tension.

"Children? *Children*?" screamed Maldon, turning around. He dropped Rawley as though he were a sack of potatoes and stalked over to the soldier who had spoken. Todd stared at Rawley's motionless body on the ground and began silently begging the Lord of the Forest to spare his life.

"You've always got to get your word in, don't you, Bates? You've always got to find your chance to play the big chap!" spat Maldon with a look of hateful contempt.

"We're running a fast trot because we're late!" replied the soldier with a sneer. "You idiots are making us even later, and for what? A few stupid laughs."

Maldon smiled with a fiendishly ugly grin and took a few steps over to Bates. "Ah, does little Batesy want to get home on time so Mummy can read him a story and tuck him in before it's late?"

A few of the soldiers burst out laughing, but others were very still, and Todd felt his every muscle tighten up.

"You made us late in the first place with all your carrying on at the camp!" replied Bates bluntly, not showing the slightest fear.

"And poor little Batesy had to wait around," snarled Maldon with ever greater aggression and less humor. "Does Batesy want to run the troop and tell us when and where to go?"

"I mounted my horse on the first trumpet blast, as did most of us. These are the sergeant's orders, not mine!" growled Bates.

"Well! Our little Batesy—he's a big man, with things to do and people to see!" hissed Maldon with such poison that there was not a laugh or chuckle to be heard. "He doesn't even have time to let his chums finish their lunch! If he's so very important, then why after all these years in the army is our Batesy still *only a corporal?*"

It was dead silent.

Bates flew with a single leap from his horse, bursting with rage. He was also a big man. Before Todd knew what was happening, both men had their swords drawn.

"I follow the orders of our sergeant—not of some half-wit private!" Todd shuddered as Bates's face blackened, and his eyes sparked with an evil hatred that seemed to come from the very depths of hell. Even his voice changed. "You can kill as many of these forest scum as you choose, but you do not mess with me, unless you want my sword through your liver!"

Maldon seemed taken aback. Todd could see the same surprise, even horror in his eyes that he himself also felt. To see this respectable soldier turn into a fiend before his eyes was rather more than he had expected. Nonetheless, with all the strength Maldon could muster, he gazed right into the devilish fire in Bates's wild eyes and growled, "Put the sword away, Bates!"

Instead, Bates started wielding his sword to the right and to the left, as though warming up for the battle. His movements were the fine, disciplined strokes of a skilled swordsman, and he seemed to take great pleasure in them.

"Come on, Maldon!" said he. "You love your sword! Oh, yes! I've seen you play with it, I have. Women and children! Yes, they're your specialty. You're a big man too, aren't you?— when it comes to women and children, and old men like this one, and your lunch!"

Bates let out a wild, sick laugh. "Let's see what you're really made of! Come on!"

"Put the sword away!" said Maldon in a slow, threatening voice that did nothing to hide his fear.

"I'll put it away once it's dripping with your blood!" snarled Bates as he started approaching his enemy.

A trumpet blast stopped him. Everybody froze.

"That's enough!" shouted the sergeant, whose half of the troop had ridden up from behind while everyone was too riveted on the duel to notice. "Swords away! Immediately! You will remount, and we will continue to our destination."

This was followed by another terrifying silence as both men stood in the ring exchanging hateful stares.

"Now!" screamed the sergeant. "Remount!"

"What about the old man?" shouted a voice from among the soldiers.

The sergeant cast a glance at Rawley, apparently noticing him for the first time. "Do with him what you want, but be fast!"

"Ha!" said Maldon, jumping down from his horse. The soldier wanted to use this to save face. But before he could reach Rawley, someone stepped in between them. It was Bud.

"Sorry about your boot," said Bud in a calm, easy voice.

"'Sorry' doesn't help me much!" replied Maldon.

"This should be more than enough to buy you a new pair of boots," said Bud as he held out a leather bag of coins.

The soldier took the bag and opened it up. A villainous smile came across his face, and he leaned forward. "You just saved Grandpa's life, you know that?"

Bud didn't flinch. He just coolly replied, "Well, that's good."

"Remount!" shouted the sergeant.

After a few short commands they were all in formation, and then they were gone, almost as quickly as they had come. Todd found himself staring down the road after them as though he were in a trance. It was Bud who brought him back into this world, as he pushed past him and knelt down beside Rawley. Bud scooped the old man up, held his head close to his chest, and uttered a few quiet words of prayer. As Bud held him and rocked him back and forth a little, Rawley opened his eyes.

"Sonny?" he asked.

"No, it's me, Bud!"

"Bud? Bud! Yes, of course," said Rawley in barely more than a whisper. "And the soldiers?"

"They're gone."

A short time passed as Bud held Rawley in his arms, giving the old man time to gather his strength and wits. After a while, Rawley glanced over at Todd and gasped.

"Owen! Owen Silas! It's you!" Immediately full of life, Rawley struggled to sit up as he stared into Todd's face. "Can it really be you, Owen?" He stretched out his hands to touch Todd's face, and gently running his fingers from Todd's ears down his cheeks as a blind man might do, he blurted, "Owen! After all these years! You're back! You're back!"

Todd had absolutely no idea what to say, and Bud, who was never at a loss for words, just sat there with eyes like saucers. Instead of correcting Rawley, he said nothing.

After a few long moments of silence, Bud cleared his throat. "Todd, bring Daisy over, will you?"

As Todd went to get his mule, he stumbled over something. It was the body of the lamb, crushed under the horses' hoofs. Stopping to look at it, Todd felt the sickness in the bottom of his stomach grow.

It seemed a lifetime ago when Todd had caressed the lamb's warm, soft wool as it lay in Rawley's arms. Something horrible had happened, and it had changed something decisively—but Todd did not know yet what that was.

They put Rawley on Daisy's back, and with Bud on one side and Todd on the other, they walked him into the village. Laying him out in bed, they were able to see that he had no broken bones, just a lot of cuts and bruises.

For Bud and Todd, it had been a singularly horrible day. But for Rawley, it was one of the happiest of his life—because on this day, *he had seen Owen Silas again.*

CHAPTER 7

Owen Silas

It was an odd evening—unlike any Clara had ever seen. Bud and Todd had come home quite late after bringing Rawley home and stopping to have a short talk with Dorn. Bud told her the story, eating heartily but nervously the whole time, and Todd sat staring blankly at the candle flickering in the middle of the table.

She had seen this expression on Todd's face many times before. It was an uncomfortable bewilderment at the world and its very peculiar inhabitants. Tonight, though, it was particularly serious. The experience of many years had taught her to make sure Todd ate enough and send him off to bed. When the questions were ripe, they would fall from the tree themselves. The secret was not to shake the tree, but rather to wait patiently in the garden.

"Come on, sleepyhead! Finish up your bread and hop off to bed," said she with particular tenderness.

"Oh, yes," said Todd distantly, never taking his eyes from the candle.

With only a few more reminders, Todd finished his supper, gave both Bud and Clara their evening hugs, and went off to bed. The evening drew to a close, and Clara was the last one up. As she walked around blowing out the last candles and lanterns, she noticed that both Bud and Todd had left things lying around in the most disorderly way. Normally they would have been yanked out of bed by the matron of the house and given a stern word, but not tonight.

It must have been shocking, she thought as she picked up bits of clothing that had been thoughtlessly dumped on the floor. Bud's nervousness and Todd's silence both spoke of the same thing—a horrible experience for which the human soul did not have a drawer or a cupboard to put it away in. What had happened was a big ugly thing that needed to be broken down into little bits and could only be put away over a long time, piece by piece.

The more she cleared up, the more she felt that she needed to check on Todd. When everything was done, she took the last lit candle over to his bed. As she expected, he was lying with his eyes wide open, staring out into the star-filled sky.

She sat down and took his hand in hers.

"You okay?" she asked.

"Yes."

Nothing more was said, but Clara knew very well that her presence was welcome.

After a long silence Todd said, "You know, Mom. I've see Gerlor the baker get mean, really mean—but he was angry. He was really angry because we knocked his woodpile down."

"Yes," said Clara.

"He's not always mean, you know. We just made him mean. We got him angry." Todd paused for a minute and added, "But these soldiers are always mean, even when no one makes them angry."

"Yes, that's true."

There was another long silence. Clara peered out the window to see the stars flickering clearly in the black sky.

"Mom," continued Todd, "Dad once told me that wolves and foxes are also dogs."

"Yes, that's what people say."

"Our dogs are friendly and happy, but wolves are always fierce, right?"

"Well, to us they're always fierce."

"And we can never make friends with them, can we?"

"No, that's true."

"Are people like dogs? You know what I mean. Are some people like dogs, and some people like wolves?"

"Hmmm," said Clara, pondering what she should answer.

"Travis says that if there are many wolves, they travel around in packs and kill all the dogs. They don't want any dogs in their territory."

Clara could sense the increasing fear and tension in his words. She knew that big fears must be attacked with a battle axe and not a butter knife, so she went straight for the point.

"And you're wondering if there is any difference between a pack of wolves and a patrol of soldiers."

"Exactly!" said Todd, breathing a big sigh of relief to have the big ugly question out on the table where everyone could see it.

Clara began speaking, although she was far from sure what she should say. "Todd, I can only give you one answer. There have been dogs and wolves for a very long time, and the wolves have never killed off all the dogs. What do you think? Here in the forest, what do we have more of, dogs or wolves?

"Dogs, I guess."

"Yes, that's right. There are lots more dogs. And you know why?"

"No."

"Because someone takes care of them. The wolves are out on their own, and have to fight for themselves. But dogs belong to someone, and someone takes care of them. In the same way, Todd, we belong to someone. And he takes care of us."

"Hmmm," said Todd rather distantly. This was certainly a comforting thought, but it didn't take away the horror of the day. "That was awful, today."

"I'm sure." Clara sensed the lostness of a child losing his childhood world and only wished she knew what to say. She ached with regret that Todd had seen such a thing. She squeezed his warm soft hand and suddenly blurted out, "I'm so sorry! I really am! We've been . . ." and then she stopped as suddenly as she had started, realizing that she was about to betray a long-kept secret.

"You've been . . .?" asked Todd, sitting up with great attention. He was well aware that there had been secrets.

"We've been trying to keep you from seeing all this."

"That's why you didn't let me go with Travis and Brody to Maywater, right?"

"Yes, it is."

"And why we never go to the east road market."

"Yes, you're right." There was a long torturous silence, after which she choked out, "I don't know if that was right, Son. I really don't." A wave of grief rolled over Clara as she thought back on all her efforts to hide the world from Todd. At the same time she was now furious with herself that she had just blurted everything out without the slightest thought whatsoever. It was all so utterly confusing. She regretted both hiding the truth and telling the truth.

Bitter memories of her childhood returned, and here she was again, in a world far bigger than she could cope with. But now it was different again, because she held in her hand that dear treasure that she cherished more than the world. He is so dear, and so fragile. Were he to fall on the ugly rocks of this world, he would surely shatter into a thousand pieces. This was a thought she could not bear.

"Well Mom, I have seen it now," replied Todd in an even sober tone.

"You have," Clara heard her own voice reply.

"I've been wondering what Travis and Brody are talking about, and why they get so angry. Everyone's angry, Mom! . . . and kind of afraid!"

"I think they feel helpless," said Clara.

"That's what Dad says."

For whatever reason the waves of grief rolling over Clara were growing stronger and more desperate and she felt driven by an earnest longing to make everything alright.

"I'm sorry! I'm so sorry!" The lump in her throat almost choked out her words, and then the first tear raced down her burning cheeks.

"It's okay, Mom," said Todd and reached forward to take his mother in his arms. Clara buried her head in the chest of the boy she had wanted to comfort. Sorrow flooded her soul and as the tears flowed she suddenly found herself not in the arms of a boy, but in the arms of a man, whose calm steady breathing and strong silence gave her great peace. The grief was somehow broken and Clara felt Todd's hand caressing the back of her neck.

"You didn't mean any harm in it," said Todd quietly. How often had she heard those words from Bud? They were often used to comfort Todd, who in his clumsiness had broken a lot of things. It was wonderful to hear these words from her son's lips, with the same affection, care and strength that his father had.

Bud had told Clara that something had happened to Todd in that evening, and now she had seen it for herself. After a long time of sitting still together, Todd said, "Mom, did you hear what Rawley said?"

"About Owen Silas?"

"Yes"

"Your father told me."

"Do you know who he is?"

"I do. He's been dead for a good long time now. I think Rawley knew him when he was a child."

"Who was he?"

A faraway look came over her eyes. "He was a hero." She smiled. "Or so they say. Owen was actually a small man, probably as big as you are now. People say he lived somewhere in this area. The story goes that he was weeding a field of barley beside a well when a group of the king's soldiers came through, supposedly looking for horses which had been stolen. Owen suddenly noticed a young man among them wearing chains on his feet. The soldiers ordered the young man to give all the horses water to drink from the well, but this was very difficult because of the short chain between his legs. Every time he fell, they mocked him and laughed at him and kicked him if he wasn't fast enough getting up."

"So not much has changed," said Todd.

"Soldiers are soldiers!" said Clara. "That's normal in the kingdom, but not here in the forest. Owen had never seen anything like it. He was burning with anger and yet trembling with fear. He wanted to step in and speak, but seeing the other villagers standing around saying nothing, he did the same.

"The patrol soon left, and as Owen remained there in the barley field, his blood boiled. How could he have stood there, doing nothing? How could his own people have held their peace? He tried not to think about it and to keep working, but he was so confused and angry that he could barely even tell weed from barley. Finally he went to the well, hoping that a drink would bring him back to his senses. As he came to the well, do you know what he saw on the ground?"

Todd shook his head, wide-eyed.

"A key! He picked it up, and as he did the voice of the Lord of the Forest spoke to him very clearly: 'Go! Now!'"

"Well, that was all that he needed to hear. He ran to his house, got his donkey, and galloped as fast as the beast could go. He caught up with the soldiers toward evening. They were still in the forest and had set up camp to stay the night. Owen crept to the edge of the clearing and watched the soldiers carefully until they had all gone to sleep.

"That night, the Lord of the Forest put them into a deep sleep. Owen crept in under the light of the moon and found the chained young man. His foot had been chained to a fat soldier who lay snoring beside him. Owen roused the young man, who watched him silently. He pulled out the key that opened the fetters, pocketed the key again, and they both crept as quietly as possible back into the forest.

"I don't know what happened then, but suddenly the dogs started barking and Owen and the young man were seen. They dashed wildly into the forest with men and dogs behind them. Something told Owen to climb the trees, so that is what he and the young man did. They went up, and up and up, higher than Owen had ever climbed. The soldiers searched for them all night and for most of the next day, but with no luck. It was then that Owen realized that when you are high in the trees in the deep forest you cannot be seen, and this gave him an idea."

"Owen knew the soldiers would come again, and many more with them, because the king would not take this affront to his power without revenge. He called his friends together—there were many young men whose hearts beat as his did—and they made a plan to chase the soldiers out of the forest.

"After about two weeks, a messenger of the king came demanding the heads of both 'criminals' to be taken back to the king. The chief at that time replied that the forest people were under the rules of the Lord of the Forest and that this demand would break those rules and was neither right nor wise. The messenger left angry, vowing that revenge would soon come upon them."

"Owen and Rufus, the young man he had saved, and all the men they had gathered together, had used the time to make treehouses way up in the trees, deep in the forest. They made a network of rope bridges from tree top to tree top and placed supplies of food, arrows, and spears in these little treehouses. They were all together with one heart to fight."

"After another six weeks a brightly colored cavalry followed by a multitude of foot soldiers marched into the forest with orders to hang the chief from a tree and take as many slaves as possible. Well, they didn't know what hit them! Arrows fell like rain upon them wherever they went, whatever they did. The forest people chased them out of the forest without even being seen. And no soldier set his foot in the forest for fifty years after that!"

"But they're here again. More than ever before," said Todd, puzzled.

"Yes, you're right. That's why a lot of people are hoping for . . ." Clara grew suddenly silent.

" . . . for another Owen Silas," said Todd, dryly, finishing her sentence.

"Yes, but you know what my Uncle Harny used to say?"

"No."

"Well, he was a great hunter, and made all his own arrows. I can still hear him like it was yesterday:

"All of my arrows are exactly the same, but you never know what the Lord is going to pull out of his quiver!"

"And, you know, Todd. I think he's right. The Lord often uses the oddest, most unlikely people."

"Why?"

"I don't know. It's his world. He can do what he wants," said Clara with a smile.

Todd could not help by smile, too. Some things were just that simple.

"There is, though, something that all of the people he uses have in common," said Clara in a sudden serious and philosophical voice.

"What?" said Todd sitting up with curiosity.

"They all get enough sleep!" said she with great triumph, unable to keep herself from laughing.

Todd let out a deep sigh, and in the faint flickering candle light Clara saw how he shook his head and rolled his eyes, doing his best to fight off a smile.

"Thanks, Mom," said Todd, giving her hand a final squeeze.

"You sleep well, Son," she said, leaning over and kissing him on the forehead. In no time the candle was out, and she, too, crawled into bed, and although they were both very tired it took them a good long time before they finally fell asleep.

CHAPTER 8

A Surprise

The next day was a day like any other, except for the fact that the village was buzzing with the news of Rawley's mishap with the soldiers, and at every delivery that Bud and Todd made, people gathered around to hear the story.

Todd was very relieved that Bud never mentioned Rawley mistaking him for Owen Silas. That was something that Bud, too, obviously wanted to keep quiet.

The walk home was unusually somber and without any mule-riding tricks. Todd felt like tricks and chatter belonged to another life—a life he had now left behind. Even the silence they shared along the way home was different.

As they arrived at the mill, Todd saw Brody and Travis down on the riverbank fishing. His eyes lit up. "Hey, Dad, can I stay outside till supper?"

"Yeah, sure you can," said Bud with a smile. "We'll call you when we're ready."

With a holler, Todd handed his mule over to Bud and ran across the grass to the river. The meadow was covered with dry, fallen leaves that crackled under his feet. "Hi, guys! Catch anything yet?"

"A couple of nibbles," said Brody, looking up with a broad grin.

"We've been waiting for you!" said Travis.

"You've got to tell us what happened!" said Brody, flattening the grass between himself and his brother to prepare Todd a place to sit.

The fishing lines were dropped in total disinterest as both brothers' eyes and ears were fixed on Todd. He carefully recounted all that had happened, and he could not help feeling older somehow as Brody and Travis hung on every word.

"This is just so terrible!" said Travis, whose eyes were aflame with emotion.

"And Dad's getting all weird again," said Brody.

"Yes, we had another one of those big elder meetings till late last night," added Travis. "Same old story—lots of talk, no action."

"They decided that this was an 'isolated incident'!" said Brody, mimicking the serious tone of some elder.

"An isolated what?" asked Todd.

"An isolated incident" said Brody, waving his finger in the air as though he were saying something profound and weighty.

"That was Georg the tanner's new word," added Travis dryly.

"Did you know that Georg is an expert on absolutely everything?" said Brody with a sarcastic grin.

"Really?" asked Todd.

"Yes, just ask him! He'll tell you. He's even an expert on things he knows nothing about."

"And the terrible thing is that Dad listens to him!" said Travis in disgust.

"What's an isolated incident?" asked Todd.

Throwing himself into the role of Georg the tanner, Brody breathed in deeply, pumping up his chest in importance: "An isolated incident, my boy, is an incident that has no relation whatsoever to anything else. It is something that happens all on its own and is not part of any trend or development."

"Huh?"

"It's something that happens alone! And because it happens alone, it has no meaning,"

"And because it has no meaning, nobody has to do anything about it," added Travis with evident frustration.

"You see, because it just happened once, out on the road, it is as if it never happened," said Brody pompously. Smugly, he added, "What could be clearer, my boy?"

Todd could not hide how puzzled he felt.

"It doesn't have to make sense, Todd," said Brody in his normal voice. "It just has to sound good. According to Georg, what happened to you yesterday was as meaningless as a leaf falling in the forest."

"But when a leaf falls, that shows that times are changing and winter is coming!" said Todd.

"Exactly! Exactly, Todd! But when you don't want to do *anything,* you can talk your way out of *everything,*" said Travis.

A cold, unhappy silence rested on all three. Todd's mind was a whirl and tumble of thoughts and images from the last couple of days.

Travis picked up his fishing rod in a renewed attempt to do some fishing and tried to get his hook further out into the river. His actions were all clumsy and tense, and Todd could see that fishing was the very last thing on his mind.

Travis finally threw his rod down, turned to the other two, and blurted out, "You know, it just won't let me go. It's getting worse and worse. Dad and the elders are never going to do anything!"

"And?" Brody asked.

"And," continued Travis, "*somebody's* got to do something. *We've* got to do something!"

"Us?" Brody asked.

"Us!"

"What are we going to do?"

"I don't know. No idea!"

Silence fell again, but this time it was a different silence. It was an *I-can't-believe-he-said-that* silence. Todd stared out across the glassy surface of the water and thought. He could only think about one thing—or rather one person. Owen Silas.

"Do you guys know the story of Owen Silas?" he asked.

"No," came the replies.

Todd told the story as he remembered it. The older boys listened intently and exchanged a loaded glance at the end.

"Why doesn't Dad tell us stories like that?" asked Brody at the end.

Travis was silent—utterly silent. He was looking out over the river but was obviously somewhere very different in his thoughts. "Come with me!" he suddenly said. Without any more warning than that, he dropped his fishing rod and started running toward the forest.

"Travis, what are you doing?" called Brody, but there was no reply. Brody jogged after his brother. Poor Todd could barely keep up.

"Travis, what's with you? Wait up!" Brody called as they ran deeper and deeper into the forest, but it was no use. Travis ran ahead without slowing. Brody lagged behind so he could keep both him and Todd in sight.

Soon enough, Travis stopped. Brody and then Todd arrived shortly after him. As Todd leaned against a great oak tree, gasping to get his breath, he looked around. They stood in a small clearing like any other, surrounded by enormous oak and beech trees and with a little brook winding through it.

"What on earth's got into you?" asked Brody, perplexed.

"Look up this tree," said Travis.

"Where? What?"

"Way up there, in the oak here, just above those beech branches." Travis pointed almost directly up.

Todd saw it first. He gasped. Way up in the oak nestled what seemed to be cut sticks attached to a kind of framework.

"A treehouse?" asked Brody.

"I think so!" Travis said. He looked at them with his eyes alight. "Let's go!"

In no time, they were on their way. Travis led them up and up and up, higher than they had ever climbed, but in the very difficult places they found notches cut out of the tree or old ropes with knots hanging from above. The ropes seemed very old but easily held their weight.

Up, up, up they went, so high that the ground was hard to see through all of the leaves. Travis and Brody waited for Todd, helping him up where necessary, and they all finally arrived at a circular platform that surrounded the thick trunk, as did a roof about five and a half feet above it. Todd was the only one who could stand up straight under it. He remembered something his mother had said—*Owen Silas was a small man, about the height that you are now.*

Todd was overcome with awe as he looked around. Bags made of leather and sealed in tar were tied to the roof and hung down in clusters. There were many of them, in all sizes and shapes, and they had lasted well over the years. He ran his fingers over the bags lightly, as though handling a sacred treasure. Images of burly, rugged men filled his mind, tying, hoisting, cutting, fitting—it must have been grand, truly grand. They were preparing for that great day, that day of all or nothing when everything they'd done would prove to be an amazing victory or a horrific mistake, and who could know?

Todd's hands fumbled with a mix of fear and excitement as he and the others starting taking the bags down and looking inside. In them were knives and spears, bows and arrows, tools, dried fruit, and flints and tinderboxes to make fires. It was like nothing they had ever seen.

Todd noticed a round piece of bark that looked somehow unusual. As he touched it, it suddenly fell to the floor, revealing a hole behind it in the tree. He reached into the hole and pulled out a key tied to a note.

They all gathered round to look at it. Engraved on the key was the name "Owen Silas." The note said:

> *Here is the key that bears my name,*
>
> *Take it boldly and do the same.*

It was on that evening that the three made a solemn promise to create a secret league. They would take the key and so accept its duty as their own. When the time was right, it would be their job to free the forest of soldiers.

They had no idea how they would do it, but they felt sure they would know when the time was right.

CHAPTER 9

The Intruder

The cool, windy days of autumn gave way to the cold and snowy days of winter. Our three heroes spent every spare minute they could find fixing up the treehouse, stocking up supplies, repairing rope ladders, and even building a few rope bridges from tree to tree. They had a lot done by the time spring came, and instead of their zeal fading away as the days went by, it seemed to grow with each finished task.

Todd loved those early spring days right after the ice and snow had fully melted. He found it wonderful to smell something again in the formerly frozen forest, even if it was mud. The birds were back in greater numbers and intent on making their presence known. The buds were swelling and bursting as the trees woke up from their winter sleep. All spring seasons are celebrations, but this one was special somehow—there was something new and wonderful in the air.

It was on one such day that Bud and Todd arrived home early from delivering flour. The day's deliveries hadn't been far, and they got home unusually early. Bud decided to putter around the mill, so Todd took the opportunity to go out to the treehouse again. The lads had met there so often lately that beaten paths were developing on the forest floor. Todd made a note of that with a frown—they would have to make a point of coming from different directions. There was no use in leaving a clear path to the fort for the soldiers to find!

As he came to the great oak, he noticed that the rope ladders going from branch to branch were hanging down in plain sight. This was unusual. Surely Brody and Travis would never leave anything like that.

Todd gave the secret cry, a repeated cuckoo call, but no answer was to be heard. There was clearly something wrong.

Todd climbed up the ladders quickly, stopping now and again to look down to the forest floor. It was a beautiful, cool afternoon, but far from enjoying it, Todd could only focus on the thought of an intruder in their treehouse. The more he thought of it, the more his stomach tangled in knots. It wasn't just a house, it was the center of a dream—the dream of freeing the forest from the king's soldiers, and maybe more importantly, of freeing the forest people from their own sleepiness and carelessness. The dream had become everything for the three lads. It was what they spoke about when together, what they dreamt about in bed, and what they thought about while walking along the way. And now an enemy was mucking around with their treehouse!

A chill went down Todd's spine, and he paused in midclimb. Had the king's soldiers found out about it? It couldn't be!

Up he rushed, getting wilder as he went. Finally he got to the platform and climbed on to have a look. His heart sank. Someone had opened up the dried fruit bags. Someone had eaten from the dried bread rations and drunk from the water and apple cider. The blankets had obviously been used.

Todd's blood boiled, and again he began searching for any traces of the enemy. Climbing out on a branch, he searched the forest floor for any clue. There! Down by the creek he saw something moving. Fixing his eyes upon it, he could make out what looked like a head of dark brown hair and a white shirt.

"Axelon!" he said in disgust. Todd could not stand the village boy, who was about his own age. Axelon and his stupid friends had called Todd every name you could imagine—the the miller's mongrel, the singer-freak's son, and the list went on. Axelon was a big and a strong lad, but that wouldn't stop Todd now. He was going to beat him no matter what it took and ensure that he and his gang would never come near the treehouse again.

The ladders swung violently as he descended, and it was only when he almost fell that he stopped and deliberately calmed himself down. He needed to proceed quietly. Should he get Travis and Brody? No! This was his battle, and despite being smaller than his enemy, he was determined to win it.

He came silently to the bottom of the tree and moved with great care over to where Axelon was sitting. He crouched behind a thick bush and listened—it sounded as though the intruder was washing his hands in the creek. This was the perfect opportunity.

Todd leapt out from the bush and flew with full force into his enemy. The two went crashing onto the sandy bank of the creek, and as Todd raised his fist for the first punch, he stopped.

This was not Axelon. Before him he saw a girl about his own age, staring up at him in terror.

Todd pulled back and toppled off the girl more quickly than you could imagine.

"I'm so sorry. I really am sorry. I thought you were . . . I mean, I didn't know you were . . . Have I hurt you? Are you okay?" Todd's face burned with shame and regret, and he wanted nothing more than for her to smile and tell him it was okay.

She didn't oblige. Instead, she looked dreadfully afraid. The girl, who had backed away and now leaned back on her arms on the bank, looked about his height, with a lovely but deathly pale face. Her thick brown hair hung in locks past her shoulders; Todd found it beautiful even though it was caked with mud and dirt. Her dress was dirty and in tatters but had obviously once been a fine garment.

"Who are you?" asked Todd, but she gave no reply. She only stared into his face, trembling all the while.

"I'm sorry. I really shouldn't have done that," said Todd. "I thought you were someone else. I don't want to hurt you. Please forgive me!"

He went to the creek and filled up his leather flask with water, came back, and offered it to her. By this time she had sat up completely, and to his great relief she took it, drank a bit and gave it back without a word. There she sat, with her eyes fixed on the ground.

"Who are you?" asked Todd again. "How can I help you?"

"By forgetting you ever saw me!" she replied without emotion. From her voice Todd sensed that she was completely exhausted. "Please tell no one."

A long silence followed in which she sat motionlessly gazing at the gound. Todd tried not to dance from foot to foot in anxiety—he didn't know what to say or do.

Finally she added, "I'll be gone before you know it. I was just stopping on my travels. Please promise me you'll never tell a soul."

"Who's looking for you?" asked Todd.

At that point she was silent.

It was obvious she wanted to be left alone, but he couldn't just leave her—she was in trouble. "Is that why you went into our treehouse? You're hiding from someone?"

"I'm sorry about your treehouse," said the girl. "I was just very hungry."

His face burned with shame. How could he have just attacked her like that? All because of a stupid treehouse! "No problem. Really, I shouldn't have become so angry."

"Promise you'll never tell anyone?"

Todd thought for a second and said, "Yes, if you promise to wait. I want to bring you some warm clothes and food."

The girl kept staring at the ground. She did not look at him at all. "Don't tell anyone you saw me. Please, promise me you won't!"

"I promise. I won't tell a soul. But you must stay here and wait, okay?" asked Todd again.

The girl just stared at the forest floor. Todd's heart bled for her—she looked so weary and weak that she could hardly raise her head to look him in the eye.

Todd knelt carefully and sought out her gaze. "Okay?" he asked with an affectionate warmth that he hoped would disarm the girl's fears.

It seemed to work. For the first time she raised her head and looked thoughtfully into his eyes. "Okay."

Todd ran off toward the mill with a mixture of feelings that he himself could not understand, hoping all the while that she would still be there when he came back.

He snuck into the house as quietly as he could, using the back door under the low thatching by the river. His parents were somewhere else, and he managed to stuff the necessary things into an old flour sack without being seen. With the sack over his shoulder, he ran back toward the forest.

The girl was not there.

With his heart alternating between hope and disappointment, Todd walked around looking, calling, but to no avail. It was soon clear that she was no longer there, and he leaned on a tree, still breathing hard after running the whole way. He was plainly and simply angry with himself.

"Sometimes you are such an idiot!" he burst out.

"It's okay! I'm here!"

He jumped, startled but happy. Looking up, he saw her far up in a stately beech tree. "I thought you were gone!" he said, unable to hide his happiness.

"I didn't know if you would come back with soldiers," she replied. "Sorry for not trusting you."

"No problem, not at all!" said Todd. At the same time, her words made his blood quicken. *Soldiers!* He should have known.

"So you're running away from soldiers, are you?"

"Yes," said the girl, shinnying down now to the ground, looking around to be sure there was no one else with him.

Todd held out the flour sack. "Have a look. I've brought you some food, and here are some of my clothes. I'm sure they'll fit you. We don't have any girl's clothes."

Her eyes sought him out this time. "You didn't tell anyone, did you?"

"Not a soul," said Todd. She had large, captivating brown eyes that shimmered with life and a longing to tell a thousand stories. He could only gaze at them briefly and then had to look away.

After reaching out slowly for the flour sack, the girl seemed to lose some of her fear. She attacked the bread and cheese and ate ravenously. Todd watched her patiently. She really didn't look well at all, and she was constantly looking around with the nervousness of a frightened rabbit.

"I live outside the village in the mill. My father is the miller."

"How do I get away from the soldiers?"

"I don't think you can, completely," said Todd. "They go anywhere they want in the forest now."

The girl stopped eating and stared at him in horror. "I thought the forest was supposed to be free of soldiers!"

"It was, once," said Todd sadly.

"You don't like them?"

"No one does!"

There was a long silence, and the girl finished a piece of bread. "I'm so afraid. I'm just so afraid."

"You can stay with us," said Todd.

She shook her head. "If the soldiers catch me with you, then we all go down to the mines!"

Todd straightened his shoulders. "My parents are not scared of soldiers. And neither am I."

The girl swallowed one last piece of bread and nodded shortly. "Okay, thank you for everything. Please, don't say anything to anyone."

She was leaving? Todd's heart tightened. "Why don't you stay in the treehouse until you have new strength?"

"The soldiers are coming."

"But you're not—I mean, are you strong enough to go on?"

She trembled as she spoke. "I can't run anymore. And sometimes when I fall, I can hardly get up again. But I must keep going!"

"Stay in the treehouse, and I'll bring you food. If the soldiers come, they won't find you there. You have to stay there tonight anyway. It's too late to travel now."

The fight seemed to go out of her—she knew he was right. "Yes," said she, staring off into the distance.

Relieved that she wasn't going to rush off right now, he asked, "Why are you so afraid of the soldiers anyway?"

"They have taken my mother, and now they want me."

Questions shouted through him. "You? What did you do?"

"I . . . um . . ." she stared blankly into the forest.

"You're very tired," replied Todd.

"I'm so tired!" she said, blinking back tears. She was barely able to hold her head up.

"I'll help you up to the treehouse. No one will ever find you there," said Todd.

"All right," said the girl faintly.

Todd suddenly wondered if the girl had the strength to get to the treehouse. Up they went together, with Todd helping her all the way. With a big push, Todd got her up onto the platform, propped her up against the trunk, and laid out a mattress with some warm blankets. She crawled onto the mattress and wrapped herself in the blankets.

"I really think you should come with me tomorrow and talk to my parents. They'll help you. They're good people."

"Let me think about it," said the girl sleepily.

"Now, over here we've got some nuts," began Todd, "and enough dried bread for one month. Over here there's some goat cheese, which is really strong but you can wash it down with apple cider or water. All the plates and cups are over . . ."

Todd glanced at her and suddenly realized that she was fast asleep. For a moment he just stood and studied the fine features of her dirty, pale face and her delicate but perfect eyelashes.

Have you ever seen anything so beautiful in all the world? Todd asked himself as he stared at her.

He shook his head to wake himself up. After putting a few things away, he made his way home.

* * *

The girl slept solidly from early evening until something woke her in the middle of the night. An east wind was rocking the tree gently to and fro. It was a fresh wind that cooled her cheeks as she stared up into the sky. The stars seemed to be shining with special brilliance. In her heart of hearts, she knew what she would do next. She would indeed go with this lad and risk meeting his parents—she just knew it was right.

This was the first chance she'd had to look back on things in the last few days. Probably the most terrible feeling she'd suffered while she was alone was just that—the feeling of being utterly alone. She had never been without someone she could trust, and she was surprised at how her heart had leapt for joy when she saw Todd coming back without any soldiers. She had a strange feeling when he was around . . . the feeling of being at home.

And anyway, what had she managed by herself? She had run herself ragged and been consumed by dread and fears. At the end of only a few days she had felt like a trembling little mouse on the forest floor, lost in a world that was much bigger and scarier than any place she had known.

The stars seemed to sparkle in a very special way tonight as she stared into their midst, and she got the feeling that they understood, or that *someone* up there understood and was encouraging her in her resolve to go to Todd's home.

Her mind went back over the wonderful days of her youth, and then to the troubles, the problems, and the horrors of late, but happily all this grew vague and foggy in her mind, and voices and scenes mixed and muddled as she dozed. Before she knew it, she was sound asleep again.

CHAPTER 10

The Girl's Story

The creaking of the tree was the first thing the girl heard as she slowly awoke the next day, followed by the birds, which seemed particularly loud. *Yes, that's right, I'm in a tree,* she thought, *and not at home!*

The reality of her last few days came back to her with a shudder. Opening her eyes suddenly, she sat upright in surprise. Someone was there.

It was Todd. He was meticulously stripping the bark off a long, straight stick. She stared at him in silence. After stripping off the last of the bark, he started making long, spiral-shaped cuts down the stick with his knife. His mouth was wide open, and his eyes scanned his work up and down with great concentration. The perfectly cut shavings fell with great regularity onto the floor, and she felt she was in the presence of a master.

Without thinking she cleared her throat, and Todd looked up with a start.

"Oh, sorry! I didn't mean to startle you," she said.

"No problem," said Todd, who felt a little embarrassed at having been so easily spooked. "I thought I'd use the time to make a few arrows. They're always helpful."

"That arrow looks amazing."

"Yes. Thanks. There's a really good sycamore not far from here. That's where I got the wood for . . ." Todd's words just sort of petered out, and he cleared his throat. "Did you sleep well?" he asked.

To her surprise, she had. "Yes, very well. Thanks. Everything feels fine until I move, and then I suddenly remember how sore I am." She gave a shy chuckle, surprised at herself for her suddenly chatty nature.

There was an abrupt silence in which neither knew what to say.

"My name's Todd," said Todd, "but I already told you that, I guess." He leaned over to shake her hand.

"I'm Dana. Nice to meet you," said the girl as she shook his hand.

"You look a lot better than you did yesterday."

She smiled. "I feel better. Much, much better. I've been running for so long. I hate soldiers. I really do."

After a pause, Todd said, "Many people do."

Dana sat up in sudden anger and cringed at the pain of this abrupt movement, "You don't?"

"I don't know," said Todd, obviously surprised by this sudden burst of emotion.

"You don't know?" asked Dana, trying to get her emotions under control. Was he untrustworthy after all?

"No," said Todd. "My mother says that as soon as we hate them, they've won."

"Hmm," said Dana, looking down in shame at the treehouse floor. The words hit her hard, for she had heard them from her own mother—before the soldiers took her.

Todd went on, "She says you can't hate and sing the song."

"Your mother sings the song?" asked Dana.

"Yes."

"Mine too. It's that stupid song that's got us into all this trouble!"

She glanced up to see Todd looking at her with great perplexity. It was an honest, unashamed perplexity, full of care, and it disarmed her of all her anger.

"Do you know the song?" asked Todd.

"No."

There was silence. After looking around awkwardly, Todd started working again on his arrow. Dana could sense his frustration but didn't know what to say. She had not meant to be harsh. His movements were not the smooth easy strokes she had watched as she woke up. They were now abrupt and haphazard.

"I'll get going," said Todd suddenly, putting his things down.

"Oh no! Don't!" blurted Dana, angry at herself for her hard tone.

"I understand if you want to be alone," said Todd, who was now already on his feet and putting things away.

"Don't! Please don't! I mean, you've only just got here!" Dana quickly felt embarrassed, knowing that she really had no idea how long he had been there. "I mean, uh . . . I just woke. Please stay a little."

"Yes, okay," said Todd. He crouched down beside his pile of arrows, seemingly undecided as to whether he should stand or sit.

"It's nice to have you here. I mean, I've always had people around. I grew up in an inn," said Dana quickly, without any real idea why she said that or what she would say next.

"What's an inn?"

"It is a big house with extra rooms. Travelers can stay the night there and get something to eat."

"Were you traveling?"

"No! No, my father and mother owned an inn in a little country village outside the city. They worked very hard to make it a success. It was their dream."

"I've never seen an inn in the forest."

"No, it's in the Kingdom. That's where I grew up."

"Okay," said Todd, "and the inn was in a village?"

"Yes. We had rooms for about twenty guests and a big kitchen and dining room. In the evenings meals were served until the shadows grew long, and people would sit and talk afterwards. Then my father would pull out his lute and play. He made that lute sing, I tell you."

She smiled at the memory, the notes dancing through her mind along with the sight of her strong, handsome father. "And when Mom was finished in the kitchen, she would come out and sing. She has the voice of a nightingale. People loved their music, and this was their way of keeping the place full.

"Mom's voice could melt the hardest heart. I still remember those evenings in a full room. I used to sit and watch the old people. Tough, wrinkled old farmers' wives sat there and for a short time forgot their anger, and those hardened stone faces grew soft, and honest, and you could see the sadness and their sense of loss. These were the bitter, mean women I was afraid of in the village, and yet when Mom sang . . ."

Dana stopped speaking and stared off into the branches of neighboring trees, lost in memories. A gust of the cool morning breeze shook the spell, and Dana came to herself again to find Todd watching her intently. "Where was I?"

"Mean, bitter old women," said Todd with a smile.

"Oh, yes. But those days were happy. Then my father got sick. I don't know what it was. He grew thinner and thinner, and weaker, and quiet— really quiet. One day a big carriage came, and I was called out to the front. Dad was there with a trunk packed with things. Mom tried to be strong, but the tears flowed and flowed. She was barely able to talk. I had no idea what was going on. They put Dad's case in the carriage and tied his horse to the back, and slowly it became clear that they were taking him away. I guess he was too weak to ride himself. He gave me a big squeeze and told me to take good care of Mom until he got back . . ."

Dana's voice began to tremble, and she stared intensely into the forest floor, but she was really looking far beyond it, into the past.

A flood of sorrow welled up in her soul as she choked out the words. "They never told me! I didn't really say good-bye! I couldn't, because I didn't know what was happening! Dad took me in his arms and told me he loved me. I didn't say anything, because I didn't know what to say! And then, before I knew it, he was gone."

Wave upon wave of grief, desperate grief, flowed over her—the kind of sorrow that time should heal but doesn't.

"Where did he go?" asked Todd.

Dana pulled herself together and continued, "A kitchen maid told me they had taken him to a special doctor and he should be back in a couple of weeks. I waited for him every day. I would go down to the bench beside the gate and wait for hours. Now and again I heard what sounded like his voice, or like the hoofbeats of his horse, Syder, but no, it was never Dad. I remember the maids coming, asking if I wanted to play a game, or the gardener coming and offering me a ride on his pony. I only wanted Dad. I wanted to stay there and wait because sometime he would come back. He had to come back. He just had to.

"Sometimes Mom would come out and sit with me. She didn't say a word. I would sit on her lap, and she would stroke my head and fondle my hair. Sometimes I would just start crying, and she would too. We would hold on to each other, and when it was dark we would go inside.

"As time went by, it slowly became clear that Dad was not coming back. We both knew it, but we didn't talk about it. We still sat outside in the evenings, and we always lit a lantern just beside the door—in case he came home in the middle of the night.

"One day a rider came with a message. The doctors had sent Dad far away. He was staying in the cottage of an instrument maker right on the edge of the forest. He had called for my mother there.

"She left right away, while I was in bed. I woke up and she was gone, and I panicked. I had already lost my father, and now where was my mother? The cook told me she had gone to bring back my father . . . and I tried to believe her. But I was so afraid I'd lost her too. I couldn't eat. I couldn't talk. I just sat for hours by the gate. After his work the gardener, an old man named Sedon, often sat with me, never saying a word . . . but it was so nice to have him there.

"And then after a couple of weeks my mother came back, riding Syder, Dad's horse—and then I knew. She didn't have to tell me anything. I knew he had died. She was happy, though, really happy. I didn't understand this at all, but it was so nice to see a smile on her face. I had not seen that for ages.

"She told me of the new songs she had learned with Dad—songs of the forest. He didn't have the strength to play the lute, but they sang together. I really didn't understand this at all—but she just shone with a kind of joy and a peace. I somehow understood that everything was all right."

Dana smiled through tears. "She brought another message from Dad to me, and it was almost the same: 'Take care of your mother until we meet again, and we will most certainly meet again. Your father loves you more than all the world.'"

At this point Dana burst into tears, and placing her hands on her face, she wept with great sobs. Todd made a movement toward her but then stopped—he didn't seem to know what to do, but she sensed his sympathy and his affection. That was comforting, very comforting.

"And then Mom told me that he had died," said Dana slowly, pulling herself together, "and she said there are some lives that are worse than death and some deaths more wonderful than a thousand lives. She said, 'He died with a smile on his face and a song in his heart. There's so much that he wants to tell you, and he will—when you two meet again.'

"That's all she said. She didn't say anymore, and I somehow didn't need to ask. It was enough."

"I'm very sorry," said Todd, who still seemed to be trying to put everything together in his mind. After a long pause he asked, "But why are you running from soldiers?"

The question startled her—of course, that was what she'd been trying to tell him!

"Oh, yes. Well, it was like this: my mother ran the inn alone for about five years. She didn't sing very often even though people asked her to. Then one evening she agreed to sing a song or two, and without knowing it she sang before a colonel in the army. He found her voice absolutely stunning and afterward spoke to her of a feast he was organizing to honor the king. My mother told him she couldn't leave the inn and that she was not good enough to sing before the king, but he insisted . . . and it soon became clear that she did not *want* to sing before the king."

"Why didn't she want to?" asked Todd.

"Because if she sings for him, she has to tell the king that he's wonderful and sing the songs of the kingdom. All of those songs are the same, and Mom told me she simply couldn't do it. The colonel was angry when he left, and we heard nothing for about a week, and suddenly in the middle of the night Mom woke me up. Someone had told her of a large patrol coming. I got dressed, and we went outside. Sedon was waiting with a large wagon full of hay. Mom told me there might be some trouble, so I should go with him until she called me back or met me in the countryside.

"I went to sit up front with him as I had always done, but he and Mom took me to the back of the wagon, where he shoved his pitchfork deep into the hay, lifted it up, and told me that I was to crawl in. He let the hay down over me, and we traveled most of the night like that. We traveled all the next day and into the next night. I still remember soldiers asking him if he had seen me—they were looking for me! They told him that they had already found my mother, and that she would receive the punishment she deserved for her disrespect."

"Sedon brought me to the edge of the forest and told me to go as deep as I could. He said the edge of the forest was the beginning of hope, and that this story was not over ... that I should run as deep into the forest as my legs could carry me, and that when I was in the middle of the forest, I'd know what to do next. In the distance I heard the bugle of a patrol. I ran off into the forest, and Sedon went back another way. And now here I am."

"You must tell this story to my father," said Todd, starting to rise. "We'll help you."

They were the words she had wanted to hear—and yet, now that she had told her story, the bitterness of everything that had happened felt overwhelming. "I don't need help; my mother needs help!"

"That's what I mean!" said Todd. "We'll help you get your mother back."

Dana almost wanted to laugh. She looked at the boy with an affectionate smile. "You don't understand. The king has tens of thousands of horsemen. Nobody stands against the king!"

She never forget what happened next. The skinny, clumsy boy straightened his shoulders, took on a confidence she had never seen before, and said, "We will go, and we will get your mother out. We must, and we will."

There was a trace of fear in his eyes, yet he spoke with total surety. Dana stared at him, amazed at his words, and yet something about him reassured her.

"Come and tell my parents your story," said Todd eagerly. "They'll know what to do."

Dana paused for a minute, but she knew very well what she would do. "Okay, I'll come."

"Really?" said Todd, clearly surprised.

"Yes. Really," said Dana. She smiled and then laughed as the boy almost burst with joy.

"Let's go!" he said happily, and they started off down the tree.

CHAPTER 11

The Gathering

Before long Dana and Todd were at the bottom of the tree. Dana jumped down onto the ground after him, and they both started off quickly toward his house.

"Wait!" called Dana.

"Huh?" said Todd, stopping and looking back.

"I can't be seen! There are soldiers looking for me."

"Oh, yeah, that's right. Okay, let's do it like this. A cuckoo call means come, and a crow call means stay. We can go together for a while, and when we get close to the main path, I'll go ahead and make sure the way is clear before you come out of the trees."

They spent a short while practicing bird calls and then continued along the way. Their idea turned out to be a very good one, as several people came unexpectedly walking down the main path. Todd chatted with them casually, and as soon as they were safely on their way, he called Dana out of her hiding place.

Finally they came to the mill, only to be met by a big black dog running out to greet them.

"Hello, Hadder! Can you keep a secret, old boy?" asked Todd as he went down on one knee and gave the dog a hearty pat on the back as it pranced around. "Dana, wait behind this tree till I call you. Come dog!"

With that, off ran Todd and Hadder to the mill. They disappeared through the front door. An instant later, Todd's head appeared out the door again, and after looking left and right, he gave the last cuckoo call. Dana ran into the house.

Her arrival was no small surprise for Clara, who suddenly saw a strange girl wearing Todd's clothes running into her house as fast as her legs could carry her. Todd quickly explained the situation, and it was not long before all four were sitting around the kitchen table, drinking tasty cups of root tea. Dana told her story again. It was longer this time, with many more details, and Bud and Clara sat and listened without saying a word.

As they listened, Clara looked at this thin, weary little girl and loved her. *What a beautiful, dear soul,* she thought—and just as the Lord of the Forest had brought Todd those many years ago to find refuge with them, he had now brought Dana. She was the daughter Clara had waited for. Bud drank in Dana's story as though it were his own.

Dana finished her story, and silence fell around the table. Silence, that is, except for the snoring of Hadder under the table.

His voice both excited and trembling, Bud declared, "We must go and get your mother!"

"Bud, you can't be serious!" said Clara with a start.

"Of course I am! This is the time!" Bud calmed his voice a little and laid a hand on his wife's shoulder. "I'm not crazy, Clara. It's time someone stood up to the kingdom—it's *past* time. You know, I've been thinking about this a lot lately. This present life is the only one full of doubts and unknowns. This is the only life in which we take risks and act valiantly!"

"Oh, Bud!" said Clara, with a shudder. It was not the first time she had feared for Bud. His bold words and deeds had gotten him into trouble many times before.

"She did what is right. We must help her!"

"But Bud, your chances are ..."

"We may or *may not* succeed," said Bud. "We may all end up in the mines. But that's the beauty of it. That is what makes courage real!"

Clara had seen this look on her husband's face before. There was no point arguing, and for some strange reason, she felt that opposing him would be wrong. But that did not take away the horror of the thought away.

Wanting very much to talk about something else, she said, "Well, dear, the first thing we'll have to do is get you some decent clothes and maybe also—"

Clara's words were interrupted by a knocking on the door. Up jumped Hadder with a start and began barking.

Bud and Clara looked at each other in shock. "The gathering!" said Clara. This was the night of the gathering. They had all been so taken up in Dana's story that they'd forgotten.

"Bud! Clara!" rang out the voice of Donger Bee, one of their very best friends.

"Be with you in a minute, Donger!" shouted Bud, jumping up out of his seat. He cast an anxious glance at Dana, and Clara nodded. They could trust Donger, of course, but with soldiers so often in the village, the fewer people who knew about her, the better.

"Over here, dear!" said Clara quickly, picking up the top half of a heap of flour sacks. "Lie down there, in between these sacks!"

Dana lay down flat, and Clara covered her with sacks, clucking a little with concern. "Can you breathe okay, dear?"

"Yes, I'm fine," said Dana.

Seeing that Dana was well hidden, Bud opened the door and welcomed Donger with a big hug.

"Am I too early?" asked Donger, somehow aware that he was causing a disturbance.

"No! No, not at all! We all lost track of time—just sitting around the table talking, you know how it is. Got your pipes?"

"Sure do. Have been practicing, I have! You know, Landa's new song."

"Well, that'll make her happy," said Bud with a smile.

Donger got to work with the others getting the room ready for more visitors.

Dana could just make out Donger's figure through the flour bags, but she wanted to see him better. She waited until he was looking in the other direction and took the chance to move a bit, pushing all but one sack away from before her eyes. Now she could see much better. Donger was a short but sturdy fellow with thick black hair, and although he had no beard, his next shave was obviously overdue.

They were all working together putting chairs in place, setting food on the table, and getting the fire going when another knock was heard at the door.

Donger opened it. "Maltin! Come in!"

In came a tall, slender older man carrying a large, bulky object. He set it down on the floor, and after hugging and greeting everyone, he placed it between a couple of chairs. It was like a long, cylindrical drum that lay on its side, covered with a wide brown drum skin and strung with ten strings stretched over it and pulled tight on an upright framework. It looked like a cross between a banjo and a harp. Dana had never seen anything like it. Maltin sat down on the drum like someone would sit on a log, with one foot on one side and one foot on the other. After making some adjustments to the strings, he said, "Donger, give me a daw."

"A daw you want?" asked Donger, pulling a wooden flute out of his bag. He took a deep breath, covered all of the holes but one, and blew. The room filled with the warm, smoky sound of his flute, much different from the shrill metal whistles Dana had known in the kingdom. The old man reached around the frame and plucked the third longest string. A rich, mellow sound filled the house, ringing for a long time after being plucked.

"And again!" said the old man. Donger played the note longer, and the old man began turning a wooden cross-shaped piece at the end of the string. Gradually the note grew higher until it was the same as that of the flute.

He's tuning! thought Dana. In her mind's eye she saw her father in their inn, tuning his lute with her mother. Such an unexpected and clear memory filled her with feelings of every kind. She listened intently, all the while thinking about her father, who seemed strangely near.

"A high daw now, Donger," said the old man, reaching to a much shorter string on the far right. Donger's deep melancholic flute suddenly jumped an octave and sang like a playful bird. Todd and his parents went about their work quietly, not wanting to disturb the musicians.

After Todd finished stoking the fire, he crossed silently over to the heap of sacks where Dana was hiding.

"Everything okay in there?" he whispered.

"It's better than okay! Don't worry about me!" replied Dana, who felt happy in a peculiar kind of way.

One by one people arrived, and the atmosphere became more festive by the minute. They seemed mostly to be farming folk, simply dressed and unrefined. They were a motley mix of young and old, fat and thin, men, women and children.

Amid the hugs, laughter, and loud chatter, Bud opened the door for a short, plump, middle-aged lady carrying something in a large leather bag. She was followed by two strapping young men, tall and broad-shouldered, each of whom had a pack on a strap over his shoulders.

"Travis! Brody!" shouted Todd. They greeted Bud, Clara, and Todd with great enthusiasm, and the affection between them all was evident. As the young men made the rounds to greet all the other guests, it became apparent to Dana that they both had drums strapped over their shoulders. As they finally took a place to sit, they took their drums down and placed them on the floor. The plump woman sat between them and pulled another instrument out of her bag. At first glance, it looked like a porcupine with bell-shaped quills pointing out in every direction. Dana recognized it as some kind of accordion with wooden horns sticking out.

In total, about twenty people crowded into the room, sitting around the room on chairs, stools, or trunks along the walls, with several of the younger ones sitting on blankets on the floor. Hadder, the dog, stretched out on the floor in the middle of the room and proceeded again to fall asleep.

The chatter grew slowly quiet until the whole group was silent. Dana peered out intently. In the light of the few flickering candles and the fire, she could see that everyone had their eyes closed. They just sat peacefully, as though waiting for someone.

After a long, unhurried silence—one of the few silences which Dana did not want to end—the plump woman started singing. She didn't really use words, but sang a pattern of "Na, na, na's,"—a slow, repeating tune whose melody soon became clear. Slowly people joined in, following the pattern but with different notes as a harmony developed, growing in range and in volume. It seemed to Dana that they simply joined in whenever they felt they were ready to begin, and some stayed silent a good long time. The sound grew richer as more of the men joined, filling the bass, and tenors and altos laid a thick carpet under the soprano melody.

Gradually, other rhythms appeared and new patterns grew out of the original one. The plump woman sang the same tune she had begun, again and again and again, and what seemed in Dana's mind at first to be a stream flowing ever greater and wider now split, with sections splashing over rocks and other sections twisting and turning in deeper waters until all the waters flowed seamlessly into each other again.

It was unlike anything Dana had ever heard. It was spontaneous but not chaotic. The music of the kingdom had the rigid, rectangular structure of a house or a building; this music also had a structure and a beautiful pattern, but it was more like a tree or a vine growing up a cliff face or the freedom of a group of swallows flitting back and forth over a wheat field, all flying alone and yet all flying together.

I am because he is

I have because he gives

I hope because he loves

I can because he lives.

The lyrics emerged out of the singing and sank back into it, never sung by everyone at once, but rather by individuals or in pairs or threes. Dana scrutinized the singers as well as she could, studying the faces of those who sang, and in the dim candlelight it seemed that all eyes were either closed or fixed on the floor. No conductor kept the whole thing intact, yet its unity never broke. Travis started slowly in with his drum, and Brody followed shortly after. The deep, dull thuds of the drums could be not just heard but also felt in the rickety old house, and everything seemed to be moving, as though the house were dancing along. Other verses could soon be heard, praising the Lord of the Forest for the tranquility of the dawn, the magnificence of the thunder, the regal voice of the wind, and the silent healing words that the Lord speaks deep in the heart of his followers.

Donger started playing his flute, and the plump woman played her accordion. The older man played the banjo-harp with such vigor and heart that Dana wondered if the instrument frame could withstand it. Now the house was full of music: deep, flowing music whose parts could hardly be distinguished. What sounded from the harp, accordion, flute, and drums flowed mystically into oneness with the voices. It was a whole spectrum of sounds, yet one voice, a voice addressed in singular praise to the Lord of the Forest.

This is majesty, thought Dana to herself, *pure majesty!* For some reason the sound made her think of the pompous sheriffs and lords of the kingdom, dressing in their bright colors, driving around in their glossy carriages with footmen before and after—how ridiculous they all looked now, like a little boy picking up a stick as though it were a sword and playing the great knight. Nothing reveals the fake like the authentic, and for the first time Dana was tasting of the authentic, of something she had never even imagined.

The one voice of the group flowed from emotion to emotion. Great gratitude, earnest longing, and deep sighs of tired hearts freely expressing their pain and grief. Tears rolled down the cheeks of some as they gladly dropped their burdens at the feet of the One who cared for them. Dana also heard bold words of confidence, confessions of trembling, confirmations of hope, and bursts of ecstasy and solid, tranquil joy. It was the uncovering of hearts to an unseen audience.

And suddenly, a new voice joined them. Dana looked for its source in astonishment. There he was! Her father sat on a small stool between Brody and an old, hunched woman. He was playing his lute and singing with a joy that Dana had never before seen in him. Although his eyes were closed, his hand moved effortlessly up and down the neck of his lute, and he sang with great passion along with the others.

Dana wanted to shout and jump out of the pile of sacks but knew she could not. She just fixed her gaze upon him and smiled—and yes, more, she wept—not only because he was alive, but because he was doing so well. It was only with great difficulty that she could wipe the fast, hot tears from her eyes, and she gazed at him, drinking in this image of her father. He opened his eyes and looked over to the pile of sacks, straight at her. With eyes beaming with love, he gave her a smile as if to say *I love you more than all the world, and everything is going to be okay. Yes, everything is going to be okay!*

It was one of those magic moments when time stands still, waiting for the heart to catch up. Amid the flood of a thousand feelings Dana could only lie there and stare at her father, drinking up the joy of the moment. He then blinked as if to say good-bye and was gone. Her eyes frantically searched that corner of the room, but all she found was a small empty stool beside Brody, who, like all the rest, did not seem to have noticed anything.

He's gone! said Dana to herself, but without the shock or horror one might expect. She somehow felt that he'd had to go, and for some reason this was good. The knowledge that her father was well, and doing far better than she had ever seen him, gave her enormous comfort.

The music continued. At times she listened, at times she thought, and at times she just stared off in a stupor, unable to take in all that was happening. The music went on for a good hour or maybe even an hour and a half, until one by one people stopped singing or playing. It all faded out as gradually as it had faded in.

After the last person stopped, there was a silence again like a quiet spell after a big meal. Everyone was sitting with eyes closed, and all was still . . . and then, suddenly, the old hunched woman sitting beside Brody cried out and sat forward.

With closed eyes but in great excitement she cried out, "I see them, I see them! Pounding of hooves! Crossing bridges, down paths, beside hedges! Captain upon captain! Each with ten men! Colonel upon colonel! Each with ten captains! A swarm! A great swarm! Defiling the Lord's forest! Searching for the tender heart! Tender heart! Tender Heart, hear my voice! Flee to the treetops and go to the high place, where I will comfort your soul and strengthen your body! Be strong and know that you are more beautiful to me than the rising sun, more precious than the soul can understand. They must get past me to get to you! Do not fear! I am with you! Flee, Tender Heart! Flee!"

The guests looked at each other with perplexity. Dana could not help but feel that this message was for her, and it aroused two thoughts, one after the other. The first was the dreaded thought of soldiers galloping after her in wicked haste and stopping at nothing. But this thought quickly gave way to the next. The Lord of the Forest had just spoken to her—as to one of his own—with the warm, cherishing voice of a father and the sovereignty of a king. By royal decree she had become his child and stepped not only into his family, but into his loving embrace. Oh, what joy! What joy unspeakable took hold of her soul as she lay there silently among the sacks!

Slowly she started to notice again what was happening around her, like waking up from a dream. Bud and Clara were serving root tea and biscuits, and the room was full of laughter again as friends spoke of the affairs of the week, their sore backs, the cow that should soon calve, and the everyday talk of any village. They gradually began leaving, in twos and threes, out into the dark but moonlit night.

As soon as the last guest was safely out of sight, Clara and Todd came over to Dana's pile of sacks, uncovered her, and pulled her out.

"Are you okay there?" asked Todd.

"I'm more than okay," said Dana with a smile, stretching her sore muscles.

"Child, I was worried you wouldn't get enough air in there!"

"Oh, no! It was—"

"Okay, now, everybody listen," interrupted Bud as he came back from the front door. He sounded more serious than Dana had heard him in the short time she'd known him. "Todd, you take Dana to the treehouse tonight, and you both spend the night there."

"You know about the treehouse?" Todd asked, clearly startled. Dana almost giggled.

"I do, but that's not important now. Your mother and I will put some food together, and you both are to go there and stay there at the top until you hear from me. Is that clear?"

"Uh, okay," said Todd. "But how did you know about—"

Bud didn't give him time to interrupt. "I could be wrong, and I hope I am, but I can't shake the feeling that this place will be crawling with soldiers tomorrow, maybe as early as dawn. Leave no trail, no broken branches. Pull all the ladders up and out of the way. Don't come down or go anywhere until Travis or Brody or I come. Clear?"

"Clear, Dad," said Todd.

"And we'll use the cuckoo's call," added Bud.

"Once? Twice?"

"Let's say three times, just to be safe."

"Okay."

Bud put his hands on his hips and surveyed the pair. "You two will need to pack your things for a trip. A long one."

"You gather up some clothes for them, dear," said Clara, "and I'll get food ready."

Soon enough, a bag of clothes and a bag of food were ready, and all four stood at the door. "The Lord protect you, my dears," said Clara with tears welling up in her eyes.

She hugged them both. Dana clung to her for a long moment, soaking up a mother's comfort.

"I'll come with you to the path," said Bud.

At the end of the clearing Bud gave them both a big hug, and while hugging Dana he said, "Be strong, Tender Heart! Be strong!"

With that, the two children disappeared into the night and the forest.

CHAPTER 12

Getting Ready to Go

The two found their way to the tree safely. They were very thankful for a break in the clouds that let the moonlight through; it would have been very difficult to find and climb the ladders without it. They agreed that Dana should sleep in the treehouse where she'd been before, and Todd would sleep higher up on a secondary platform used as a lookout. The sway of the wind troubled him a little as he settled into his high place. But as soon as both of them had pulled up their blankets and put their heads to the pillows, they fell into a deep sleep. They were far more tired than they had realized, and no amount of wind would keep them awake tonight.

It was early the next morning when Todd woke up to the clatter of hasty hoofbeats. He couldn't see anything through the leaves, but he tried to imagine how many there would be. This was the first time he had ever heard so many horses together.

Going down the ladder, he saw Dana wrapped in her blankets, sitting up and listening. He saw the same expression of fear on her face that had been there when he met her. When she was at the house with him and Bud and Clara, she had somehow come alive, with a sparkle in her eye and a smile on her lips. These were now gone.

Dana didn't look at him but just stared like a stone into a neighboring tree. "I hate soldiers!" she whispered suddenly, as though no longer able to hold it in. "I really hate them, Todd!" Her lips trembled as she fixed her gaze on the tree in front of her. A look of dread and almost panic darkened her face, and she drew a deep breath, trying to control her emotions.

Todd, not knowing what to do, took her hand in his and squeezed it. She clung to his hand in return, and he thought she seemed comforted.

They sat together for a long while in silence, listening to a seemingly endless number of horses passing by. After a long time, the clatter grew fainter until the last horse was gone. The children still sat, without moving, waiting for the next wave, but it didn't come. Todd found himself back in the silent forest he had always known, as though the horses had just been a dream.

Todd slowly turned to Dana, who was nervously looking all around. "Let's pack things for the trip," he said, feeling that if he got Dana busy doing something, she would begin to relax. Within a few minutes they were comparing bags and discussing who could carry what.

Todd pulled out a trunk of supplies and opened it in front of Dana.

"What on earth is all this?" asked Dana, who was unable to keep a smile off her face as she looked at the mass of hooks, knives, forks, long pieces of rope and short pieces of string, bits of leather and cloth, and other tools and materials of every shape and size imaginable.

"Uh . . . supplies," said Todd, whose face reddened as he spoke.

"All right," said Dana, laughing. She found Todd most endearing when he was embarrassed.

All this activity was indeed just what Dana needed, and she felt the new lightness of heart return. Over breakfast she told some funny stories from her life in the inn, and Todd had to quiet her laughter down several times so that no one would hear. It was just so nice to have someone who listened with such interest and care, even if he obviously could not picture it all in his mind.

When they finished eating they packed everything away and started to discuss the next steps. "You look very tired," said Todd.

"Silly me . . . I ate too much!" said Dana, rubbing her hand over her very full stomach.

"Why don't you lie down and close your eyes for a couple of minutes? You had such a terrible journey to come here; I think you need all the rest you can get."

She nodded. "Maybe you're right." Having said this, she lay down, pulled her blankets around her shoulders, and was asleep in an instant.

Todd got busy packing their backpacks, and when that was finished he took some straight sticks to make arrows. This was by far his favorite pastime. He had developed a very precise method and a steady, skilled hand. More than anything else, he had learned to slow down and use unrushed, deliberate strokes of the knife to fashion the perfect arrow. Sometimes he could work for hours, not even feeling the passing of time and only noticing the ever greater pile of finished shafts that lay beside him. At other times, thoughts and concerns would drag him out of his concentration after only a few shafts were finished.

This was how it was today. Those waves of soldiers filled him with an uneasy tension that threatened to explode as hateful anger. The images of Rawley were as fresh in his mind as on the very day the old man had nearly been killed, and only in his late-night talk with Clara had he realized how deeply the presence of soldiers affected her.

Where was Dad anyway? He'd said he would come! "A promise made is a debt unpaid!" That was always Bud's motto! A chill came over him, his anger giving way to fear. Maybe the soldiers had got wind of something. Maybe they'd searched the mill. Maybe they'd taken Bud and Clara away.

Just as he felt himself tensing up, he chose to heed the words he had so often heard from Clara: "Tell it all to him who always hears." In doing so, he soon noticed that he returned again to peace. It may not be the peace necessary to shape shafts, but it was certainly enough to break and file the flint arrowheads.

Dana slept into the afternoon past sunset and only woke up shortly after the stars started to appear.

Todd smiled at her startled expression as she realized how late it was. "All is well," he said. "Keep sleeping." And so she did, falling asleep again immediately.

Todd did not want to light a lantern for fear of being seen, so he climbed up to his bed in the lookout in the darkness. He lay down thinking about all of the details for their trip and wondering where they were to go, but the slow swaying of the tree had its effect, and he was soon sound asleep . . .

"Hey, Sleepyhead! Wake up!"

Todd rolled over and opened his eyes to the blurry image of someone familiar beside him. "This is the good life, eh? Just hanging around at the top of a tree!"

It was Brody, whose smiling face slowly became clear under the moonlight.

"Brody, hi!" said Todd, overjoyed.

"Come down below. It's time to make a plan."

"Okay, I'm coming," said Todd, wiping the sleep out of his eyes. He came down to find Travis, Brody, and Dana sitting and whispering together.

"Oh, so you've met," said Todd, a little surprised to see them talking with Dana.

"I wasn't afraid of them, because I saw them at the meeting," said Dana.

"She was well hidden, eh?" said Brody. "I had no idea she was there."

"Me neither!" said Travis.

"How's everyone?" asked Todd.

"Everyone's fine!" said Travis.

"Lots of soldiers!" added Brody.

"Yes, really. Lots and lots," added Travis, "all walking around like they own the place—but they haven't done anyone any harm. Bud didn't think he could get away without being seen."

"Well, that's good!" said Todd who for some reason always wanted to protect his father. There was something wonderful about being with his best friends high up in the treehouse at night, hearing good news. The weather was remarkably mild for spring, and the moonlight seemed much brighter in the treetops.

"What's your father doing?" asked Todd.

There was a short silence, and Todd realized he had hit a sore spot.

"He's doing what he does best!" replied Travis cynically.

"He's doing nothing! Absolutely nothing!" said Brody. "He called the elders of the village together for yet another secret meeting. A secret meeting in our own village! Can you believe it?"

It was quiet for a few moments before Travis added, "It's really bad. The soldiers set up a large tent in the marketplace. They have been asking everywhere for a young girl, the daughter of a certain singer."

Dana moaned.

"Don't worry, Dana, you're safe with us!" said Travis. "It's those soldiers I'm worried about, because they've picked a fight with the Lord of the Forest! If they want to grab a bull by the nose, they can. I won't stop them." He smiled.

Brody was still storming over the thought of his father. "I just don't know what's got into him. They call this secret meeting in the shed behind Willard's henhouse. Travis and I were there to serve . . . and all this talk of being careful not to provoke anger, and of waiting it out until they leave. And then Markus got talking about the new weapons the soldiers now carry—pretending to know what he's talking about—"

"He is such a phony!" added Travis.

"He is," continued Brody, "and you know, they didn't mention the Lord of the Forest once! Not once! It's all too crazy, I tell you."

"And the worst thing is," said Travis with unusual emotion, "that they determined that if anyone knew where the girl was, she should be handed over."

"No!" said Dana suddenly, shaking her head. The day was slowly dawning, and all could now see the fear on Dana's face.

Travis put a comforting hand on Dana's shoulder. "Don't worry, Dana, only over our three dead bodies will they get to you! And then Brody—"

"I was so angry," said Brody, "that I shouted out in the meeting, 'I can't believe it! I can't believe what I'm hearing! You are going to hand over someone who has fled to the forest for refuge? You're going to give her over to the king? Are you mad?' And then Dad got really angry, and he told me to leave the meeting immediately, and I said, 'This is why those soldiers respect the chickens on the side of the road more than you and your feeble group of elders!' Then Dad really got really angry—angrier than I've ever seen him. He got up and screamed at me, 'Get out!' And then—"

"And then I shouted at my father. . . for the very first time in my life," said Travis. "I said that Brody was right, and he said, 'How dare you talk to the chief of the village like that!'—you know, shaking his fists around like he does—and I answered, 'You were once the chief of the village. Now you're just one of the king's deputies!'"

"And then we left," said Brody, "and we stood together outside in the forest, not knowing where to go or what to do."

"So we decided to go to the mill," added Travis, "and we got Clara and Bud out of bed. We went inside and told them everything, and then they told us about Dana."

"Bud told me he has never been so proud of us as now," Brody said.

Todd could see the enormous grief in the faces of both Brody and Travis, and his heart went out to them. They both loved their father very much, and they'd never had a conflict like this with him before.

"We're all in this together," said Travis. "None of us really has a home he can go to right now." After a pause he said, "Bud told us the way up to the high plains, where the mountain people live. Our task now is to take you two up there and leave you with the mountain people until Bud comes to get you."

"You're supposed to stay there until Dana regains her strength and the situation here calms down," said Brody.

"But people who deal with the mountain people get killed!" said Todd.

"This is true," said Travis. "But Bud had a dream . . . and this is the plan."

"And remember the prophecy," said Brody. "The one in the meeting: 'Flee to the treetops and go to the high place, where I will comfort your soul and strengthen your body.' Where else could it mean but the high plains?"

"We talked about it and want to do it like this," started Travis.

"You guys walk with Travis, and I'll walk ahead," continued Brody. "I'll give you the signal. What would you like? Robin? Cuckoo? Crow? Blackbird?"

"Let's say a double cuckoo means come, and a robin means wait there," said Travis. "And we'll do a blackbird if it's not clear. A blackbird means you should repeat the call."

"Double cuckoo, come. Single robin, wait. Your blackbird, repeat. Got it."

"Anything else before we go?" asked Travis.

"How are you guys for food?" asked Todd.

"We're fine. Backpacks are full. Clara really loaded us up!" said Brody.

"Wonder what Bud's going to get for breakfast tomorrow?" laughed Travis. "She gave us almost everything!"

"Yesterday I made a bunch of new arrows, if anyone needs any," said Todd, pulling out the arrows he had made.

"Man, no one makes them straighter than you!" said Travis, holding an arrow up toward the red sunrise and looking with one eye down the shaft. Todd swelled with pride. Praise from Travis was something he valued very greatly indeed.

"Oh man! That means if I miss it's only my fault now!" said Brody with a cheeky smile.

"You never miss, Brody," said Todd, who despite the dangers of the moment felt utterly happy to be with his friends. The brothers had always been his best friends, and he felt sure that was what they would always be.

Together they packed everything in the treehouse away and got a bow out for Dana. Brody and Travis were excellent archers and hunters, and Todd was learning fast. Off they went down the tree, everyone with a pack on his back and a bow over his shoulder.

Bud had told them to travel up the river to the great white rock about nine miles upstream. At the white rock, a small creek flowed into the river. They were to follow the creek until the first set of waterfalls. There, they would see two jagged peaks toward the setting of the sun, and they should constantly walk toward the larger one, on the left. They would come to the high plains at the end of two days, provided they left early and traveled constantly until sunset both days.

Their bird call system worked very well. Brody set off ahead, and when the way was clear, he called with a double cuckoo and the others came. They didn't walk along the paths but traveled parallel to them a good fifty yards away. They made it to the great white rock by noon and turned up north, parallel to the path beside the stream.

The constant, silent walking gave everyone time to think. Dana, for whom the forest was very new, just soaked up its beauty, its smells, and its impressions. It was surely the most beautiful place she had ever seen. She enjoyed the warmth of the flickering rays of sun through the leaves and the gentle, constant breeze, although she could never tell where it was coming from or where it was going.

The spongy, leaf-littered forest floor, the soft moss over trunk and stone, and the rough dry bark around the waists of great stately trees—they all seemed to caress her soul as one strokes a cold kitten coming in from the rain. A couple of days ago, as she was running for her life, she had noticed none of this. The forest had seemed a cold, hostile place she somehow had to get through.

How different it all seems, she thought as she walked single file between Travis in front and Todd behind. *But I'm still running for my life.* She felt perplexed, but everything, yes, everything was so very different, even the life she was scrambling to save. She had seen something absolutely new in the eyes of her father during the meeting, and this very thing was now bubbling up within her own heart.

She looked intently at Travis, who was walking directly in front of her, and admired the ease and energy with which he found his way through the obstacles of the forest floor. His thick thighs and blocky, muscular calves jumped silently over trunk and stone with the agility of a deer. *They're friends,* she thought with a smile, *friends like I've never had, and now all of a sudden when I need them the most . . .*

"Get down!" said Travis suddenly, and all three were suddenly flat on their bellies on the forest floor.

"What's up?" whispered Todd.

"I don't know, but I heard a robin, and then another one quickly after it. Brody wants us to stop and wait."

They all lay silent for a while.

"How's your pack, Dana? Do you want to give me anything?" asked Todd. "You've seemed a little tired."

"Oh, no! I'm fine!" whispered Dana. Having said that, she felt how lovely it was to lie on the forest floor. She was more tired than she had noticed.

"Get your backpacks off and bows and arrows out," said Travis. "There's something wrong here."

It was a great relief for Dana to take off her backpack and let her shoulders move freely. Behind her, she could hear Todd doing the same. Travis also slipped his backpack off, and putting his quiver back, he took his bow in his right hand.

"Wait here and don't move. If I don't come back, don't look for me, but wait until sunset and continue the path until night."

"Okay," said Todd, and Travis disappeared silently into the forest.

CHAPTER 13

The Patrol

Travis crept forward under cover to see why Brody had signaled. They had entered a wide valley of tall, slender hardwoods, and the morning sun, which had risen quite high now, filled the forest with light. After about thirty yards Travis saw a road they had to cross. Brody was there, surrounded by a group of mounted soldiers. Travis crept up silently to hear the conversation.

"And where are you going?" asked the sergeant.

"I'm going from my village to another village, as I often do," replied Brody.

"And you're travelling alone?"

"Oh, no! The Lord of the Forest goes with me everywhere I go!" said Brody cheerfully. Travis shook his head a little— Brody knew well the provocation he was causing.

"I see," said the sergeant coldly. "And how long do you intend to travel?"

"More or less until I come home again!" said Brody.

Travis gasped. *Not now, Brody! Stop being such an idiot!*

"Listen, boy! Do you realize who you are talking to?" shouted the sergeant.

"I'm talking to a man of flesh and bone, who like everyone else receives his every breath as a gift from the Lord!" said Brody coolly, although Travis could see the dangerous way his brother was starting to cook inside. It was clear in the set of his shoulders and his jaw.

Travis stared, astonished, hoping that Brody would just shut up. He unconsciously pulled an arrow out of his quiver and placed it on the bowstring.

"Enough!" screamed the sergeant. His corporal pulled out his sword, and the soldiers encircled Brody and cut off any escape.

"I am here as first-class sergeant of the Royal Elite Cavalry Second Division, under special commission of King Erduarl III, and I will be spoken to with respect!" The sergeant's face turned red with rage.

Brody said nothing but stared the sergeant right in the eye with a gaze of steel. He didn't flinch a muscle, even as he heard the soldiers' swords being drawn all around him. Travis drew his bow and aimed at the sergeant. If the conflict got violent the sergeant would be the first to hit the ground.

"And I am Brody, a freeman of the forest," he said with the dignity of a conquering king.

"I will not tolerate this insolence!" roared the sergeant. Travis's arm began to tremble with the strength it took to hold the bowstring for such a long time. "Shut up, Brody!" muttered Travis.

The sergeant nodded to his corporal, who nervously got down from his horse and held his sword high to strike Brody down. Travis changed his target. Everything had gotten out of control.

"You want to be the first to spill the blood of innocent forest people? Go ahead! You will pay for that, if not from my people, then from your own generals," said Brody in a cool, steady voice. "After the latest massacre you are under orders to spill as little blood as possible."

Brody's steadiness unnerved the sergeant, as did the evident uneasiness of his corporal and soldiers. Brody had hit a nerve.

"We are looking for a young girl," said the sergeant quietly, clearly aware that he'd made a mess and was now frantically trying to find a way out of it. Travis breathed a huge sigh of relief, but he kept his aim on the corporal. Brody remained silent.

The sergeant seemed to recover a little of his arrogance. "When you arrive at your next village, inform the people that His Majesty is looking for a girl about fourteen years old, named Dana."

"I can do that," replied Brody coldly, never for an instant taking his piercing gaze from the sergeant's face.

The sergeant nodded again at the corporal, who with evident relief put the sword into its sheath and mounted his horse again. As he did, all of the soldiers again put their swords away, and Travis finally relaxed his arm.

The sergeant addressed his men. "The squadron will continue on the southeast patrol, Marnicks at scout, Klintney at rear guard, others in position as drilled. Steady trot; we've lost enough time already. Understood?"

"Yes, sir!" came the reply.

"Ride!"

At that, the soldiers got themselves into position and rode off at a quick trot toward the southwest. The sergeant took one last glance over his shoulder at Brody, and for an instant the stern expression on his face disappeared, replaced by a look of helpless defeat. He shook his head, turned around, and rode off.

Brody smiled as he saw the soldiers disappear around a bend in the road. Soon enough there were no more hoofbeats to be heard. They were gone.

"Brody! Come! We'll go back to the others," said Travis. He was burning with anger but did not want to speak so close to the road. All his fear and tension turned into anger as they walked back together.

When they got to Todd and Dana, Todd asked, "Everything okay?"

"You should have seen it!" said Brody triumphantly. This patrol came and—"

"Why do you have to be such an idiot?" roared Travis, unable to control himself anymore.

"Huh?" blurted Brody, eyebrows shooting up in surprise.

"What on earth did you think you were doing? I can't believe how stupid you are!" It took all of Travis's control not to throw his brother to the ground.

Brody reddened. "But Travis, he—"

"You're not traveling alone! This is not a game!"

"Aw, come on, Travis, did you see how he talked to me? I'm a freeman of—"

"I don't care who you are! We have a mission to bring two people to the high plains, and we are going to do that *without* getting anyone arrested or killed!"

Brody stopped, and surprise gave way to anger on his ever redder face. "Look, Travis! He has no right to talk to me like that in the forest!"

"It doesn't matter what right he's got or not. We have a mission!" said Travis. He stabbed his finger toward Brody's chest. "You provoked him, and that is just plain stupid!"

Brody jutted his chin out, looking every bit the stubborn, temperamental little boy who had filled Travis's childhood with both joy and frustration. "Hey! I'm not going to take that. If you want to play the sweet little mommy's boy, you can, but I'm not."

"After our mission, you can do what you want. They can hang you from a tree. I don't care! But I don't want *Dana* hanged from a tree because you played tough guy. Now get out there in front of us and do your job, and stop being an idiot!"

"But Travis!" shouted Brody angrily.

"No buts, just go!" shouted Travis. He pointed to the mountain they were heading toward and repeated, "GO!"

Brody shook his head and went, giving Travis an ugly look as he went. Travis could just hear the words "He is such a moron" as Brody muttered to himself, and from behind Travis could see that he was walking far too fast and too loudly. He dared not call him or run up to him.

It'll only make him wilder, said Travis to himself. *When is he ever going to learn? When is he going to grow up?* He looked ahead in angry contempt at his brother, who was thoughtlessly crashing through the forest.

Every few minutes, Travis looked over his shoulder to see if Todd and Dana were keeping up. They seemed to manage all right, but both looked very sheepish and concerned. "You do something stupid like that and of course it's going to affect the whole group!" muttered Travis to himself, although slowly he began to wonder about the wisdom of talking to Brody as he had in front of the other two.

They covered several miles without saying a word. Brody always went out in advance, and when he saw that the path was clear he gave the cuckoo call, and then the others came. It was not fast but it was certain. Travis noticed that Brody barely looked him in the eye, and when he did there was no smile. This suited Travis well, as he had no smile to return.

Minutes turned into hours, and they found themselves trekking through increasingly rolling hills, with lots of oak and beech and the occasional sweet-smelling thicket of pine, especially on the northern slopes. The valleys between the hills abounded in moss and mushrooms, and thick, tangled vines made the way very difficult at times. Travis could not help but be impressed by Brody's knack of finding the best way.

While Travis walked, the scene of Brody and the patrol came back again and again. As time went on Travis began to see it differently: he saw a brave young man take on a whole squadron of soldiers and a sergeant who just didn't know what to do with him. How stupid that sergeant looked when riding away! Like a dog with a tail between his legs!

He suddenly found himself smiling at the thought. That was the courage that made Brody Brody, and the poor sergeant had never seen anything like it.

If only Dad had been there! This is exactly what Dad has to see. Dad is just too . . . too, I don't know. Is he too scared or too cautious? He's just too . . . too much like . . . like me.

The thought gripped Travis suddenly, and he stopped in his tracks. Dana and Todd, who were close behind, instinctively went down to their hands and knees between the bushes. They looked at each other bewildered as Travis just stood there, without crouching down to stay out of view and without pulling out his bow.

After waiting a minute Todd whispered, "Travis! What's up?"

"Oh . . . nothing. Sorry, I was just thinking," said Travis in embarrassment. "Brody's just up ahead."

As the journey continued, Travis felt a growing pride in his brother and began regretting the words he'd used when telling Brody off. He would have to set it right sometime. Brody was also obviously rethinking it all—he had given Travis a couple of shy smiles, which Travis was glad to return.

They had to stop a couple of times, once for a hunter and once for an old man carrying firewood. They made a small detour for an old woman and child collecting mushrooms and berries. None of these caused any great delay, and Travis felt confident that they had managed to stay out of view.

As it began to get too dark to travel, Travis asked Brody to find a place to spend the night. Brody's next cuckoo call came from a small valley to the south, surrounded by a thick stand of spruce trees.

"What do you think?" asked Brody.

"It's perfect!" Let's spend the night here," said Travis.

"It's fine!" said Todd admiringly.

"Perfect!" said Dana, who sounded very weary and extremely happy to stop.

For the first time that afternoon, Brody looked into the eyes of his brother. There was no trace of anger or frustration. Drawing close to Travis, he said, "I'll . . . uh . . . try not to do that again. You know, um, with the soldiers . . ."

A smile covered Travis's face. "Sorry I was so hard on you," he said. "I didn't mean to get so angry."

"Oh, no. It was absolutely—" began Brody.

"You just keep being brave. I hope that one day I'll be able to stand beside you with the same courage."

"Come on!" said Brody, looking to the ground in seeming embarrassment.

Travis interrupted. "Did you see the look on that sergeant's face as they left?" He could not hold back a big smile that bared all his teeth.

"Yeah," said Brody, letting out a deep sigh of relief.

"That sergeant looked like Molly-Ani! Remember when she saw the flying pig?" Travis said with a sudden twinkle in his eye.

"The flying pig?" asked Dana in a puzzled tone.

"Tell her, Brody!" said Todd, grinning from ear to ear.

"Oh, come on!" said Brody, who was still embarrassed and earnestly trying to look away.

"If you don't, I will!" said Travis with a mischievous smile.

Brody laughed. He knew when he was beat. "Okay, okay! So, Dana, there is a girl in the village. Her name is Molly-Ani—"

"And she's pretty!" said Travis with a sly smile.

"Yes," said Brody, not wanting to discuss that. "Anyway, this girl said she would never be friends with me. 'Pigs will fly before I ever think of calling you a friend of mine!' she said."

"So on that very day Brody went to the butcher's," said Todd.

"Yes, and I secretly took a big pig's head. I went to a clearing beside the path where we'd set up a swing, and I tied the pig's head to the rope and waited for Molly-Ani to come home in the evening. Well, she was on her way home carrying a bag of wool."

"I remember! She was walking along whistling without a care in the world!" added Travis, who was already laughing.

"She didn't see us. We were hidden in the trees. And then when she was just under the swing I threw the pig down with all my strength and screamed like a pig!"

"The only thing she saw was this screaming pig flying toward her out of a tree," laughed Travis. "I tell you, I've never seen anyone run so fast in all my life!"

"I almost fell out of the tree laughing!" Brody said. "And then, you know, she let out a shriek, dropped everything, and ran home screaming all the way!" He burst out laughing as though it had just happened.

"Brody, that is mean!" said Dana, shaking her head but unable to hide a grin.

"You're right," said Brody, trying in vain to look serious. "And I knew it, too. So that evening I carried the bag of wool and a couple of other things to her house. She looked at me kind of funny, but was, you know, friendly until—"

"Until he passed on *greetings from the pig!*" said Travis, who was almost rolling on the ground with laughter.

Dana looked at the two with a broad grin and just shook her head. Todd was laughing too, his whole face lit up with pleasure.

"And for some strange reason she still doesn't want to be friends," said Brody, pretending to be puzzled at the thought. This brought a loud chorus of laughter, which slowly drew down to silence.

"Hands!" called Todd, holding out his right hand toward the brothers.

"Hands!" shouted Travis, and he, Brody, and Todd all joined hands in the middle of a three-way handshake. "Three souls, one Lord, one heart!" said all three in unison.

Dana looked on curiously.

"That's our secret league greeting," said Brody happily.

"Yeah, but now we'll have to change it," said Travis.

"What?" blurted Todd.

"How's this: *'Four souls, one Lord, one heart'*?" said Travis cheerfully. "Dana, are you in?"

The boys all looked at her in hopeful expectation. Tears sprang to her eyes—but even Brody, not the most sensitive soul, could see they were tears of joy. "There's nothing that I would love more!" she said, wiping a tear away.

"Okay, once again lads! Uh, I mean, lads and lass . . . you know what I mean!" said Travis, laughing at himself.

"Hands!" called out Todd again. All four placed their right hands in and said, *"Four souls, one Lord, one heart!"*

Despite her great tiredness Dana felt happier than she could ever remember feeling.

"We need to celebrate," said Todd. "Why don't I make some root tea?"

Brody looked around. "Yeah, I think it's late enough that no one will see the smoke."

"I agree," said Travis. "Look, Brody and I will hang out the hammocks before it's too dark and hang all the bags up in the trees while you two take care of the tea."

This seemed to everyone like a good idea, so that was what they did. Brody and Travis hung the hammocks and the backpacks high up in the trees in case anyone came in the night—they wanted to be high enough that no one would see them unless they looked up. By the time they got back, the tea was ready and a small but welcoming fire was burning brightly. They sat around eating hungrily from their rations, drinking their tea, and chatting. Soon afterward they put out the fire and covered it completely with leaves and sticks to hide all traces. Up they climbed into their hammocks, and all, without exception, fell asleep in an instant.

CHAPTER 14

The High Plains

It was the loud singing of the birds that finally woke Dana. Slowly she became aware of the cool morning breeze on her sun-browned cheeks and the rocking of her hammock as the branches swayed back and forth. It was so comfortable. Up above, through the treetops, she saw a deep blue sky with only a few wisps of cloud.

It must be late! she thought suddenly, sitting up straight. As she did, she felt the pain of her sore, stiff muscles. Looking down, she saw the three boys below sitting and chatting, and she rushed as quickly as she could to join them.

"You should have woken me!" she said sharply, angry more than anything at herself for having slept so long.

"Come, Dana, don't be angry," said Travis. "You've had a very difficult time lately, and we wanted to let you rest."

"We're a long way from anywhere now," said Brody. "We don't have to rush like we did yesterday."

After eating their breakfast and packing the last of their things, they continued their journey. It was just a matter of walking toward the left of two great peaks, which rose grandly from the mountain range before them. They made good progress, only changing course twice to avoid a shepherd boy with a group of goats and couple of anglers at the river they needed to cross.

Dana got the feeling that they were going uphill more than down, and indeed she was right. After going up gentle hills for most of the morning, they found themselves climbing steeper and steeper slopes. There were fewer great oaks and beeches now and more and more pine and spruce trees. The ground grew rockier and the sand coarser. Indeed, some hills before them were so steep that they lost sight of the mountain peak. It was only at the crest of a hill that they would see it again, and so they quickly decided to choose other points they could see toward the mountains so that when they dropped down into the valleys in between, they always had a marker.

This land was like nothing any of them had ever seen. The forest was sparse, made up of mostly spruce and birch, and some tall pines rose above the forest only to grow bent from the constant wind. The woods were full of life. Fluffy little rabbits and animals that looked like a cross between squirrels and groundhogs were about their day's work, all disappearing as soon as they saw the group coming and yet peeping over the edges of their holes as soon as they could, curious at the rare sight of people. Out of the coarse sand rose great white rocks which were themselves spotted with large, thick tufts of dark green moss.

At first they tried to stay under the trees to avoid being seen, but as there were fewer and fewer trees, this became more and more difficult. Ultimately they came to a huge mountain slope, with only a very few trees and a large, serpentine path heading to the top. Brody kept walking ahead as a kind of scout, staying about forty yards in front of the others as they all climbed the long, winding path.

The sun was intense and warmed their faces. It would have felt much warmer were it not for the cool, fresh wind that blew all of the time, whistling in their ears. It was a long, hard walk to the top, and if not for the almost magical beauty of the place, they might have lost heart. Up and up they climbed to the top.

Brody was the first to reach the top and get a glance at what lay beyond.

"Wow!" he shouted in delight.

"What?" shouted Travis back, slowly coming to the top. But no answer came. Brody was lost in his gaze over the landscape.

Great, slightly cup-shaped plains stretched before them in a rich green that seemed almost to glow under the deep blue sky. Here and there, roundish outcrops of rock jutted from the grass, partially covered in moss, and small, bent trees were scattered as far as the eye could see. The place was dotted with small ponds of greenish-blue water from which great tufts of grass grew high into the sky, each tuft crowned with a big, brush-like flower.

After looking long and hard at a cluster of white rocks on a distant hill, Todd suddenly saw some move. Then he realized they were animals, and the more he studied, the more he saw that they were some kind of sheep.

"Look at that!" shouted Dana excitedly, pointing over to the right. It was a herd of yaks, grazing in the evening sun.

"Those are the hairiest things I have ever seen!" said Brody, laughing.

"If it weren't for the horns I wouldn't know which is the front and which is the back!" said Todd.

They all laughed loud and free, and all understood, without saying a word, that they had arrived. The time for crawling around and whispering under cover was over. Theirs was a great feeling of relief. This was something to celebrate.

So it was that as they laughed and joked and sat down on the warm moss drinking in the wonderful scenery, nobody noticed a pair of eyes from behind a high tuft of grass not far away. It was a little shepherd boy, staring at these unusual creatures in wonder.

After thinking for a minute, he shot off down the hill toward the left. Travis saw him going and suddenly felt stupid for letting everyone be so loud and silly in such a high, exposed place. He pointed the boy out, and all of them followed his little black head until it disappeared over a ridge and was gone.

"Should we hide?" asked Travis with uncertainty.

"No, I'm sure we are among friends here," said Brody, and something in his voice reassured Travis.

"Let's just wait here and see who comes," said Todd, and that is exactly what they did.

The little boy had been tending a herd of what looked like fuzzy, curly-haired rabbits, but bigger than rabbits and with much smaller ears. Large white sheep grazed near them, and unusually hairy donkeys sauntered casually here and there on the dense green turf. There were so many new sights that the four could barely take them all in.

Travis, who was rather nervously glancing over the crest where the little boy had disappeared, suddenly saw something approaching. He could make out a person's head, and as that person drew closer, his neck and shoulders gradually appeared. It was an unusually tall man with a large mane of black hair, bleached red by the sun. Looking at his red-brown complexion and his great, bushy black eyebrows, Travis knew him at once.

Without saying anything, he poked Brody and pointed to the man, who was now fully visible. At the end of his long right arm they saw the little boy holding his hand, running to keep up with his long strides.

As he approached, the four stood up and brushed themselves off, trying to show as much respect as they could. *Of course that's him!* thought Travis as he studied his face. The mountain man standing before them looked Travis in the eye with such intensity that he had to look away to the grass. Looking up again, he saw a face beaming at him with affection, in the way someone looks at a dear relative after a long absence. The mountain man then looked at Brody, and the smile on his face grew into a grin of deep satisfaction.

As the man's gaze came to Todd, the smile disappeared. For an instant he looked puzzled and perplexed. Then, with a sudden gasp, he stepped back with eyes wide open. "Deribo!"

The boys and Dana looked at each other, uncertain.

"Deribo!" the man said again. Taking a step toward Travis, he made the motions of one taking off a backpack and giving it to someone.

"Yeah! Yeah!" said Travis excitedly. He also made the action of taking a backpack, and he pointed to it and then at Todd. "Deribo!"

The great man's eyes filled with joy, and in wonder he just kept repeating, "Deribo! Ah . . . Deribo!"

The mountain man's two immense hands took Todd by the shoulders and shook him with glee.

"Deribo?" answered Todd with a questioning look.

While the mountain man was giving instructions to the little shepherd boy, Travis turned to Todd and quickly asked: "Do you know the story?"

"What story?"

"The story about how you came to Bud and Clara."

"They just told me the Lord of the Forest brought me!"

"Well, that's true, but—"

"Todd, this man brought you," interrupted Brody excitedly. "We were there!"

"You were a baby in his backpack!" added Travis.

"Him?"

"Yes!" said Travis.

Todd's face grew white, and he was almost wobbly with shock as all eyes turned again to the mountain man.

The man had gone down on one knee to speak with the boy. He clapped his great hands, and the shepherd boy turned and ran as fast as his little legs could carry him, calling "Deribo!" all the way down the hill until he disappeared behind the crest. The man motioned that they should join him, and they picked up their packs and followed him down the hill.

Walking over the crest, they saw the village that lay behind it. It seemed to be made of circular dwellings with cone-shaped roofs. Were they houses or tents? It was all very hard to see from this distance, and it was all the harder because of the crowd of people coming up the hill from the village. Barefoot children ran up the hill like a swarm of bees, crying "Deribo! Deribo!" in great excitement.

They were followed by a group of about fifty or so adults, men and women of all ages who surged toward them with equal excitement. The word "Deribo! Deribo!" was often to be heard in their enthused conversation.

"Man, Deribo, you were really popular in this village, eh?" said Travis, laughing.

"Let's just hope that Deribo is not something to eat!" said Brody.

"Not funny!" said Todd rather earnestly, somewhat unnerved by all of this attention. The children, arriving first, started dancing around the visitors, laughing and singing as they went. As they grew bolder, they would run up shyly to Todd, touch him, and then run away as though they had gained something of great importance.

When the adults arrived, all of the visitors were grabbed by the shoulders and shaken in welcome. Todd especially was shaken more in ten minutes than most saltshakers in ten years. He could barely walk after the affair.

The people impressed Travis very much. They seemed as light afoot as deer, springing through the spongy thick grass with great agility and poise. The women were beautiful—stunningly beautiful, almost all wearing their dark, sun-bleached hair tied behind their necks. Their brown, leathery faces and large black eyes took his breath away. Both men and women wore square, loose-fitting shirts made of a kind of woven wool. These shirts were tied around their sleek waists by leather belts of every color imaginable. Unlike the men, whose shirts were a kind of milky white, the women's shirts were dyed all sorts of different colors and mixes of colors.

All the people without exception wore a kind of trousers going down to their knees, revealing thick, muscular calves that were likewise browned by the sun. Over their trousers, the women wore a skirt that flung around as they quickly paced up the gradual slope.

After watching the mountain man with them, Travis came to the conclusion that he must be their chief. He received a special respect and seemed to be constantly giving out short, quick orders as they walked. And there was joy—joy bursting from every face, celebration coming forth from every step and gesture. This was a feast in the happening. When was the last time Travis had seen anything like this in the village? He couldn't recall.

Travis found himself fascinated by the chief, whom everyone referred to as Varsal. His easy, friendly manner and yet natural authority were a wonder to behold, and Travis could not help thinking of his dear father, who was forced to pump himself up with an air of fake authority before going out the door. His father's leadership survival tricks were nowhere to be found here. Travis, who was next in line for village chief, found himself constantly thinking about these things in the same way that a man lost in a labyrinth is always looking for the way out.

Varsal escorted the travelers into the village and brought them into a large tent in the center of it, and pointed to large fur beds arranged in a square formation in the middle of the tent. In the middle of the square were cups and a great variety of ornately painted gourd pitchers.

Varsal told them to sit down, and a short, middle-aged woman filled all of their cups and gestured for them to drink. The drinks had a delightful rich fruity taste, and they gave the four weary friends a boost of new strength. Varsal gave the woman instructions, smiled warmly at the guests one more time, and disappeared out the door.

Minutes later, a stream of ornately dressed young girls came into the tent. Unlike the women out in the fields, these girls wore colorful headbands from which bright beads hung down, forming a row of beads right across their foreheads. They also wore matching armbands and a waistband, all of which carried the same hanging beads. With the girls' quick, lively movements, the beads clicked and clacked as though dancing on their wearers.

The girls quickly laid plates, bowls, and spoons before their guests, followed by a vast selection of food, from little sticky-sweet pastries to wonderful chunks of spiced meat. They brought in some of the food on grids over basins of burning coals. Some of the food itself was burning, with great flames jumping out of the pots. It was only just before serving it that the girls put a lid on the pots to put out the fire. This food had a delicious creamy, smoky taste that seemed to melt on the tongue and warm their insides.

The food was all wonderful, simply wonderful. Travis looked up to see the others eating in pure delight.

"Is this ever good!" said Brody without even looking up from his savory meat morsels.

"All the king's cooks with all their diplomas could never make anything like this!" Dana agreed.

Travis sat there secretly admiring his brother's ability to simply enjoy the moment and forget all the other burdens of life, even if just for a minute.

There was so much excitement and noise and cheer, and so much that was totally foreign, that it could have overwhelmed the guests, but there was also something kind and peaceful about these people, and our travelers felt as natural and uncomplicated with them as they might when stroking a playful little puppy.

After a while Todd lay down his spoon in his plate, looked up with a boyish grin, and said, "I ate too much!"

"Me too," replied Travis, who had also just stopped eating.

"But I don't regret it," added Todd.

"Me neither!" said Travis with a smile.

"I think we've all eaten too much," said Dana.

"Not me!" said Brody with his mouth full. "I'm still eating! And yes—I am eating too much!"

"You know," said Travis, "I think these people are speaking a dialect of our language."

"That's just what I was thinking!" said Todd. "Now and again I get the feeling that I understand what they are saying. Dad once told me that we all spoke the same language several hundred years ago."

"I'm really going to listen hard and see if I can figure—"

Travis stopped in surprise as an arm reached over his shoulder and took his plate. The girls had come back in and started taking things away. While they were doing so, a strange drumming began. The girls looked at each other and smiled. The drumming grew louder, and the girls began dancing to the rhythm. As they did, their beads became a kind of musical instrument. They kept working, but every move and every step was somehow animated by and in step with the drum. Something was happening. The girls were getting livelier and happier as the drumming got louder.

Without saying a word, Dana looked nervously over to the others. They obviously had the same uneasy feelings. There is something spooky about being in a place where something is happening and you have no idea what it is. More drums gradually joined the first one, playing different rhythms but all related.

"I guess this is the next thing on the agenda!" said Travis with a somewhat forced smile.

Varsal came in and called his guests to follow him. They went out to a large, grassy area—a market or a meeting place in the midst of the many house-tents—where seats had been prepared for them. The large red sun was casting long shadows as it set. After motioning for them to sit down, Varsal called out with a loud voice, and villagers started to gather and form a large circle. All of them, without exception, were dancing to the beat—not in the sense that we might think, but rather, whether they were walking, or just standing, or carrying little children, the beat was going through them like a wave, and they were moving to it. Some people were swaying with great vigor while the dancing of others was just barely noticeable, but they were all doing it.

As the villagers gathered together, Travis noticed that they began dancing as a group, all swaying left and then right together, all up and then down together—a bit like two people who unconsciously begin to walk in stride when they walk together. A sense of ease came over him. He had the feeling that everything was okay, and as he looked around, it was clear that the others felt this too.

More and more people gathered until there was a great crowd indeed, and at the far side, a few people pushed through to make a kind of opening in the circle. In came six girls, each carrying branches in both hands, and they took up positions in two rows of three in the middle of the large clearing. The crowd went wild with happy cheers. Dana and Todd exchanged smiles of delight. Some kind of festivity had just started.

The girls all lifted up their branches, holding them in both hands over their heads, and started a strange kind of swaying dance.

"Now that's clever!" whispered Brody to Travis as he watched the girls sway. They all swayed perfectly parallel to one another and so beautifully that they seemed no longer to be people with bones and joints but rather trees swaying in the wind.

Four boys entered into the ring and took positions in four corners outside of the swaying tree-dancers. Each carried a burning pole that looked something like a javelin. The crowd cheered with excitement. At the exact same time, each of the boys threw his pole like a spear up and over the tree-dancers, across to the other boy in the opposite corner. What is more, they all caught the flaming poles out of the air, turned them around, and with perfect timing threw them back. They all stayed in a perfect rhythm and kept this going in harmony.

The travelers stared in amazement. They had never seen anything like it—swaying branches, flying fire, a great crowd dancing to the beat, and all this with perfect timing.

Now a young man and a young woman entered, juggling ten balls between themselves. The crowd roared with pleasure as these two took their position at the far end of the clearing, behind the swaying girls, all the while juggling. Eight more boys and girls came in, forming two lines down the sides outside of the fire throwers. At this point the young man and woman started throwing their balls, one after the other, out to the lines of children at the side. The young woman threw to the left side and the young man to the right. Soon all the balls were flying between the rows at the outside and the two in the middle. Shortly afterwards, the two jugglers in the middle went down to their knees, still juggling with tremendous skill.

When they had made themselves as low as they could get, they somehow changed their juggling pattern. The children from the outside threw their balls in high arching paths so they would fall down into the middle behind the swaying girls, and the jugglers threw them low and almost secretly back to the rows behind the swaying girls and the fire throwers. The effect was the impression of balls raining endlessly down behind the swaying trees.

It is at times like this that you forget everything. You forget time. You even forget yourself as you stare at things that are just too wondrous for the imagination. This was certainly true for Todd, Dana, Brody, and Travis, who couldn't take their eyes off this amazing spectacle. As fire flashed across the sky, it rained balls behind what looked like beautifully swaying trees.

No sooner was the scene established than two boys carrying baskets came dancing in among the girls. Unlike the others, they were running—running in a dance, again in a perfect beat. The boy in front had a red piece of wool on his head, with curly red locks hanging over his ears. The boy behind had black wool over his head, and he followed the first in a wild running scene around the swaying girls.

Suddenly Varsal entered the ring with a backpack on his back and walked around the outside until he came to the front. The boy with the red locks ran straight into Varsal, bounced off him, and landed flat on the ground. Varsal stood straight and strong, and suddenly the second boy, with black hair, jumped between Varsal and the boy on the ground. He roared like a lion, threatening to fight Varsal. The crowd cheered with glee as Varsal dropped down on one knee in front of the boy to give him the honor he deserved.

Varsal quickly picked up both boys and carried them over to a place in front of the jugglers. He sat them down on the ground and threw his cloak over them. The balls fell over them like rain . . . and suddenly Travis got it.

"That's us!" he shouted to Brody.

"Yeah!" shouted Brody back, immediately understanding everything. The flying fiery poles were the lightning; the swaying girls were the trees of the forest; and the balls were the intense rain of that day, long ago, when the mountain man and his strange gift had changed their lives. Travis and Brody looked at each other in wonder.

Suddenly Varsal threw back his cloak and stood. He held the hands of both children up, and the crowd cried out in praise. He then raised his hands as if to say stop. In a very short time all of the flaming poles had been caught, the balls stopped flying, the girls stopped swaying, and the drums ceased to beat.

Everything and everyone was still.

Varsal walked in the almost thunderous silence over to Travis and Brody. It was so quiet, they could hear his footsteps on the thick grass as he approached them. He signaled for them both to stand, and as they did, he took them both by the hand and raised their hands up as he had done with the children.

The crowd broke out in cheers, and out of the corner of his eye, Travis saw Todd and Dana cheering as well—as though they had become part of the crowd without realizing it.

Brody and Travis could barely keep the tears back. They were being celebrated. For many people in their own village, they had become an unwelcome and disliked nuisance. They were too odd, too radical, and too dangerous for their neighbors. But here, up in the mountains, there was a group of people who saw them, understood them, and loved them for who they were.

Varsal grabbed Brody's shoulders and gave them a mighty shake of approval such that Brody would have fallen had Varsal not held him up. And then he came to Travis. Instead of shaking him, he gave his shoulders a squeeze and looked deep into Travis's eyes. Varsal's great black eyes shone with warmth and acceptance.

Suddenly, Travis knew something for the first time in his life. He knew that he was not alone. The incredible feeling of aloneness that had gripped his soul for years on end suddenly let go, as though shattered by a greater power.

Now it was clear! Someone had always been there, sharing his grief and celebrating his victories. Nothing had escaped this Person's eye, and when Travis found himself persevering through the moments of deepest darkness, there the celebration was the greatest.

It all became clear in an instant. The love beaming out of Varsal's eyes spoke of the far greater love of the Lord of the Forest, who at that moment spoke to him the words he had never heard from his own father:

I am pleased with you and love you dearly, my son.

Travis fell into Varsal's arms with great sobs and tears as waves of joy and of grief and all that his heart had locked up over the years rolled over him. Varsal held the young man like his own son. The crowd was utterly silent, but they seemed neither shocked nor distraught. This great event had obviously fulfilled a higher purpose, and a deep sense of joy filled the air, as though a lame man had just been healed and could walk, or a blind man had been made to see.

Travis slowly regained his composure, and the crowd gradually broke into small groups of people, standing around chatting informally. It was loud, and lively laughter filled the cool night air.

Travis left Varsal and turned to his companions, who all glowed with joy for him.

"We've got to come here more often," said Brody, giving Travis a slap on the back.

"We do," said Travis. "You're right."

Now that the spectacle was finished, the four guests suddenly felt the weight of their tiredness and wanted nothing more than to get to bed. Varsal saw this and called the middle-aged woman to come and take them to the tent where they would sleep.

She led them to a dwelling where a thick woolen mattress was laid out for each one of them, covered with a large blanket of densely knit wool and yak hair. Each bed had a large yak skin to pull over top, and beside each bed sat a huge, white, hairy dog. In the middle of the room hung an oil lamp, which shone a gentle light throughout the room.

Very little was said as the four took off their boots and crawled in their clothes into their beds, and after a round of "good nights," they all fell quickly into a deep, joyful sleep.

CHAPTER 15

Fetching Eggs

Travis and Brody left early the next morning. They were concerned about their father, who would soon be sending out men to look for them if they did not return. Todd and Dana and a large group of mountain people escorted them up to the crest of the hill where they had arrived, and after some sorrowful good-byes, they descended back toward the forest.

Todd especially felt a great lump in his throat as he saw them slowly disappear behind the brush at the lower part of the serpentine path. When they were around he felt like a king on a stallion, and nothing was impossible. But when they were gone, he suddenly felt like a little boy in a big bad world, expecting only to fail and feeling afraid of everything that moved.

Dana noticed the troubled look that came across his face as their friends left. She herself knew only too well what it was to fear. She had never expected to see it in Todd. *How can it be that the person who gives me so much courage must himself battle for his own courage?* she wondered.

"Come, Todd, let's go back," she said, giving his arm a friendly squeeze.

"Yes, let's!" said Todd.

"Do you have any idea how long we'll stay here?" asked Dana as they walked the gentle descent to the village.

"No, no idea at all," replied Todd. "A few weeks maybe."

"I don't mind staying for a while. There's something about these people I really like!"

"Yes, me too. I think Brody and Travis were sad to leave so soon."

"Yes . . ." said Dana absently. Her eyes were scanning the magnificent landscape from one end of the horizon to the other. "Have you ever seen so many ponds?"

"There must be thousands of them," responded Todd.

"And each more beautiful than the next!"

"Yes," said Todd. On the broad grassy slope going down to the village they were free to raise their eyes and view the stunning panorama without worrying about stumbling over anything.

"Are those trees beside the ponds?"

"They are as big as trees but somehow look like grass," said Todd, cupping his hand over his eyes to see against the sun.

"Yes," said Dana. "In the wind they dip back and forth like huge stalks of wheat. Look at that one over—"

She stopped abruptly as she saw two figures walking toward them from the edge of the village. It was Varsal and a tall, dark, beautiful girl about her age or a little older.

They approached Dana, and Varsal pointed to Dana and then to the girl. "Dana—Pian. Pian—Dana."

Pian stepped in front of Dana and looked deep into her eyes. With her thick wild hair tossed by the wind; her noble, high cheeks; and a beautiful smooth red complexion, Dana thought she had all the makings of a mythical heroine. Her large black eyes danced with a playful friendliness, and a serene grin grew across her face.

What a beauty! thought Dana, who felt a smile appear on her own face in return.

"Come," said Pian, taking Dana's hand and giving it a slight pull. Dana looked warily at Varsal, who simply nodded with a smile. Dana threw a fleeting good-bye glance at Todd, who did not at all seem happy to be left "alone," but before she knew it she was being whisked off at great speed by this strange and wonderful girl.

Pian pulled a rather reluctant Dana quickly down the hill into the village. Dana looked repeatedly over her shoulder for Todd, but he was gone, and she concluded that she should just cooperate and accept her fate. Pian was going at quite a pace, and it was all that Dana could do to keep up. Around and between the dwellings they hurried, along narrow alleys, through grassy clearings, around tables and tall frames with meat hanging to be dried in the sun.

They suddenly found themselves in a large clearing where a number of older women were huddled around a table sorting through berries and small fruits.

With a shout, Pian ran into their midst, and after a lively exchange with a lot of laughter, an older woman pointed to two large backpacks leaning against a wall.

Pian signaled that Dana should come and stand with her arms in front of her. Dana did, and before she knew it she felt the weight of a backpack on her shoulders. She put her arms through the loops, and Pian tied Dana's belt around her waist and threw her own backpack on.

After exchanging a few quick good-byes with the women, the girls were on their way out of the village. They marched between dwellings and through clearings until suddenly they were out and standing before the vast expanse of the high plains.

The cool, refreshing wind tingled in Dana's face as she squinted to gaze over the horizon. "Come!" said Pian, and off they went. The morning sky was a beautiful blue, with only a couple of wisps of cloud stretched high and long over the vast horizon. Majestic mountains rose to the left, and directly in front of them lay a flat, grassy plain dotted with lakes and ponds as far as the eye could see. The occasional tree rose out of the plain, bending in the wind. Great stands of grass rose out of the banks of the ponds and stood upright for fleeting minutes between gusts of wind. The larger tufts of grass bore large silky white flowers that bobbed left and right in the breeze.

It was all as wondrous as it was strange, and Dana found herself stopped in her tracks, staring at the grandeur of the place and wanting to spy out every detail.

"Come!" cried Pian, who was now quite a few paces ahead.

"Oh, yes. Coming!" called out Dana as though waking from a dream. She was delighted to see that Pian was heading directly toward a distant pond, and she hurried to catch up.

Little rabbit-like creatures peered over rocks and tufts of grass, and Pian greeted them all without exception. "Don't worry about her!" shouted Pian to a badger and pointing to Dana. "She's new here! She's my sister!"

Her sister? thought Dana to herself. *This crazy girl thinks I'm her sister?* Dana was quite sure that she had understood her, for Pian spoke clearly, and Dana had already made some progress in understanding the dialect of the mountain people. It wasn't so very different from her own language.

The pond proved to be further than it had seemed, and Dana was ready to drop by the time they got there. "Come! Come!" called Pian, going down to the edge of the water. For a small pond, it was a noisy one, teaming with life. Cicadas were chirping amongst the reeds, large leathery frogs were in full chorus, and a flock of duck-like birds were protesting, outraged at the sight of the intruders.

Dana stumbled down to the water with the last strength she could muster. She stood before Pian but was ashamed to look in her face. *This girl dances through the grass with the ease of a deer, and she's being slowed down by me, a weak city kid. How pathetic I am!*

Feeling Pian's two strong hands gripping her shoulders, Dana slowly raised her eyes to look her in the face. As she did she saw eyes like great coals and a lovely face shining with great concern. "Oh! Dana! Dana tired! Pian running! Pian very sorry. So very sorry!"

Dana had to look away. "It's no problem. No problem!"

"Forgive me," said Pian. Dana looked up again—looking into Pian's eyes was like looking into the eyes of love itself.

Dana could not help but smile, and as she did, a great smile appeared on Pian's face. "Stand there!" said Pian. She undid

Dana's belt and disappeared behind her, lifting the pack from Dana's back and laying it on the grass. *What a relief!* thought Dana. Her tired back suddenly felt light as a feather.

With one heave, Pian pulled off her own backpack and laid it beside Dana's. After digging around inside, Pian pulled out what looked like a large ball of big leaves. She sat on the lower frame of her backpack and called for Dana to do the same. Dana had never been so happy to sit down in her life. She could feel her legs throbbing with fatigue, and her shoulders felt wonderfully free.

Pian opened up the ball of leaves and pulled out a clump of sticky black stuff that looked like dates or maybe figs. She held it up to Dana, who cautiously took a bit and examined it in her hand.

"Not for looking! For eating!" said Pian, putting a piece in her mouth and chewing on it heartily. Dana did the same and was rewarded by a nutty sweet taste as she chewed. Without a word, the girls polished off the contents of that package in no time, and now Dana felt very much better indeed. They then kneeled down at the edge of the water and with cupped hands took a drink.

Sitting down again on their packs, they bathed their faces in the warm sun, which was now quite a bit higher.

"You like it here?" asked Pian cautiously.

"Very much!" said Dana, who indeed felt as though she was sitting on the threshold of heaven itself.

"I am very happy you are here with me," said Pian with breathtaking honesty.

"Thanks," replied Dana shyly, not knowing what else to say. Everyone she had known in the kingdom was guarded and cautious in their speech. Pian was so open, so truly free. But before she could think further she suddenly realized they were being approached. Maybe a hundred duck-like birds were slowly and very deliberately walking towards them. They were something between ducks and geese—but not as friendly as ducks nor as elegant as geese.

Dana's chest grew tense as it always did when she felt threatened. And threatening they were! Spitting and hissing, they were probably the most mean-looking, unfriendly animals she had ever set eyes on. They were definitely coming right for them, like an angry mob determined to eliminate intruders.

Pian glanced up at them with a bored, unimpressed look and said, "You really are idiots! The whole lot of you!" With that she burst to her feet and charged them, shouting, waving her hands in the air as though she were attacking. Suddenly there were ducks and feathers everywhere, and the air was filled with the sound of panicking birds who didn't have the foggiest idea of what they should do next. Tripping over each other on land and flying into each other in the air, they all fled back to the water in one totally disorganized flop of a military maneuver.

"Let's get to work!" said Pian, bending over her backpack to get some things out. She pulled out a big bag and walked down to the water. She then started throwing what looked to Dana like bits and pieces of food into the water. The ducks went wild, diving and jumping after them. They had utterly forgotten their common enemy, and it was now every duck for itself in a huge battle for the tasty morsels being thrown into the pond. The pond exploded with squeaks, yelps, hisses and groans. Feathers flew in every direction, and Dana wondered if any of the ducks would survive this out-and-out brawl.

"Come with me!" shouted Pian over the wild splashing and squawking of duck greed, and she led Dana to the rear of a tall stand of grass. There Dana saw long rows of perfectly ordered nests, furnished with thick layers of feathers and filled with large eggs.

"For each nest take all the feathers and all but one egg!" shouted Pian. The girls went hastily to work, picking up hundreds of eggs and countless handfuls of feathers. Within a few minutes they were done and carried two big bags full of eggs and feathers out with them to their packs beside the bank.

The ducks were only just beginning to calm down and sat looking overstuffed and sickly on the surface of the water. A couple of them were still fighting over the remaining bits and pieces here and there, driven far more by greed than hunger. Dana was amused to see that the frogs and other birds had all retreated to the banks, not wanting to meddle in duck affairs.

"I think I've seen trees that are more intelligent than those ducks!" said Dana.

"You probably have!" laughed Pian and then added, "You stay here and rest, and I'll be back very soon."

Dana nodded, delighted at the thought of a rest, and watched as Pian went around to the tall grass and selected long leaves, which she cut off with a knife and collected under her arm. A shorter, blockier kind of grass grew beside the tall grass, and Pian chopped away at the bottom of the thicker stalks and added them to the cut grass. Dana watched her in fascination as she returned and with great skill rolled up the grass and put it in her backpack, attaching the thick stalks to its sides.

Where does she get the energy and the skill? said Dana to herself.

Soon they were on their way home. Pian was carrying everything in her backpack, and Dana carried nothing but her own pack. This was hard for her pride to accept, but she was exhausted. The way back was full of laughter and fun, and instead of greeting the animals, Pian took the opportunity to introduce them to Dana.

The descending sun was already casting long shadows on the final stretch before the village. It was a breathtaking evening. Pian looked at Dana and said, "You know, there's only one thing nicer than a beautiful spring evening. Do you know what it is?"

"No," replied Dana.

Pian stopped, looked Dana right in the eyes, and said, "Spending it with you!"

Dana looked down at her feet, overjoyed and at the same time at a loss of words. "Thanks."

As they continued toward the village, Dana's mind went back to a proverb her grandmother had once told her: "What's better than finding a treasure in the field? Finding a friend for life."

On they went, chatting and laughing and joking. The badger they had seen earlier poked his nose out of his hole and stared at the two girls making such a racket in the quiet evening hours.

"Don't worry about her," shouted Dana, pointing to Pian, "she's my sister!" Both girls burst out laughing. Totally confused, the badger did what all wise badgers do when life becomes unexplainable. He went down his hole again, sprawled out, and had a snooze.

CHAPTER 16

The Outer Huts

Seeing Dana disappear with the tall village girl threw yet another weight onto Todd's sad heart. He had just said good-bye to Travis and Brody, and now he watched Dana get whisked away. He and Varsal continued the long descent to the village without saying a word. The crowd that had accompanied Travis and Brody to the ridge were cheerfully chatting in their quick pace toward the village. The bright sun shone higher now, and Todd enjoyed its warmth on his cheeks.

As they approached the village, Varsal signaled that he and Todd should leave the crowd and walk around to the left of the village. On the way Todd peered amidst the dwellings to see a great commotion of activity. Both women and men were cleaning and cooking and tending fires and doing any number of other morning chores. Village life boomed with busyness and purpose.

At a certain point, Varsal turned abruptly into the village and came to a clearing with lots of people and about six large yaks. The yaks all wore bright harnesses and carried large leather bags on their backs.

A teenager came and greeted Varsal. He stood a little taller than Todd, and although he was quite slender, his deep chest swelled with every breath. His arms were thick and agile, and he had the bulging thighs and calves of a well-trained runner. His hair sat like a thick black mane going down his back just below his shoulders. Although he bore the noble high cheekbones and grand leathery face of the others, one thing set him apart. Not even the faintest trace of a smile could be seen upon his face. With great earnest eyes, he looked at Varsal.

"Everything's ready for hut seven, Uncle," said the boy.

"Six yaks?" asked Varsal.

"They've done a lot of shearing, so we're taking two extra," reported the boy.

"And Basdar?" asked Varsal.

"He's still sick, Uncle."

"And Zivra?"

"Zivra isn't ready," said the boy nervously.

"Not ready?" cried Varsal in alarm.

Todd was listening as intensely as he could. Both Varsal and the boy spoke slowly and clearly compared to the other mountain people, and Todd was beginning to realize that Travis had been right—their dialect was very similar to his own language.

"Don't be angry, Uncle. Zivra was really shaken by the wolves. He needs time. He needs to gather his strength."

"Gather his strength . . ." repeated Varsal thoughtfully.

"Uncle, I need a man—a strong man who can wield a heavy spear. I myself, I am just a boy—"

Varsal stretched out his hands and laid them on the boy's shoulder. "You are the *man* I have chosen!"

The boy looked away, but Todd could see the great honor that Varsal was giving him. "I now choose two men for this mission," continued Varsal. "You and Deribo."

The boy gasped and stepped backwards, glancing at Todd with a desperate look. "But Uncle! He's never—"

"Trust your uncle, Jarod."

"But Uncle! There are—"

"I have seen many wolves and many bears, my son. They gave me new eyes to see. Trust me," said Varsal.

"Yes, Uncle. As you say," replied Jarod, who bowed in respect but was unable to hide his look of desperation. Todd was suddenly gripped with fear. *What on earth were they talking about? What are we going to do?*

Varsal took Jarod by the shoulder and gazed into his eyes. The chief told the boy something Todd didn't understand and shook him, as the mountain people did to show affection. He then came to Todd and grasped his shoulders. Unable to return his gaze, Todd looked away. "Be strong, my son. Go and succeed." With that he shook Todd with the vigor of a bear, turned and shouted a few short instructions, and was gone.

Feeling a little awkward, Todd turned to Jarod and smiled, hoping in vain for a smile in return. The boy walked around the yaks, one after the other, checking the bags and bridles as if Todd were not there. He exchanged a few short words with the people who had loaded the yaks, and then they moved them to make two parallel lines of three yaks each and tied each line together, leaving about three yards distance from tail to nose.

An old man took Todd to the first yak in the row on the right and placed Todd's hand on its neck. Jarod appeared to Todd's left with his hand placed on the front yak of the left row and suddenly, as if by magic, Varsal stood before them. He raised his hands to the heavens and called out with a loud voice as though giving a blessing. All was quiet except for the constant drone of the wind, and Todd gazed in fascination at Varsal as he slowly lowered his view to the boys. He nodded, and Jarod and his yaks started walking forward. Todd's three yaks followed instinctively, and off the party went toward the northern horizon.

Will nobody ever tell me what's going on? What is with these people? In his confusion, Todd found himself being led by a yak somewhere he didn't know. *Where are we going? What are we going to do there? What's wrong with this lad? Why doesn't he like me? Why won't anyone ever tell me anything?*

Helplessness turned into anger, and Todd could feel his blood starting to boil. He took a few deep breaths and lifted his eyes to the horizon before him. His eyes feasted on a view that was more magnificent than anything he had ever seen. An enormous plain of lush green grass, dotted with innumerable ponds, stretched out in every direction till it met the vast grand sky above. The bright sun caressed his face with warmth and soothed the chill of the strong breeze. What with birds and distant flocks of sheep and the occasional donkey, the plain was teeming with life. Behind him clattered the harnesses and bells of yaks as they plodded through the deep grass.

Todd looked over at his companion, who was staring solemnly out in the direction he was trudging. *Very well then! If no one tells me what I'm doing or where we're going, I'm not going to let that bother me. No sir! I'm just going to keep going and enjoy the scenery!*

Todd gazed off into the great mountains to the left, trying to make out what the little green dots on their brown flanks were. But the more he determined not to think about his anger, the angrier he got. It was useless. He had to talk.

"My name's Todd!" he blurted out, rather more aggressively than he had wanted to.

"I know," came the reply. The boy never took his gaze from the horizon.

"What's your name?" asked Todd with all the restraint he could muster. He'd already heard it from Vasal, but he wanted to make a proper introduction.

"Jarod."

"Where are we going?"

"Hut seven."

"Why are we going there?"

"Supplies. They need supplies."

"They? So there are people there?"

"Yes." The peculiar boy seemed to skirt along the edge of unfriendliness without ever really being unfriendly. Not once did he turn to look at Todd, but his voice didn't sound annoyed.

"What are they doing there?"

"Keeping animals."

Well! That's progress! thought Todd happily. His anger was strangely gone. *Amazing what a little information can do.* He now felt free to lift his eyes up and drink in the grandeur of all that lay before him. And it was grand—fantastically grand. With the distant cries of birds, the howling of the wind in his ears, and the swaying and dancing of the enormous grasses scattered over the plain, it was a banquet for the senses.

Glancing over at Jarod, though, Todd clearly sensed that something was eating away at his companion. He might not exactly be unfriendly, but he was definitely troubled.

"When will we get there?" asked Todd.

"Just before sunset if we keep up this pace."

"So we'll stay overnight?" said Todd. He felt a pang as he missed Dana.

"Yes."

Todd pushed his hand into the hair of his yak and was surprised to see it totally disappear in the warm oily strands.

"And you normally travel with Zivra?" asked Todd, hoping he'd remembered the name right.

"Yes."

"And he's not well?"

"Not really."

"What happened?"

"Wolf bite, on his hand."

That was startling. "Is his hand better?"

"Yes, what's left of it." A look of ugly torment overshadowed Jarod's face, and for the first time he turned to Todd and continued, "Had I only thought faster, he would never have lost his fingers."

Todd said nothing. He suddenly found himself scanning the ends of the horizon rather than returning Jarod's glance. How often he himself had been hit by waves of regret and frustration! He suddenly saw Jarod through new eyes. This was a boy struggling to walk in a man's shoes.

"You were hoping that Varsal would send a man with you."

"Yes."

"Why doesn't he?"

"I don't know. He sees something in you, Deribo."

"Which you don't see," blurted Todd without thinking.

"I'm not the chief," said Jarod calmly.

"But you would rather I didn't come," insisted Todd.

"Deribo, I don't dislike you."

The simple honesty of the boy was disarming, and Todd couldn't help but like him.

"This plain is the most beautiful thing I've ever seen," said Todd, trying to steer the conversation to lighter things.

"Deribo, the plain is beautiful, it's wonderful, but it is brutal and it is terrible. It fills you with joy, and when you least expect it, it can break your heart. There are horrible creatures out there, lurking behind the tall grass."

Jarod's eyes suddenly flashed with a tormented terror. His gaze dashed restlessly to and fro, and his voice dropped to a strained whisper.

"You wouldn't believe what I've seen. I wouldn't wish that on you, Deribo. I wouldn't wish it on anyone. . . There are beasts out there who may well be watching you right now. All they want is to fall on you and make you unable to fight. And then, no matter if you're dead or alive, they go for your belly and rip it right out and throw it to the side. And then the whole frenzied pack together—they plunge their heads into your bowels and just rip out what they can. Blood sprays in every direction, and the air is thick with its scent. And you just lie there gasping your last breaths, little tiny breaths until you're still."

Todd swallowed hard, but Jarod wasn't done.

"And then the beasts go for the ribs, pulling from both sides with enormous force, and the ribs crack and break. I tell you, you can hear that a mile away! They rip and swallow. In their wildness they don't even chew. They chomp and slobber and that's all you hear. It's as if the wind stops and the whole world stands still. Within a minute all that is left is a big bloody patch on the grass, with fur and broken bones scattered around. And then they pull back as though drunk with blood and swagger off to some cave or hole, leaving the rest for the birds."

Todd fixed his eyes on the swaying horns of his front yak, without any idea whatsoever as to what he should say or think. So he said nothing, and the two walked on together. They seemed to be following no path at all, wading all the time through the thick grass of an apparently endless plain.

By early afternoon, though, they came to a gradual descent toward the colossal mountains that rose from a distance. As they continued, it became clear to Todd that the land was dropping away to the left and the right and they soon found themselves walking along a narrow grassy ridge.

As the ridge grew yet narrower and the drop on both sides steeper, they had to walk in single file. The grass gave way to stones, and every now and again a yak knocked a stone free, and Todd could hear it falling what seemed to be an immense distance till it could be heard no more. The wind was picking up, and its distant groaning seemed to Todd like the howling of some gruesome beast.

They came to a small widening, and Jarod stopped his yaks and walked back to Todd. "How are you doing?"

"I'm okay," said Todd, shouting over the wind and trying to hide the fear which had slowly gripped him.

"For the first time you're doing very well," shouted Jarod. "The wind's picking up, and I fear there's a storm brewing."

"So what do we do?" asked Todd.

"Tie yourself to your front yak. If you fall over the side, he will hold you up."

"And if he falls?" shouted Todd.

"Then you're dead," said Jarod in a very matter-of-fact way. He walked back and pulled two long sticks off the second yak. "Here, Deribo, you need two walking sticks!" shouted Jarod. "You need one on each hand!" By this time he had to shout directly into Todd's ear for Todd to hear anything at all. The wind was no longer blowing but was wailing and raging as Todd had never heard a wind do.

"If you feel a gust," shouted Jarod, "drop to your knees, or even your belly! Grab hold of the ground and hug it. Don't let go until the wind dies down!"

"Okay!" shouted Todd.

Todd watched as Jarod's nimble figure moved forward, past his own yaks, clinging to their hair with every step. When he got to the front of the train he also pulled out two walking sticks, and bending down as low as he could, walked on ahead.

The screaming wind and wild flapping of their clothes was all they could hear. Walking had become very difficult, for the wind pushed with an enormous sideways force. Todd could hardly see as his eyes watered against the blasts, and he felt how the stormy wind pushed the tears sideways onto his nose and then just licked them away. He peered over the edge and gulped in fear as it disappeared to an endless fall. He had to fix his eyes on the path before him and keep struggling for every step.

A sudden gust threw Todd off the ridge, and he dangled helplessly on the rocky face. He heard the grunt of the first yak as it struggled to hold him. As if in a dream, Todd saw himself scrambling for rocks to hold onto, sending many tumbling down the cliff face. Finally one held, and he heaved himself up with a panicked strength. Then another held, and up he got to the ridge again. The wind seized him, but he struggled desperately against it and forced his way to the ground.

There he lay, face in the dirt, gasping for precious air. He clung to the ridge with both hands and feet. Both walking sticks were gone. Walking was out of the question anyway. As he looked up, he could see that Jarod and his yaks were quite a distance ahead. All he could do was crawl on all fours. Looking down, he saw many cuts on his hands and fingers but felt nothing. The only thing he saw and felt now was the ridge and the wild wind wickedly trying to pull him off it and hurl him to a certain death.

Gust blew after gust, and Todd found himself clinging to the rocks underneath him. The little progress he had made crawling along was swallowed up in the horror of the moment. Up ahead he saw that Jarod had reached the other side and brought his yaks into a sheltered area. They were only about thirty yards away, but never had thirty yards seemed so far.

Stumbling, and veering left and right in a kind of drunken stupor, Todd went on. Sometimes the gusts seemed to cry with such a frenzied rage that he all could do was lie face-down in the dirt, clinging to the rocks as though they were his very life.

He was getting ever closer, but also ever weaker. A whole new fear gripped him as he realized that he barely had the strength to move. Then a gust grabbed him and he fell onto his face, holding the rocks for dear life.

The wind let up, but Todd couldn't bring himself to let go of the rocks. He held them. He clung to them. He couldn't go on. There he lay, unable to loose his horrified grip. He had somehow become prisoner to his own terror.

Suddenly he felt something warm on his cheek. It was Jarod, who had crawled out to get him. "Deribo, come! You're nearly there!" he screamed.

"I can't!" cried Todd.

"You must! Otherwise you will certainly die!" screamed Jarod. "I'll tie a rope to you. When you feel the rope pull, crawl! When you don't, just lie down and hold still."

"Okay!" said Todd. The coming of his friend somehow gave him new courage.

Jarod tied the rope to Todd's belt and with great difficulty turned himself around on his belly on the narrow ridge. The wind calmed, and he tugged on the belt. He and Todd crawled a few yards, and a savage gust almost whipped them both off the ridge. They both lay down tight, clinging to the rocks until it subsided. Again Todd felt the tug, and again they crawled a few yards. This went on until Todd was surprised to see the ground below him widen out. They had made it to the other side. Now all that was left was to crawl along to the shelter.

Almost drunk with joy, Todd scrambled through the soft grass on his hands and knees. The ground dropped suddenly into a large, bowl-shaped hole beside an enormous stone that rose out of the side of the mountain. Inside, it was calm. Todd lay gasping for air in the thick grass. He slowly came to himself and looked up to see Jarod standing by his yaks, undoing their ropes. Todd looked on with admiration as Jarod calmly took the packs off and laid them down in the grass.

How much happier he'd be if he didn't have to drag me around with him! thought Todd. *I'm a coward, and that's the last thing he needs.* He cast only fleeting glances at his companion, feeling too ashamed to look in his eyes. No wonder Jarod hadn't wanted him along. Jarod did not once ask Todd how he was or even give him a passing smile.

Gradually the howling wind died down, and the sun came out in all its splendor. The boys reloaded the yaks and tied them together again, all without a word. Jarod led the way out. They climbed out of the bowl and up to a narrow cut path that snaked its way around the winding contours of the mountain face.

Jarod tossed the occasional emotionless look behind him to see how Todd was doing. It was no easy path, with thorny bushes to the right and an eternal drop to the left. The utter lack of any communication between them lay like a cold black cloud over Todd's soul. How much he would cherish that boy's friendship! Jarod radiated a strong, noble character, and Todd felt drawn to him. *I can't blame him for not wanting me. I wouldn't want me either!* What could Varsal have been thinking?

Todd struggled around a large stone that leaned out from the mountain side, and coming around it saw a large meadow that hung between two mountain faces. At the foot of the far cliff face stood a ramshackle hut with smoke climbing out its chimney. Jarod didn't even look back as he continued it, and Todd hurried to catch up. Then his eyes caught a figure running out of the hut in their direction. As he approached, Todd could make out a young man in shabby loose clothing.

The man walked for a while with Jarod, and Todd could sense the excitement of their conversation from the broken bits he managed to hear.

When they got to the hut the young man came running back to Todd and shook him violently. "Great to have you here, Brother Deribo! I put some tea on when I first saw you, and it must be almost ready. I'll help you with your things, and we'll go in."

The young man's broad smile revealed several missing teeth and a deep scar that rose from his lip up to his half-closed left eye. Despite his slender frame, he heaved the packs off the yaks with the strength of a man twice his size. When all the packs had been put under shelter and the yaks had been sent out to graze, he led them inside to a warm kitchen with a happily crackling fire.

CHAPTER 17

A Hot Discussion

The kitchen was a cluttered room in the heart of the hut with a mud stove to the side and a rough-hewn wooden table with a few stools scattered around it in the center. Implements of every size and description hung from the ceiling, and Todd had to be careful not to knock his head against a hammer or get a pitchfork in his ear.

Todd stared at Jarod as he opened a box behind the stove, pulled out cups, and then reached around a corner and lay hold of a bowl of honey, as though this were his own home.

The young man brought the clay pot off the fire and poured tea from it into their cups. "Deribo, sorry!" he said, handing Todd his tea. "I didn't even tell you my name. I'm Cusharok, but everyone calls me Sharo."

"Nice to meet you!" said Todd, unable to hide his pleasure in Sharo's friendly cheer.

"Oh, Jarod, There's so much to tell you! All the ewes lambed, and we got sixteen twins! So that's fifty lambs in all, and we lost only one to a fox. Dameen then got the fox with an arrow— he is such a lucky shot, I tell you—and he skinned it and has been wearing the most ridiculous fox hat on his head. You've got to see it!"

Todd grinned as he watched Sharo dance around the kitchen, organizing bits of food and keeping the fire going. He reminded him of Bud, who always loved to entertain visitors.

"And we got so much honey, we ran out of leaves to wrap it in. We've also got loads of cheese and a fair bit of smoked meat. Can't offer you many eggs, I'm afraid." Sharo brought a large, sticky cake of berries and beans to the table and cut it up with a knife. "The geese took the east wind and disappeared early one morning. Let's see if the storms drive them back. Deribo, here!"

Sharo pushed a big piece of cake to Todd on a wooden plate. Then he pushed another to Jarod.

"Here, Jarod. You're going to have to take a big skin back. One of the yaks in the south face broke her leg, and there was nothing we could do. She hadn't been milking well anyway. We got a lot of meat out of her. I was surprised . . ."

Sharo stopped and gazed at Jarod in sudden wonder. "What's up, Jarod?" he asked.

"Nothing," said Jarod without taking his gaze off the cup in his hand.

"How are Marita and Dooley?"

"Everyone at home is okay."

"But you are not. Jarod, what's with you?" Sharo gazed at Jarod with deep concern.

"Nothing."

Sharo turned to Todd and asked, "Can you tell me anything, Deribo?"

"I don't know," said Todd tensely. He felt too uncomfortable to say anything, and didn't know what else to say.

"Varsal put you two together?"

"Yes, but that won't last long!" retorted Jarod tensely, fidgeting around with his cup. His words sent a chill down Todd's spine, and he desperately wished he could get out of there.

"I don't understand," said Sharo.

"Jarod needs someone else," said Todd quietly.

"That's right," said Jarod.

"Did you fight?"

"No!" said Jarod.

"What happened?"

"We got caught in a storm going over Raykal Ridge."

"Sharo," said Todd, "I was so scared. I could barely move! Jarod needs someone else. A man with courage."

For the first time Jarod looked up at Todd and stared into his eyes. He seemed surprised. "But Deribo, you have courage."

"I lay there like a stone. I was so terrified that I—"

"Sharo," interrupted Jarod, "Deribo made it over even after getting thrown off the side and climbing back up again. I have rarely seen such courage. Now I know what Varsal sees in him."

"Yes, but . . ." began Todd, hardly knowing what he would say next.

"I saw the storm in the east sky," continued Jarod, "and it seemed so far away. And then I decided to cross. How absolutely stupid! Deribo came within a hair of losing his life because I was such a fool."

"But you were brave enough to crawl back for me!" said Todd hotly.

"It doesn't matter!" shouted Jarod. "You want to go with someone else, and you should! I can't blame you for not wanting to continue with me."

"Who says I don't want to?" yelled Todd, getting to his feet and hitting a hanging pan with the back of his head.

"Now, you two just calm—" began Sharo, but it was no use.

Jarod stood and barked, "Of course you don't! I nearly killed you! Don't you get it?"

"But I was a coward!"

"You had the courage of ten men out there!"

"Who are you to tell me if I was courageous or not?" Todd's eyes flashed with rage. "I lay there like a baby, and you risked—"

"STOP IT!" hollered Sharo, pounding a hammer with a mighty crash on the table. "I refuse to allow my guests to shout this way under my roof! Let me make this clear. Both of you, sit down!"

Both Todd and Jarod returned sheepishly to their stools, staring only at the cake before them.

"Jarod, you say that Deribo should not work with you because you are not worthy of him."

"Exactly!" huffed Jarod.

"And Deribo, you say that Jarod should not work with you because you are not worthy of him."

"That's right," replied Todd.

"Our tradition has a solution for this," said Sharo, more calmly, sitting down again in his chair. "In such a situation, the guest chooses what he wants."

Todd looked up. "What I want?"

"That's right, Deribo," Jarod agreed.

"What do you want, Deribo?" asked Sharo.

Todd almost smiled. "There is something I want. I want it more than all the world!"

"Well, ask," said Sharo.

"Yes, I'm sure we can find someone else who—" began Jarod.

Todd cut him off. "I want to work with Jarod!"

"You what?" gasped Jarod.

"I do! I really do! With Jarod and only Jarod!"

Jarod gazed at him with eyes like saucers.

"But only if Jarod wants to have me," added Todd.

"Of course! Of course I do!" shouted Jarod, leaping to his feet. "I thought you would never want to see me again in your life!"

"Well, you thought wrong," said Todd, beaming with joy.

"It seems we have an agreement," said Sharo with a wry smile.

"But Deribo, there are more dangerous places than this," said Jarod gravely. "I am not—"

"I want to work with you, and that's final."

"Now that that's settled, let's eat our cake," said Sharo, and they sat down to eat. The boys ravenously consumed their pieces only to receive a second helping right away from their helpful host.

The room was filled with lively chatter, and cake and tea disappeared at amazing rates. Todd couldn't help notice, though, how Jarod gradually became more solemn. Sharo noticed Todd's quiet thoughtfulness and asked, "What's up, Deribo?"

"Jarod, what are you thinking?" asked Todd.

"There is one more thing I have to tell you, Sharo. A message from Varsal. It's not sure . . ." Jarod paused. "But they think they saw Ethero at hut two."

Sharo gasped as though gripped by great fear. His anxious eyes stared at the tea cup in his hand, and he slowly said, "So he's back."

"Well, they're not sure."

A thunderous silence filled the room, and Todd looked around in confusion. "Who is this Ethero?"

"He's a wolf," Jarod told him. "What we call a great wolf. He's huge."

"He stands head and shoulders above all other wolves," added Sharo. "He's already killed six men."

There was silence.

"Some say he can fly," said Sharo, "and others say—"

"Oh, come on Sharo!" blurted Jarod, "You can't believe that stuff! He's a wolf. Just a wolf."

"A wolf with a large pack," said Sharo, turning his gaze to Jarod. "What's Varsal going to do?"

"He's preparing reinforcements, but it isn't easy. Basdar is sick, and Zivra's not ready."

"Well, tell him to hurry! We're only three out here."

"He knows that, Sharo."

The conversation continued but never really regained the cheer it had before. The other two herders came in from their work on a remote meadow, and after a meal together, everyone retired to bed shortly after sunset.

CHAPTER 18

Catching Up

A hand pushed the door open a crack, and the brilliant outside sun burst in to fill the tent with light.

"Todd, are you there?"

Todd's heart leapt at the sound of Dana's voice. For a moment he couldn't remember where he was—he thought Dana had come into the dangerous regions where the herds grazed. But then he remembered. He and Jarod had come back down to bring provisions to the village. "Come in! Come in!"

"Were you sleeping?" asked Dana in surprise, "at this time of the day?"

"Well, I . . . um," said Todd, trying to shake off his drowsiness, "yes, sort of."

"Sort of? So I've sort of woken you up?"

He laughed. "No problem! Come in!"

"Okay." She came in and sat down beside a big woolly dog snoozing on the floor. She leaned on his back, making herself comfortable by snuggling up to the sleeping dog the same way the mountain people did.

"I heard you got back last night."

"Yes, it was really late," said Todd, sitting up and stretching his sore muscles. "There was no moon. We basically followed the stars home."

"How are you doing?"

"Great! I really love it here."

"Yes. Me too."

"Are you having a good time with Pian?"

Dana laughed. "She's crazy, you know that?"

"That's what Jarod says."

"She's just a thousand little girls all wrapped up in one. She is so much fun. She really is. I just love her."

"Everyone seems to like her."

"Yes, and rightly so. And how are you?"

Todd grinned. "Sore!"

"Ha, you too? I tell you, in the first couple of weeks I was sore all over. Everything hurt—to the tip of my nose. Even my eyelashes hurt!"

"But I do love it here," Todd said more solemnly. "You wouldn't believe the places I've seen, and the people way out in the outer huts are just the salt of the earth."

"The ones I've seen all look so beaten up," said Dana.

"Yes, it's true!" laughed Todd. "They've all got teeth knocked out or chunks of their ears or fingers or toes missing, chomped off by some beast."

Dana shuddered.

"And the men in hut seven. They are so funny. They want to have a bear scar competition. They're convinced that they have the best collection of bear scars of all the huts!" said Todd, laughing.

"My goodness!" said Dana, who was unable to share his laughter.

"Zagar out there told me that in the outer huts you have to be a bit crazy to stay normal."

Todd looked up to see the shock on Dana's lovely face. Feeling suddenly ashamed he added, "I found it shocking at first, but somehow you get used to it."

An uncomfortable silence filled the room, only to be broken by Dana's soft voice, "I love it here, Todd. I really do. I love the people. I love the plains. I would never leave if . . . if my mother didn't need me."

Todd looked at her in the light of the sunlight coming through the door. Her berry-brown face beamed a strength and peace that he had never seen in her before. Her black hair now had streaks of red as it flowed down to thicker, more muscular shoulders. He could hardly believe this was the same delicate white girl he had found in the forest, trembling like a flower petal you could crush with your fingers.

"You're looking great!" said Todd in a thoughtless dreaminess, quickly blushing as he realized what he had just said.

Dana laughed uneasily and looked at the ground. "Thanks." But she couldn't help but beam with pleasure at the spontaneous compliment. "Pian prays all the time, you know?"

"Jarod does too."

"We're walking along, and I think Pian is talking to me, and I suddenly realize that she's talking to the Lord. She does it all the time!"

"Jarod does the same. The people in the huts trust him, and they tell us everything. They can be desperately lonely, you know. And although they joke about scars, I've found that every scar on the skin leaves a scar on the soul as well. And every now and again they lose a colleague—forever. Jarod has this wonderful way of listening. He takes it all in, and then on the way home it all comes out again. I've learned so much from him."

"You know," said Dana, pulling her knees up under her chin and wrapping her arms around them, "there's nothing in the world more normal than walking under this vast mountain sky with Pian and just talking to the Maker of everything around you."

"And nothing more wonderful."

The silence that followed found them both staring at everything in the tent other than each other.

"Todd?"

"Yes?"

"What on earth are we doing here?"

"No idea. Bud wants you to get strong again before we go to rescue your mother."

"There's something big waiting for us."

Finally, he met her eyes. "Yes, I know."

CHAPTER 19

Ethero

The long, seemingly endless treks over the mountain plains gave the boys lots of opportunity to talk, and Jarod was very curious about Todd's life in the forest. A place in which the thick leaves of great branches blocked out the blue sky seemed terribly foreign to him: he could barely conceive of a place without a vast sky and a steady, strong wind. A flour mill powered by a wheel in a river was just one of many unimaginable things contained in Todd's stories, and Jarod found himself struggling to keep up, with only a foggy understanding of what Todd was talking about.

Todd was often far too engrossed in his story to notice this—a common weakness of all storytellers—but that was okay. Jarod enjoyed his bounding enthusiasm and evident love of his family. It was a bit like listening to a song you barely understand but nonetheless enjoy.

"My dad and mom love each other dearly, but they are very different," said Todd one day as they were on their way out to the farthest and most dangerous hut.

"How so?" asked Jarod.

"Well, Dad loves adventure and risk, and Mom wants safety," said Todd. "Above the mill the river widens and deepens, and there the water is still. It's a wonderful place to go swimming in the summer. As a little boy, I asked Dad to throw me out in the water, and he did, but it was never far enough. I always wanted to go further. So we developed a way where he would grab me around the ankles and swing me around and around, and then with a great heave he would throw me into the water. You can imagine that Mom didn't like this one little bit, but I called them my 'flying lessons' and begged and pleaded to have more. Finally we came to a deal. I got a flying lesson every birthday and certain festival days."

Jarod smiled and shook his head.

"When I was a little kid," continued Todd, "I thought like this: my Dad really loves me, and because of that he gives me flying lessons. I really liked our cat, and therefore I took it by its hind legs and gave it a flying lesson! Mom came out of the house to see this screaming cat flying halfway across the river. Poor Mom. I'm sure I turned many of her red hairs grey."

Todd wiped a tear of laughter from his eye and asked, "Did you do things like that with your dad?"

"My dad died when I was very young," replied Jarod quietly.

"Oh, I'm sorry," said Todd, suddenly realizing how utterly he had been taken up by his own thoughts and life.

"Killed by wolves," said Jarod, staring without emotion at the path before them.

They followed the rest of the long and winding path up to the hut in silence. It was midafternoon by the time they got there, and strangely enough, the hut was empty.

"They're expecting us today, aren't they?" asked Todd.

"Yes," was Jarod's only reply. With a look of concern, he walked inside. Everything was in its usual order, and a few things lay on the low table in the middle of the room.

But then Todd saw it: a piece of birch bark lay on a piece of moss along with eight round stones.

"This means they're up at the middle pass. They left to go there eight days after the new moon. They should have come back yesterday, then," said Jarod. He stared at the table, deep in thought, and after a couple of seconds said, "We've got to go!"

They quickly went back to the yaks, took their loads into the hut, and sent the animals out to the pasture to graze. Then they packed their backpacks with food and some long leather straps that Jarod handed Todd without a word.

"What is this for?" asked Todd.

"I'll tell you when we're there," answered Jarod.

Within ten minutes they were ready to go. "We'll need to take these," said Jarod, pulling two thick hardwood poles out of the yaks' saddles. Off they went together, up and down winding paths. At times they crossed cliff faces along the slender paths. Todd kept his eyes focused on Jarod's feet just to keep his eyes away from the seemingly endless fall to the side. It was scary, and Jarod's unusual silence did not help.

The path finally led to a gentle, grassy mountainside, and when they got there, Jarod pointed with his stick up to the right. High up, Todd could see a stone corral beside a cliff face.

In this last stretch they had to tie their poles to their backs and crawl up on all fours. Jarod led the way through a set of bushes that they could hold onto while climbing, which made the ascent much easier.

At last they came to a stony path leading up to the corral. In front of the entrance Todd saw a broad, flat area beside a seemingly endless cliff, and when they got there, they immediately saw a man lying between the large stones of the entrance.

"Nareb!" shouted Jarod as he ran up to the man.

"Jarod! Am I glad to see you!" said the man weakly. Todd was surprised to see a man as old as this up here—and his stomach turned at the sight of him. His gray, wavy mop of hair hung in bloody clumps, and a fresh, bloody scar crossed his left cheek. Ripped, bloodstained rags were all that was left of his clothing. He sat propped up against the stone wall.

"What happened?"

"Wolves! Lots of them. We lost three ewes but held them off. Jarod, I can't walk."

As Nareb raised his head to look at Jarod, a look of crazed panic flashed across his bloody face. Jarod reached out, and without saying a word, squeezed his shoulder.

"I've lost a lot of blood, Jarod. This morning as I woke up, I was so cold I thought I'd die. I told stories, sang songs, did everything I could to stay awake, because I was afraid that if I fell asleep I'd never wake up again."

Jarod gave him a reassuring smile. "I'm sure the sheep enjoyed that! Where's Ebner?"

"I sent him to Blue Peak to bring help. He should come sometime this afternoon."

Jarod gave him a puzzled look. "Why did you do that?"

"Jarod," wheezed Nareb as he tried to sit straight, "Ethero is here."

Jarod shuddered. Todd felt a chill rush down his spine.

"We saw him, across the pass. He's coming this way, and he's got four or five wolves with him."

Jarod breathed deeply, and every trace of humor and laughter vanished from his face. Todd had never seen Jarod like this.

"That's why I sent Ebner to Blue Peak," said Nareb. "I told him to get four men. We need at least five to hold him off."

"Now we just have to wait," said Jarod.

"Look!" shouted Nareb suddenly with a squeal of panic. "There he is! There!"

Jarod and Todd looked up to where he was pointing. In a distant clearing up the mountainside they saw four wolves and one great white creature that seemed as big as a pony leading the way. Todd gulped in horror. He had never seen anything like this in his life. The beast was enormous.

"Come quickly," said Jarod.

Todd wasted no time obeying. They went to the clearing in front of the corral and opened their packs. Jarod took out one of the long strips of leather, told Todd to stand still, and wrapped the leather like a long bandage around his neck. After looping it around many times, he tied the ends together and put the knot under Todd's jacket.

"Now you do the same for me," he said in an almost military tone. Todd sensed that this was no time to ask questions and started wrapping the leather around Jarod's neck.

"The wolves will fight and push and pull you, always looking for their chance to jump at your throat. This leather will stop their teeth once or twice. Now listen, Todd. Listen very carefully. We will stand here in front of the corral door. We must always remain back to back. Always! And if we get knocked down, then we must get up again as soon as possible and stand back to back again."

Todd nodded, but Jarod didn't seem satisfied. *"Always* back to back," he said again. "If the wolves pull us apart, we're dead. You don't worry about what's behind you. I'll take care of that. In the same way, I'm trusting you to take care of everything behind me. Take the pole and hold it, with both hands wide apart. Use it to block attacks. The wolves will jump at your throat, and you have to push your pole with all your might into their mouths, between their upper and lower teeth. Push back with all the force you've got. Don't worry about falling over backwards; I'll hold you up. In the same way, you must hold me up!"

"Okay," said Todd, who was hanging on Jarod's every word. He felt his pole trembling in his hand and hated himself for it.

"If you get the chance, you can drive the ends of the poles into the wolves' ribs," said Jarod. "That is their weak spot. But whatever you do, always keep both hands on the pole and keep them well apart."

"Okay, I'll—" began Todd. His words were interrupted by a bloodcurdling scream from Nareb.

"Jarod! Jarod!" shouted Nareb. The wolves were charging.

"Hide behind the wall, Nareb! They have to get past us to get to you!" shouted Jarod, taking position in the clearing in front of the corral. "Take courage! Todd! Get in position!"

Jarod and Todd stood back to back. Out from behind a bush came the most horrific monster Todd had ever seen. It had an enormous head, with immense jaws that hung open, dripping with slobber and foam. Todd caught a whiff of its hot breath and only just managed not to vomit. Ethero stood studying the situation, beady black eyes flashing with a crazed pleasure. This would be an easy game against two boys.

"Turn! Turn with me!" said Jarod. "Let me face him!"

Todd forced himself to turn his back on the creature, and Ethero disappeared from view. No sooner had he done this that he saw the other wolves circling around them, waiting for orders to attack. They all looked savage and half-crazed, with long, wet tongues hanging down from between their enormous teeth.

"Stand strong, brother! Stand strong!" shouted Jarod.

Ethero let out a mad scream, and the wolves stopped circling and turned inside to attack. Up jumped the first, and Todd managed to block it with his pole in its mouth. The weight of the beast threw him backwards. His back hit Jarod, who stood like a wall, and with a mighty heave Todd was able to push the wolf back down. No sooner had he done so than Jarod's back flew into his own. It took all the strength he had to stay upright, but this he did, and he kept Jarod on his feet as well.

And so it went—circling, jumping, shoving, blocking. It was clear to both boys that they couldn't keep this up long. They were just barely holding on, and Ethero had not even begun to fight. The white wolf was just sitting there, watching how its younglings handled the situation.

The attacks became fiercer, and Todd stumbled away from Jarod, who quickly ran over to him and resumed their back-to-back stance as another wolf leapt at them. Their strength was going quickly, and they were stumbling more and more. The wolves were wearing them down.

Todd just managed to block an attack from the side, but he fell to his knees doing so. A wolf sprang high at Jarod's throat. Jarod managed to block it, but the great weight of the wolf threw him backwards, and because Todd was on his knees, Jarod rolled right over him.

Then everything went wild. In attack after attack, the boys were hopelessly separated. Up, down on their knees. Sometimes blocking. Sometimes half-blocking. They reeled like drunken men, just reacting wildly to the next motion or attack. Clothes ripped, and Todd saw blood flowing from both his legs and arms. He couldn't feel pain—it was all happening too fast.

Now that they had separated the boys, the wolves gave Jarod special attention. Three wolves surrounded him, harassing and attacking him from every side. His defense was getting weaker all the time. One wolf sprang at his side, and he just managed to block it from biting off his left ear. In a fit of desperation, Jarod dropped his defense against the other two wolves and plunged the tip of his pole with all of his might into the wolf's side. The wolf let out a terrific scream as blood sprayed from his side.

When Ethero saw this, the monster let out a scream beyond all screams. It was time for the great wolf to enter the fight. Todd's heart sank within him as he caught sight of the monster advancing on his friend.

One last wolf was still harassing Todd, trying to keep him away from the others. Todd scrambled to hold it off, but it was getting closer and closer all the time. He was just flailing wildly at it. He had lost all sense of strategy and become like a madman swinging a pole around.

From the side, he saw how the other two wolves had brought Jarod to his knees. The leather strip had been fully taken from his neck, and his bloody chest was bare behind his ripped shirt. He was struggling right and left with wolves that wouldn't leave him alone, and Ethero was moving in for the kill.

Nareb was screaming to Todd that he must act . . . and somehow he heard. The words broke through the chaos, and his heart leaped to his throat. *Jarod!*

At that moment of distraction, the wolf sprang at Todd, knocking him almost down the cliff. He rolled over on the ground, and his pole flew over the edge. The wolf came to finish him off. In desperation, Todd grabbed a loose stone and threw it with all his might. The stone hit the wolf between the eyes and sent it to the ground—dead or just stunned, he didn't know. Rolling over, Todd looked up to see Ethero crouching to pounce on Jarod, who was still hopelessly struggling against the other wolves.

There was no time even to think. Todd took two steps and dove at Ethero's back legs just as it sprang to kill Jarod. All Jarod saw was a huge set of teeth flying at his face and suddenly falling short just in front of him. Todd had the monster by the hind legs.

The beast reared around in rage, and Todd held on for dear life. The wolf lunged at Todd again and again but could not reach him. Todd was flung around by its great strength, desperate to hold on. Jarod struggled to get to his feet and help, but he was just too weak, and the two wolves weren't letting up in their fierce attacks.

In a mad attempt to free himself, Ethero jumped again at Todd, throwing him with great force into the stone wall of the corral. Everything went fuzzy. In a fit of dizziness, Todd saw a picture of Bud swinging him around and throwing him into the river. Not far away, Jarod screamed.

Suddenly, a rage like he had never known came across Todd. In Ethero's wild writhing, he threw Todd again to his feet, and Todd stood and gripped the wolf's legs harder than before. With all the strength he could muster, he swung the beast around and around until Ethero's front legs no longer touched the ground. The beast screamed in rage and scrambled to get free and kill Todd on the spot. Todd swung and swung with all the strength he had, and with a frantic heave, he threw the brute over the cliff.

The monster let out a scream that sounded as though it came from the depths of hell itself—a long, desperate scream that ended in certain death.

The other two wolves ran away in a frenzied panic, gone from view in seconds. In no time, the wild battlefield had become silent except for the words of Nareb, peering over a stone from his hiding place. "You did it! You did it! Thanks be to the Lord!"

But Todd didn't hear. He just looked around in a stupor. There was blood everywhere, bits of fur and clothing, and two dead wolves on the ground. He staggered over to Jarod, who was sitting against the wall, gasping for air. Todd collapsed at his side, and they both sat there leaning on each other, gasping for air and staring blankly into the sky.

That was how Ebner and the others from Blue Peak found them when they arrived about twenty minutes later.

They were carried back to the hut, where they stayed a couple of days to gather their strength. After that, the men put them both on yaks and carried them back to the village, where their story was received with great interest.

On that day Todd got a new name. His old name, *Deribo,* had meant "the weak overcomes the strong." Now his new name, *Deriboni,* meant "the lamb that slew the wolf." This was a wordplay so clever that the wise had to wonder whether those who had given the first name knew something special. It seemed almost prophetic.

CHAPTER 20

Todd's Story

It was a good week before Jarod and Todd were on their feet again—a wonderful week of being pampered by older ladies and young girls, getting sweet treats and savory soups and lots of attention. Dana could not help noticing the enormous attention and honor given to Todd—and not only because he had slain the wolf. She had noticed it from their very first day with the mountain people and had often wondered why it was this way, but she had never had the courage to ask.

Asking questions was generally no problem for her, but this one was different—different because it revealed a fondness for Todd that she herself didn't know what to do with.

In this battle between her hesitations and her even greater curiosity, curiosity was slowly gaining the upper hand. The person to ask would be Pian. On their long walks to collect eggs they often found themselves talking about anything and everything with a freedom Dana had never known with anyone else.

Walking out of Todd and Jarod's tent after a visit she asked Pian, "What does 'Deribo' mean?"

"It means the weak overcomes the strong," answered Pian.

They walked along together in silence until they got to a clearing at the edge of the village, where Pian suddenly stopped and with a cheeky grin looked into Dana's eyes.

"What?" asked Dana.

"Well, go ahead!" said Pian, grinning ear to ear.

"Go ahead what?"

"Go ahead what! You know exactly what!" said Pian, whose big black eyes looked searchingly into Dana's. "Ask!"

"Ask what?" asked Dana, as though she had been discovered with her fingers in the cookie jar. She knew very well what Pian was talking about. "Well, I was sort of wondering . . ."

"Sort of wondering? You call that 'sort of wondering'? You're bursting to ask! You've been wanting to ask for days now!"

"Oh, come on," said Dana, blushing. "It's not that important!"

"Oh, no! No, not that important! Not important at all, really!" said Pian. She shook her head, laughing, and said, "You drive me crazy, you know that?"

"Yes, I know," said Dana who was desperately trying not to smile. By this time she had given up trying to hide anything from her friend.

"Every time you want to know something but don't know if you should ask, you press your lips together like this," said Pian, pressing her own lips together in a comical, childish way.

"I do not!" said Dana indignantly.

"No, never! Not you!" said Pian now, laughing almost uncontrollably.

"Well, not as much as that!"

Still laughing, Pian continued, "Let me ask for you." Standing beside Dana, Pian took on her friend's posture, pulled her curly hair down over her forehead as far as she could, took a deep breath, and said in a remarkable imitation of Dana's voice, "Pian, why does everybody think Todd is so special? Where did he come from? How did he end up here on the high plains? I've been lying awake at night thinking about it!"

"Lying awake thinking about it!" said Dana, rolling her eyes. "You're taking this all a little far, don't you think?"

Pian just continued her imitation. "And you know, Pian, I even asked my dog!"

Dana could only stare at her in amazement. It was true—it was perfectly true. For whatever reason, Dana had started talking to her dog, and it always listened to her with great attention and affection. "How do you know that?" she asked, flabbergasted.

"He told me himself!" said Pian triumphantly.

The cheeky young girl was beaming with victorious playfulness, and yet more, beaming with affection. Dana had never loved Pian so much as at that moment—it was the sort of feeling you get when someone sees right through you and loves you just the same.

She gave Pian a lighthearted slap on the shoulder and said, "You are ..." But she couldn't find the word to finish the sentence.

"And you are really cute when you're embarrassed!" said Pian, laughing all the while.

Dana rolled her eyes in resignation. She gave up trying to hide anything, let out a deep sigh, and said, "Okay, tell me!"

"Well, I thought you'd never ask!" said Pian with a triumphant twinkle in her eye. "Come, let's sit down." They sat down together on a large stone outside the village with the warm sun at their backs.

"Around fourteen years ago there were many problems in the village. Varsal's father, Ondo, was the chief of the village and had a very bad problem with his legs. He was in a lot of pain and could barely get around. Before that, he had been a mighty man, strong as a yak, and he had done a lot to build up the village and the outer huts. But as he lost his great strength, it became more and more difficult to control what he had built up. And what is more, his brother Ikar was doing all he could to win the power of the chieftainship to his own line. It was a very difficult time for us indeed, because Ikar was a clever, scheming man, and he and his sons were constantly at work to drive a wedge between Ondo and the people. On top of that, there were thieves, disease among the yaks, and a wave of wolf attacks. Ondo found himself with great responsibility and less and less support. Ikar saw to it that Ondo was blamed for everything that went wrong.

"Well, the sons of the chief always have to spend a certain time in the outer pastures, taking care of the sheep and yaks, and Varsal was placed in the furthest one, toward the east. He knew very well that his father was dying and that it would only be a matter of months before he would have to go and take up his position as chief of the village despite Ikar's schemes. He also knew that this would be very difficult, and even dangerous, and it all felt like too much for him. He is a gentle, peaceful man, is Uncle Varsal, and he hates conflict."

"Too much for Varsal?" asked Dana in surprise.

"Yes, he was different then. He couldn't stand the thought of going back and facing all the trouble his father faced. He had heard stories from travelers about other things he could do. He thought about going down to the sea and fishing, or maybe farming on the islands far off the coast.

"These thoughts didn't leave him alone but kept going through his head, and shortly before he was supposed to come back, he went to the very furthest pasture of that post. It was a place where you could see the sea.

"He was at a loss as to what to do. He felt that it was right to come back to the village, but at the same time, he was surrounded by people who were tougher than himself. They weren't stronger—that's not the right word—he was physically the strongest. They were harder . . . or more aggressive. Yes, that's the word, aggressive."

Pian shrugged. "He just didn't have it in him to come back and stand his ground. The thought of standing up against his uncle and cousins was too much for him."

"Did he have any brothers or sisters?" asked Dana.

"No, he was Ondo's only son, and his mother had died when he was a boy. He was very much alone, and this didn't help. He was torn between returning, which seemed right, and running away, which seemed a lot easier.

"One night he had a dream in which he saw a small young woman. She was really not more than a girl, but she was already married and had a baby boy. Her husband, who was also very young, worked in the mines, far away in the Kingdom. They were very poor and struggled just to live. Every day he left home early in the morning and arrived home late at night. His health suffered, and in their short talks, he told her several times that he was very concerned about his work. He said the mine shafts were unsafe and could collapse at any time. Well, this went on for some time, until one day when he didn't come home. Soldiers came to her and told her that her husband had been killed in an accident in the mine."

Pian shook her head sorrowfully. "This was terribly difficult, and what made it worse was that it was almost time for the tattoo, whatever that is."

"I know what that is," Dana said softly. "Pian, in the kingdom there is a group of people who work like slaves in the mines. They must tattoo the mark of the mine on their children on their first birthday. Everyone who has this tattoo must do a certain number of years of work in the mine."

Dana's voice quivered at the memories this brought back. "After working those years they are free to go, but only a few live that long."

"Okay, that explains some things," said Pian. "Varsal said that this girl had only two loves in her life: her husband, whom she had loved dearly, and her child. She determined that the mine was not to get both. One night she wrapped up her baby in a big red sheet, tied that over her back, and set off to the mountains without any idea of where she was going. She was small and weak from years of poverty, but she was determined to get away—anywhere but the mine.

"She walked through the night, and when night turned to day she left the road to avoid being seen by soldiers. She knew well that in the countryside they would stop a woman wearing the clothes from a mining camp. She walked all through the night and all through the next day. Then, just as she reached the foot of the mountains, a group of soldiers on horses saw her and came after her.

"She did everything she could to get away. In desperation she entered the narrow, steep crevices going up the mountains. She was afraid—terrified really—but that child meant more to her than the world, and she had to go on.

"She found herself on all fours climbing up the rocks in the crevice. Then suddenly she heard a song. The song was calling her up the mountain, and she felt a new confidence and strength that everything would be all right."

"I think I know that song," said Dana with a smile.

"Really?"

"Keep going!"

"Okay. When Uncle Varsal told me this story, he talked again and again about her face. She was determined and resolute, and though in the beginning it was all a mad scramble, now it was one step after the other. She was so tired that she couldn't feel her arms and legs anymore, but that didn't matter. She must reach the top, and she would reach the top.

"The soldiers had long since gotten off their horses and were on foot behind her. They were gaining ground fast. She stumbled and fell several times, leaving a trail of blood behind her. She had no idea how badly she was hurt, and she barely perceived her frantic breathing and constant gasping for breath. She grew dizzy, and her climbing became a kind of blind stumbling, but the song was always there, telling her that she must and she would reach the top. She somehow knew she would. She knew this absolutely.

"Indeed, just as the soldiers had almost caught her, she stumbled out of the crevice onto a flat area on the side of the mountain. She staggered forward and fell into a big bed of moss.

"Now she was too weak to get up again, and the soldiers came: one, two, three, four, up and into the clearing. They were angry, very angry, and they approached her with evil in their eyes. She could only lay there helplessly clutching her child, yet she was still convinced that this was not the end.

"Suddenly, two bears leapt out from behind a large stone and attacked the soldiers. They made quick work of them, killing a couple and chasing the others away. The girl lay where she had fallen, seeing this but falling asleep under the warm sun on the soft moss. She felt no fear and did not even try to run from the bears. In her heart of hearts she knew that she had done what she had to do, and in the joy of that thought she fell asleep, carried away by the melody, never to wake again.

"While still dreaming, Uncle Varsal asked, 'What is the name of this girl?', and in his dream a voice responded, 'Maragana,' which means 'love overcomes everything.'

"Then Varsal woke up. He found the dream confusing and thought perhaps it had some meaning he could not understand. Before this he had decided to leave the mountains at the break of dawn and head to the sea, and that was what he would do. He set off, but as he was walking the face of this girl returned to him again and again. He couldn't help but feel that he was being spoken to. He tried to shake it off, but her face kept coming back. This went on for an hour or so.

"As he was on his way, he heard something like a song, getting louder and louder. For the first time he gave up fighting and stopped to listen. A voice came through the tune: 'If you go down to the sea, you do it in your own strength. If you return, you do it in my strength. Shall I stand by you, or will you face your life alone?'"

"So he turned around?" asked Dana.

"No! Uncle Varsal didn't want to hear. He had decided in his heart of hearts. He wanted to leave. He rushed ahead. He was sure that the girl's face would disappear and the voice and the song would stop, but they didn't. Suddenly, two bears came out from behind the rocks, one before and one behind. He was trapped. But the bear behind him was carrying something in its mouth—a bundle wrapped in a bloody red sheet."

"Todd!" cried Dana, with her eyes opened wide.

Pian nodded with a smile. "Deribo. That was Deribo, who you call Todd. Uncle Varsal had a decision to make. By this time he was really broken. He decided to stop running away and took the child in his arms. And you know, as soon as he did, he knew what he had to do—and he knew he could do it. That expression he'd seen on the face of the girl suddenly appeared on his own, and he has borne it ever since."

"I know what you mean," said Dana, who had always seen something special in Varsal.

"Uncle Varsal's peaceful smile has carried this village through horrible times, and it has also carried me. Uncle Varsal loves Deribo so much. He once told me that Deribo saved his life before taking his very first step."

"So that's Todd's story," said Dana, deep in thought.

"That's Deribo's story," answered Pian, and then after a long pause she said, "And you know what?"

"What?"

Pian peered around, looking very serious and concerned. She leaned over to Dana, and whispered in her ear, "I don't want to tell you here!"

"Why not?"

"It's too important!" said Pian with a very solemn look. "Where can we go and be totally, totally alone?"

"We're alone here," said Dana.

"Not alone enough. I don't want to take the chance of anyone else hearing." Pian paused and changed her tone. "Actually, Dana, maybe I had better not tell you. There are some things in life that are better left unknown."

"That's nonsense! You have to tell me!"

"Why?"

"Because you said you would!"

"You may not be old enough!"

"Of course I am! I'm as old as you!"

"You may not be strong enough, you know, inwardly!"

"Well, that'll be my problem! Leave that to me! Look, are you ready to talk or what?" asked Dana who was about to explode with aggravation and excitement.

"Well, I'm . . . are you sure no one's around?"

"Absolutely sure!" said Dana hotly. "You can tell me!"

"Dana," said Pian gravely, "this is something that I can only tell my very best friend for all time. Are you my very best friend for all time?"

"Of course I am!" said Dana without hesitation.

"And you must swear never to tell another soul. Never! Never! Never! This is to be sacred."

"I'll never tell a soul, I promise!"

"Okay," whispered Pian, "come near!"

Dana drew near, trembling. Pian leaned over and cupped her hand around Dana's ear.

"I talk to my dog too," she whispered. "Everyone does!"

At that, Pian burst out in laughter and rolled on the ground with glee at her trick.

Dana stood there in a kind of stupor, shaking her head in astonishment and unable to fight a grin.

"I am going to kill you!" she said.

"You can't! You can't kill your best friend for all time!" said Pian, bursting with cheeky triumph.

"Just watch me!" Dana went after Pian, who ran with all her strength out toward the plain. But Pian proved faster, and finally Dana gave up trying to catch her and flopped down in the grass, laughing. Pian came back and flopped down beside her.

"You are impossible, you know that?" said Dana.

"People have been telling me that for years. But come on, Dana. You don't want a *possible* friend, do you? A normal friend would be boring. If you are going to have a very best friend for life, she really should be a little impossible, don't you think?"

"I guess you're right. You win again," said Dana.

And there they lay for a while, looking up into the ever redder sky as the sun set. Pian then told Dana many things she had only ever told her dog; and even more, she told Dana some questions she had asked herself—and we all know that the questions we carry around with us every day are often our greatest secrets.

CHAPTER 21

A Welcome Visitor

Within a week the boys were on their feet again, and after three weeks they went on their first new mission to the outer huts. The death of Ethero was wonderful news for the village, and people were cheerful and festive for weeks on end.

Indeed, days turned into weeks, and weeks turned into months. Over time the novelty of the two new young people in the village wore off, and life took on its normal rhythm. For Todd and Dana, this life which had at first looked so strange and magical was becoming normal, and as they reflected on life elsewhere, everything seemed like a dream. This was especially true for Dana, who somehow could not imagine how the kingdom with its unfriendly drabness could exist in the same world as these people on the high plains.

Was it only a dream? she wondered. *I've only been here a few months, and yet I feel that this is where I belong and have always belonged.* It became normal to wake up with a cold nose in the chilly air of the early morning, or even to wake up unable to move because a couple of big hairy dogs had wandered in in the night, flopped down on top of you, and fallen asleep. These things and a thousand more became the most normal things in the world. Only the thought of her mother kept Dana connected to the world she had left behind, and at times, even the need to rescue her felt faraway and fuzzy.

Just as Dana and Pian had become very close friends, Todd and Jarod had also become the best of buddies. Jarod, who by nature had often treasured time away on his own, was surprised by how much he enjoyed Todd's company. Todd drank in all that Jarod told him—about the high plains, their inhabitants, the animals they raised, and wildlife. Other people had helped Jarod in his tasks, but Todd was different from them all. Others had walked, and carried packs, and fixed huts, and cared for animals, and done many other tasks. They had come and helped and left. Todd had come, and he had watched with his big blue eyes and listened with eagerness to the stories of the hut dwellers. With great quietness of heart, he took it all in, his experiences falling like seeds in the soft soil of his heart, and those seeds took deep root indeed. Todd was the very first helper to really share Jarod's heart. He had somehow stepped into Jarod's life and taken away the loneliness he had often felt before.

Todd was equally fond of Jarod: this strong, wise boy who had been given a man's job and did it well. The elders knew what they were doing when they assigned Jarod to the work of herding. The care of the hut dwellers had become his whole life. Nothing burdened him more than their struggles, and nothing thrilled him more than their happiness. It was a burden that Todd was learning to share.

It was evening, and the sun was just setting. After eating a large meal, Dana and Todd were busy packing their bags for the next day.

"Indura gave us a bunch of her dried pears for the journey tomorrow. Man, they are good!" said Todd.

"You should try her dried berries. They taste like raisins," added Dana.

"I wonder how she does it," said Todd reflectively.

"Pian says she's so clever that her fruit dries out even when it's lying under the rain!" said Dana, laughing.

"How are your ducks?"

"Stupid as ever. I sometimes wonder if it takes work to be as stupid as they are. Hey, Todd. Did I tell you about the antelope that—" Dana stopped as Pian and Jarod suddenly burst into the tent.

"There's a visitor!" said Pian eagerly. "He's just come over the crest!"

"At this time?" said Todd, jumping to his feet. "It's almost dark."

"Uncle Varsal is calling for you to meet him," said Jarod. "Come!"

And with that, they all went quickly out toward the crest of the plain. Many people had already come out of their dwellings, and village chatter was at a high pitch. The four went quickly up and over the first ridge, barely talking as they went, and as they did so they could see about five people coming toward them in the very last light of the setting sun—four village scouts escorting someone.

Drawing closer, Todd recognized the walk of the smallest person in the group, and he began to run.

"Dad!" he shouted and ran with all his strength.

After just about bowling him over, Todd hugged Bud with all his heart. When the others arrived, Todd was still holding the miller from the forest like a treasure he would never let go. "Oh, I've missed you so much. So terribly much!" said Todd, with tears of joy streaming down his cheeks. "How's Mom, and the mill, and the village? And how—"

"Now, just a minute," said Bud, trying to wipe away his own tears, "one thing after another. Hello, Dana!"

"Hi, Bud!" said Dana, who also gave him a big, hearty hug.

"My goodness, you kids just about broke me in two with these hugs. Let's have a look at you."

Bud gave Dana's arm a squeeze and whistled with approval at her large, rock-solid muscles. She had indeed gained a great deal of strength over the last few months, and she stood before him like a well-trained athlete. Not only that, but peace and happiness radiated from her large, vibrant eyes. He lifted his rough, dry hand and tenderly caressed her soft cheek.

"You're looking great! Just great! Just as I had hoped!" He turned to Todd, who felt the pride in his father's eyes. "Both of you! You're both looking great. The Lord be thanked!"

Indeed, Todd was surprised by how small Bud suddenly seemed among the large, robust mountain people. Todd also felt that his father looked much older, and burdened with care.

Together they walked back to the village. Varsal hastily organized a meal for their new guest and prepared a table in his own tent where Bud could eat in the company of Dana and Todd. Jarod and Pian offered to take care of bedding and all the preparation for Bud to stay the night, and Varsal agreed thankfully. Then he withdrew. He thought it best to leave the three forest dwellers together to speak undisturbed. Celebrations and feasts could wait till tomorrow.

Bud dug hungrily into the food that was placed before him, even though he could barely see it in the dim candlelight. While he was eating, Todd and Dana told him of their last several months in their new home. They burst with excitement as they recounted story after story of life on the high plains. Like two adventurers returning from a great mission, they spoke of yaks, ducks, great storms, close friends, building huts, crossing mighty rivers, climbing mountain peaks, going hunting, smoking meat, making cheese, and of course, Ethero, who failed his flying lesson—all the while interrupting each other and finishing the other's sentences.

The stories were wonderful, but what made Bud happiest was their lighthearted laughter and joy. They had come as children, but they were not children anymore. Their obvious love for the high plains and their people shone from every word. This village stood in stark contrast to the one Bud had left behind, and he tried not to let his sorrow show.

As Bud finished eating and just sat listening and sipping his hot tea, Todd asked, "And how's Mom?"

"Your mother has a heart as soft as a young lamb's fleece, not to mention the strength of a bear. Not a day goes by without her saying, 'I wonder how the boy is' . . . five or six times! But I've got to tell you, I was really angry with her last week."

"You were?" asked Todd in surprise.

Bud winked. "Yes, well, I was coming home from delivering flour, and there was your mother sewing up a sandal for a young soldier. I was furious! I told her these people had no right to be here and that his sandals had been bought with dirty money taken from some old girl like herself and made by some miserable slave." Bud pointed his finger in the air like a warmed-up preacher.

"And she said, 'He'd like to learn medicine but must first serve four years in the army to pay off his father's debts. His father's in the mine right now.' And she told me about his lame brother and his two sisters. I tell you, that soldier boy broke all the rules and told her everything!"

"So," said Todd with a big grin, "Mom is just being Mom."

"Exactly!" said Bud. He leaned forward and poked Todd in the shoulder. "And she told me that you've got a great new friend who you travel with."

"How does she know that?" asked Todd, surprised.

"She's been talking to Someone about you pretty intensely," replied Bud.

After a pause he added, "And she thinks about Dana all the time too. Before I left she said, 'Some people lose a daughter after ten years. I lost mine after one day.'"

"She didn't lose me," said Dana. "She'll see me again."

"Yes . . ." replied Bud, and there was silence.

After a long pause Todd asked, "So there are still soldiers in the forest?"

"More than when you left! It's tough, Todd, really tough. You know the camp they set up beside the well?"

"Travis told us about it."

"Well, it's still there, and it's bigger. It looks like it's going to be there for a while."

"Are they really going to look for me for so long?" asked Dana uneasily.

"I think they've given up looking for you, young lady. But it seems they have decided to set up permanent posts in the forest."

"Oh, no! I can't believe it! They can't do that!" cried Todd with a start.

"I know, I know. It is unthinkable, but it's exactly what they're doing," said Bud gravely.

"Well, what's Dorn doing about it?" asked Todd.

"Huh! Dorn! He's doing what he always does! He's meeting with his elders. I don't know what's wrong with that man!" Bud shook his head in disgust. "His father was made of steel! He would never have tolerated this, but Dorn is different. The king's generals know weakness when they find it, and they're making the most of it. There was a time I thought Dorn was strong inside, that he just needed time and he would pull through. But now . . ."

"What are Travis and Brody doing?" asked Dana.

"They are very angry, as you can imagine," said Bud. "There have been great arguments with Dorn, and the boys are more often gone—up in the treehouse, that is—than they are at home. I think they're preparing for something.

"Should we go back and help them?" said Todd, a little surprised to hear the words coming from his own mouth.

"Oh, no. I'm sure they've got everything under control," Bud said with a wry smile that Todd could just make out in the dark tent. "We've got another plan: we've got to get Dana's mother back!"

"It's time," said Dana resolutely.

"Yes. It's time," said Bud gravely.

"But Dad, if the forest is full of soldiers, is this really the best time?" asked Todd.

"I'm just following orders," replied Bud in a matter-of-fact way. Both Todd and Dana knew exactly what he was talking about.

Then there was silence again, and quite a long silence at that. Dana had no idea what to think. The thought of seeing her mother again filled her with joy, and yet the idea of returning to the kingdom filled her with a sudden horror. And then there was Pian. How could she ever leave Pian? They had lived and worked so closely that she could hardly imagine not having her at her side.

She sat in silence and breathed deeply as she always did when she needed to calm herself down. How many times now had life simply felt too big for her? It was all too big—too much. And yet she had always come through, as though some protective, helping hand hovered over her.

She also thought of her mother, and as she did, a big lump formed in her throat. Every time she tried to speak of her mother, it was as if waves of sorrow broke over her—waves that threatened to break her in two. By this time, her mother had almost become a kind of storybook character in her mind. It was clear to her that she couldn't keep this up any longer. The time to act had come.

As the moments passed, it all became clear. She knew well what she was to do.

"There's only one way to go," said Bud, as though reading her thoughts, "and it's forward."

"Yes," said Dana, pulling herself up from her thoughts.

"Are you in?" asked Bud.

"I'm in," replied Dana.

Todd gave her hand a squeeze, and the silence returned.

After a short while Todd said, "And me? You didn't even ask if I'm in!"

Bud laughed. "You're always in! If anything just smells of adventure you're in!"

"Yes, but you didn't ask me!"

"Okay, son. Are you in?"

"Of course I'm in!" laughed Todd.

"Listen you two! This is no laughing matter! We're going to a place with more perils and dangers than you have ever known!" Bud paused in a serious silence and continued, "I struggled and fought, you know. I don't want to take you there, and I told him so. But as I said, I am under orders."

* * *

Soon afterward they called Varsal, Pian, and Jarod, and the Todd and Dana told them their plan. Pian and Jarod were both horrified at the thought of losing their friends, and both asked Varsal if they could join them in the adventure. But it wasn't to be. Bud told them that they would be recognized very quickly as mountain people in the kingdom, endangering the whole mission as well as themselves. He would be pleased, though, if they could accompany them down the steep mountain slopes to the foothills. They begged Varsal for permission. The chieftain didn't like the idea, but he ultimately agreed that he and a few select men would give them an escort to White Ridge, at the edge of the high plains, and then Pian and Jarod could descend with them through the foothills to the great river, where they should build a raft. The next day was to be a day of rest, and on the following day the mission would begin.

Although Bud only understood a few words, he could not help but notice that Varsal spoke with the authority of a king and yet with the warmth of a brother or friend. Thoughts of Dorn came to his mind. Despite his enormous physical strength, Dorn was a great man crumbling before the task in front of him.

He could only hope that things would change somehow, some day—before   it   was   too   late.

CHAPTER 22

Down to the Kingdom

The next day was a relaxed one. Dana, Pian, Todd, Jarod, and Bud went for a long walk together on the high plains. Todd and Dana were bursting to share with Bud all they had seen and done up there. They led him to duck ponds and distant shepherds and had a picnic on a high ridge with a great view. Bud found the high plains wonderful, but he struggled against exhaustion from the trip and his cares about the village, and probably most of all, his missing Clara.

It had been a difficult time in the forest. The permanent presence of soldiers near the village filled Bud with a ceaseless concern. It was like walking around with a stone in your shoe, a stone you can't take out. The whole thing had worn him out enormously.

Clara, on the other hand, saw the world through very different eyes. She remained her joyful self and had become a pillar of strength for Bud. Oh, how he loved that woman—more than he had ever thought he could ever love anyone in this life. As the years passed, the love between them had grown deeper, and quieter, as fewer words said ever more and the twinkle of an eye spoke volumes.

Their good-bye had been painful. Bud felt terribly torn as he left, as though he had left part of his soul behind. The soldiers, Clara's absence, the enormity of what lay before them—all these things lay heavy in the heart of this man, who was no longer as young and strong as he would have liked to be. It was a struggle to listen to all the things the children so eagerly shared. Todd and Dana were so keen to share and show their new world that they barely noticed Bud's weariness. Jarod, however, saw it very clearly, and he did his best to stretch out periods of silence just to give Bud a break.

While walking, they spent a long time talking together and to the Lord of the Forest, trying to finalize a plan. Bud had a clear idea of what he wanted to do, but Dana knew the place and the people of the kingdom. They agreed to first go the cottage of Sedon, the gardener at the inn who had originally helped Dana escape. He would certainly know where Dana's mother was.

There was a welcome feast in the evening with some singing and dancing, but not too much. Varsal had also noticed how tired Bud was and wanted to get them all to bed early. The next day's trip would begin at sunrise, and everyone had to be well rested.

All but Bud lay awake for a long time that night. Pian and Jarod were both struggling with the thought of losing their very dear friends. Todd had come to love the high plains, and in his heart of hearts he really regretted leaving it. Dana had all of these feelings and more. If she never saw the kingdom again for the rest of her life, she would be happy, but then, of course, there was her mother. Sometimes, your head is so full of thoughts that you don't really know what to think. Your biggest plan is to get through tomorrow, and that is basically how she felt.

The next morning was a flurry of activity. Several of the women had gotten up very early to prepare a breakfast fit for a chief. They ate hurriedly, and everybody met at the east side of the village. A party had already gathered to wait for them. Eight yaks were ornately decorated and loaded down with wood, sacks, and tools. They stood in a line of four pairs, each yak led by one young man with a spear. Four elders in ceremonial dress oversaw the party, each standing between a pair of yaks. There were three young men in light yellow clothing, two at the front and one at the back.

"Who are those guys in the yellow?" asked Todd.

"They're scouts. They run out ahead and behind," replied Jarod.

Varsal wore the same colorful robes as the other elders, but he was right at the front. Soon the whole village had come out, gathering at the eastern edge of the village, and the women raised a hauntingly beautiful song in which they placed their guests into the hands of him who carries all things. As they sang, they shed great tears of sorrow, which flowed freely and unashamedly down their cheeks. It was only then that Bud realized how great a love had grown among the kids and these people in the last few months. Pian cried a river of tears, as did Dana, but unlike Pian, Dana did her best to wipe hers away.

As soon as a sliver of sun appeared over Goat Horn Ridge, Varsal turned to the people and raised a pole in his hand. There was a long, eerie silence in which nothing but the faint dawn breeze could be heard. He stood like that for a while as though waiting for some kind of inner signal, and everyone stood silent and expectantly still.

Suddenly, with the butt of his pole, Varsal beat a strange, repeating rhythm on the ground. After several repetitions, one man began to sing, and then more until all the men were singing. To Bud, it sounded as though the song repeated itself—almost. It was always the same and yet always a bit different.

Soon the women joined in, not singing the same melody but rather a totally different one as a response to the men. The men sang out, the women replied. Two different tunes in the same rhythm, but they fit together like a hand in a glove. Bud felt sure he had never heard anything so magical in his whole life.

Varsal turned around, toward the east, still striking his pole to the beat, and started walking. The whole traveling party—the elders and scouts, yak drivers, yaks, and visitors—all followed, leaving the crowd behind as though they had heard a silent command. The song continued behind them, and everyone walked in its rhythm. Bud looked around, amazed to see how well they all kept in step, and suddenly realized that he too, without trying, was walking to the beat.

It was magical, simply magical.

As they continued, the sound gradually grew quieter, but it was clear to everyone that the people kept singing until they were too far to be heard.

Bud, Todd, Jarod, Dana, and Pian walked at the front with Varsal. Little was said as they walked down the grassy plain and toward a large outcrop of rock known as the Lonely Needle. The sky was crystal clear, with only a few wisps of red cloud in the western sky, and as the sun hit the dew-drenched grass on the slopes, they took on a mystical glow. The mountain shadows dropped lower and lower as the sun rose until finally, about two hours after they had set out, the sun's warm rays hit the floor of the plain.

They journeyed in silence except for the words of the scouts as they came to report to Varsal. A scout would run out and disappear in front of the group. As soon as Varsal saw him returning, he would send the second, and as soon as he could be seen returning Varsal would send the first again. So it went, again and again. Todd was amazed at the strength of these young men, running as tirelessly as gazelles through the thick wet grass.

No one spoke. Even Pian said nothing, which was very unusual indeed.

After about three hours they arrived at the Lonely Needle and stopped for a pause and a snack. With military discipline, the young men pulled down wood, foodstuffs, and utensils from off the yaks, and soon everyone was sitting on the mossy stones around the Lonely Needle, drinking tea and eating tasty morsels caringly prepared in the village. The yaks were unloaded and allowed to graze.

Bud watched in wonder as such effort was made to unburden the yaks. Todd came over, and seeing his father's thoughtful look, said, "You know, Dad, they say that he who loves his yak loves himself."

"Have you ever seen such happy, peaceful animals?" asked Bud in amazement.

"No, never," replied Todd with a grin.

The tea did its trick, and soon the group was full of chatter. For the mountain people, drinking tea without chatting was about as ridiculous an idea as swimming without getting wet. After a while Varsal gave the order to load the yaks again, and they started the long decline to the edge of the Spoon—a long, winding, grassy decline shaped a bit like a curvy food-trough and meandering between outcrops of mossy rock.

In single file, the whole group navigated their way slowly and carefully down the precarious slope. The further they descended, the more trees and bushes they passed, and the sounds of birds became ever louder.

After a long hour of slow progress, they arrived at a wide gravel base that looked like a large bowl. In the middle was a beautiful blue pond with a few ducks and moorhens. The yaks were brought to the edge of the pond, and they drank with such gusto that the noise of their great gulps made the waterfowl flee to the other side. Everyone knelt down and drank from this lovely clear cool mountain water. The elders stood guard until all had drunk, and then, upon Varsal's nod, they themselves drank while the others stood guard.

The party continued to the edge of the bowl, a cliff dropping down into a large, rolling forest. They had reached the edge of the high plains.

As soon as they got there, the yaks were unloaded with great speed, and everybody jumped into action. The young men who led the yaks unloaded the wood and made fires on which they prepared food. Two elders stood watch with spears in hand, and the other two worked with Pian, Jarod, and Dana to prepare backpacks. With the help of Bud and Todd, Varsal set up a system of ropes going down the precipice.

A thick and hearty soup was soon ready, and when the jobs were done, everyone but the elders on watch came to eat in a circle. It was quite unlike the usual loud and drawn-out meals of the mountain people, who loved to sit long around food and talk. Varsal had said they needed to leave as soon as possible to be back on the plain before sunset. Before long, the unwashed dishes were loaded into packs on the yaks, and preparations to return were already underway. The elders changed roles, giving the two on watch the chance to eat something, and all the yaks but two were loaded. The two remaining yaks were placed in a harness.

When everything was done, Varsal called everyone to the edge of the cliff. They linked arms in a circle, and the great chieftain pronounced a blessing on them all. Bud, who could not understand his words, gazed at his face as he blessed each one individually. The great hulk of a man shone with loving pride as he spoke out blessings on Jarod and Pian. They stared at the ground as he spoke, but the delight on their faces was not to be hidden.

And then he turned to Todd and Dana, and he beamed with a compassion so intense that Todd almost wanted to hide his face. His solemn words were mixed with sorrow.

"Deriboni, I knew you would come, but I didn't know when. You came as a boy, and you leave as a man. You are indeed the lamb that slew the wolf. His love has made your heart great. Follow your heart. In our tradition, a man must kill a fox before he can fight a wolf. You have killed your fox, but a much greater wolf lies before you. You must be strong, not in your strength, but in the strength of the Lord."

Todd nodded, and Varsal turned to the girl beside him. "Dana, you are that great rock that holds the tent through the storm. Deriboni will need you, as you need him. Tender hearts do break, but they heal and go on to great victories."

Varsal placed his fist on his chest. "You will take my heart with you wherever you go, and not just mine but the hearts of us all, and yours will also stay with us. When we look at the mossy stone on which you used to sit, and the tools with which you worked, we shall think of you, and we shall love you as one of our own."

He turned his gaze to Bud and said, "Oh Great Man of Small Stature, what you have long been waiting for will come. You will feel alone but will never be alone. You will feel weak, but the day will come as the dawn breaks through the morning sky. The night cannot hold back the day."

He then spoke the word of final blessing: "You are with us wherever we go, and we are with you. May the Lord be with you, and bring what he has started to completion."

After a moment of silence, the group broke up and set out again to the tasks at hand.

The yaks in the harness were placed a fair distance from the cliff edge, and a long rope was drawn from them to the edge. Jarod put a loop in it and threw it over the cliff. Varsal tied another rope around Jarod's waist, and it was taken by the young men. Helped by Varsal, Jarod climbed over the edge and placed his foot in the loop on the rope attached to the yaks. When he was ready, Varsal called out a command. Some of the men slowly led the yaks toward the cliff edge, lowering Jarod down the cliff. Down and down he went until the yaks were right to the edge.

"It's okay, I'm at the bottom," he called.

In the same way they lowered Dana, Pian, and Bud, as well as the backpacks and other sacks. Finally Todd came to the edge. Before he could step into the loop, Varsal grasped his shoulders, and looking into his eyes, said, "Good-bye, Deriboni!"

Varsal gave Todd a hug and helped him over the edge, down into the thick forest. When he came to the bottom, the others were waiting for him. There were no calls of farewell from above, so as not to attract attention, and the escort party returned in silence to the village.

Jarod now took the role of a scout. He went ahead, checking that the way was clear, and returned to where they could see him and the flags he carried. A white flag meant "follow," and a red flag "wait." In this way, he led the group slowly through the forest. They were carrying so much gear that they could not go quickly and had to rest fairly often. There was not a soul to be seen.

It was not long before they came to a wide, gently flowing river. Jarod and Pian opened up their sacks, which were full of everything needed to make a raft—hatchets, bands, and ropes. Into the evening hours they cut wood in lengths and collected any suitable pieces beside the river's edge.

In the last remaining daylight, Todd and Dana set up hammocks high in the branches. Bud called everyone to come and sleep.

"You want me to sleep way up there?" asked Pian uneasily.

"We do it all the time," said Dana with a smile. She was so used to receiving instruction from Pian, and now she could be the instructor. Mimicking Pian's voice with words she had said on the high plains a thousand times, she said, "Ha! This is what people do!"

"You, my sister, are impossible!" said Pian, trying to hide a smile.

"Everything I learned, I learned from you!"

"Ha! Ha! Ha!" said Pian sarcastically as she started up the rope ladder Todd had made.

All went well that night, and no one fell out of his or her hammock despite both Pian's and Jarod's fears that they would wake up on the ground with a broken leg.

The next morning they all ate a special breakfast prepared for them in the village and quickly got to work on the raft again. They had decided to make the raft "one Bud wide" and "two Buds long." Now and again Bud had to lie down beside the logs so they could mark the place to cut. For the long pieces, he had to lie down twice.

"Life would be so much easier if we had two Buds, eh?" said Bud jokingly.

"Two Buds! I can't imagine it! Ha! That would put Dorn in an early grave!" laughed Todd.

"And how would Clara cope?" added Dana, laughing.

"You two are very cheeky indeed!" said Bud, pretending to be offended.

By midmorning, their heap of wood was starting to take shape. Bud was amazed at the complex looping and tying done by Pian's nimble fingers, and by Jarod's quiet strength, which seemed to move mountains of wood.

By lunchtime, the raft was finished.

"Let us eat something quickly, and then we must go," said Jarod, looking up at the sun moving across the blue sky. "We need to get past the Lonely Needle before sunset."

Todd and Dana hurriedly prepared something to eat, and the two ate heartily. At last the moment all had dreaded finally came—the time to say good-bye.

Pian took Dana in her arms and said simply, "I will be waiting for you, dear sister."

"And I will come," replied Dana. "A hundred yaks could not keep me away."

Jarod turned aside with Todd and said, "Take the raft until the birches turn to beech; then you must get off very quickly and continue on foot."

He took Todd's hand in his and said, "You have been better than ten brothers. I could never thank you enough."

Todd could do nothing more than choke out a "thank you" of his own, and looking at the ground, he did not manage to raise his eyes to look into Jarod's. It was all too difficult.

Jarod simply put his hand on Todd's shoulder and said, "Remember Varsal's words. There is a great wolf waiting for you, greater than Ethero. Be strong, brother, be strong. I am with you in heart."

He gave Todd's shoulder a squeeze, and without a word he and Pian picked up their packs, turned around, and were gone. In a kind of stupor, Todd stood, staring at the place where they had just been as a crushing sense of loneliness fell upon him.

He felt a hand move up his back and clasp his shoulder. It was Dana, whose face said she understood. She gave his hand a silent squeeze. The time had come. This was something they both knew. This chapter must finish and another must begin.

Bud got lunch ready without asking for their help, and they ate more or less without saying a word. He left the two to clean up and pack their things while he went into the forest with an axe. A few minutes later he returned with three long poles to be used on the raft.

With all their strength, the three lifted the raft into the water, put their things in the middle, and pushed out into the gently flowing river.

The sun sparkled on the water—it was an ideal autumn day. A gentle breeze was blowing out of the eastern sky and swirling between the trees on both sides of the river. The splashing and gurgling of the river could be faintly heard below the cheerful singing of birds, and everything seemed to be fine—not just fine but wonderful. The beautiful river reminded Todd of his own, beside the mill, and slowly but surely the pain of saying good-bye to Jarod was losing its sting.

Dana and Bud, however, knew something that Todd did not. They knew the brutality of the place that lay downstream. They knew that this was a voyage into the jaws of a lion—a lion that had devoured many people before them and seemed to exercise unchallenged power. Only a miracle would bring them out alive. Bud was especially troubled at this thought, knowing that he was putting these two dear children in danger. The struggle that raged within him was greater than either Todd or Dana knew, but he also knew that all of history's great acts looked utterly impossible and ridiculous right up to the end. That was what made them great.

Yet even Bud, with all his insight, did not truly realize what lay before them—one truly greater than Ethero, and the fight would be a great one.

CHAPTER 23

The Raft

The odd ray from the early morning sun darted through the forest leaves and sparkled on the still water. Indeed the only ripples on the glassy river were made by their raft, which they shoved along with long poles. Bud watched the kids maneuver the raft between the muddy banks. Todd, on the left, had become a burly, brown fifteen-year-old with a deep chest and thick, strong legs. Dana still bore the beautiful face and tender eyes that had fascinated Bud when they met, but she too had become unusually muscular, a girl who now radiated strength of both body and mind.

The magnificence of the perfect autumn morning, though, could do nothing to calm his troubled mind.

Am I an absolute fool? These two beautiful kids have put all their confidence in me, and I'm feeding them to the lions! It's crazy!

He watched them poling down the river toward the kingdom and the dangerous task before them—rescuing Dana's mother from the mines, snatching her out from under the wicked oppression of the kingdom. *Of course it's crazy—but so were all the mighty deeds of history!* The splash of a kingfisher diving into the river interrupted his thoughts, and he noticed a large stream flowing into their ever-widening river.

He shook his head. *Where are the "valiant men" of the village? A camp of soldiers is swallowing our freedom bit by bit, and only a handful of kids have the courage to stand against them.*

His thoughts flashed back to the soldiers overrunning his home village with growing brutality. The elders, including the chief, Dorn, cowered more and more by the day. That was why he was here. *Bud,* he told himself for the umpteenth time, *you must stand with these children! You dare not let courage stand alone!*

Dana glanced over her shoulder and gave Bud an affectionate look. "I can't wait to see Mom, Bud! I've got so much to tell her, so many dear friends for her to meet."

Bud cast her a fond smile, trying to hide the worry he felt. "I'm looking forward to meeting her myself."

Do these kids understand at all how difficult it will be to free her? The mines are a far crueler taskmaster than anything they have ever seen . . .

Swirls and eddies caught his attention, and he realized that the current had become so fast that no more pushing was necessary. Dana and Todd now only used their poles to keep the raft away from rocks and branches as it freely drifted down the river. Bud struggled to see the banks, but they lay hidden behind trees, bushes, and vines hanging low over the water. Birches and poplars stretched branches from one side of the river over to the other, forming great leafy tunnels for them to drift through. The only sounds to be heard were the squeaking and creaking of the branches in the raft, the gurgling and splashing of the water under the raft, and the singing of what sounded like an army of birds.

Bud saw how the kids enjoyed the ride, and he felt this was the perfect remedy for the sorrow of their recent good-byes. The gentle ups and downs on the sparkling water could soothe the aches of any soul, and he himself sensed a new lightheartedness as they were carried along.

About an hour later, the gurgling water quickened its pace. Bud noticed that the kids pushed off with more effort than before, and more often, as the raft bobbed ever faster between large rocks rising out of the water. Even the forest seemed to change. The birch trees which had once dominated the forest gradually gave way to other trees, especially beech. Large, mossy vines hung down from their mighty branches, and the forest seemed to be getting darker.

Dana let out a shriek at a sharp bend, and Todd rushed over to help her push them away from a large stone in the increasingly violent water. After the bend, the river seemed to drop down quickly, and suddenly the forest was gone.

They found themselves in a large, sunny clearing with a small grassy field to the right, in which they saw two older farmers sitting and talking while seven oxen were drinking at the bank of the river.

"Get down!" said Bud quickly, "And don't say a word!" He didn't think the farmers themselves were dangerous, but he didn't want word to get out that they had arrived.

They all lay as flat as they could, forced to leave the raft at the mercy of the rushing waters. As the water grew faster and faster and the raft began to spin, all they could do was lie flat and hold on for dear life. Bud lifted his head just enough to catch sight of the farmers. It was clear they had not seen them. Only a little further and they would be out of sight.

"They didn't see us!" said Bud. "In just a second we can get up and slow this thing down."

Water splashed in over every side, and now their raft was well and truly out of control. Then it happened—with a great crash, the corner of the raft struck a large stone, and they all lurched forward.

Dana screamed as she flew over the side. Todd grabbed her arm as quick as a flash and pulled her back to the raft. She managed to climb on again, but struggled to get her footing.

"Look, Dad!" Todd pointed to the side of the raft.

To Bud's horror, a broken rope was pulling away from the logs. The raft began falling apart. "We'll have to get off!" shouted Bud. "Throw the packs on shore!"

With a heave, Todd threw the packs one after the other onto the shore. Now the water was all white in every direction, and the raft tipped and rocked with violent force. Struggling to keep his footing on the slick wood, Bud peered ahead and noticed a calm spot off to one side.

"Todd! There's a pool up ahead. Take this pole and jump over that rock, and then hold on to the pole!"

"Okay!" said Todd as he crouched, ready to jump. Bud grasped hold of one end of the pole and gave Todd the other.

"Now!" shouted Bud, and Todd sprang with all his might onto the rock and scrambled over it, falling into the pool on the other side. Bud barely kept his end of the pole from getting yanked out of his hands, but as Todd got to his feet, together they used the pole to steady the raft. Slowly it came to a halt and remained in one place, bouncing fiercely and smashing against a rock.

"Dana, grab the pole and pull yourself toward Todd!" shouted Bud above the wild white waters.

"Okay!" shouted Dana. She grabbed the pole and climbed along it toward Todd. Bud held tight to the pole, desperate to keep it from slipping even as he tried not to lose his balance and pitch into the water. Her body freely floated in the fast-flowing water, but with great strength she managed to get to Todd and grab his forearm. With an enormous heave, he pulled her up onto the rock, and she crawled over and fell into the pool.

In a flash, she turned around and grabbed the pole with Todd in order to pull Bud in as well. But he had nearly lost his grip. The wet, slippery pole was slipping further and further through his hands. He saw Dana's eyes go wide with horror.

"Come on, Bud!" she shouted. The raft was tossing wildly and falling apart under him. A wave pitched him, and as he fought to stay on top of the raft, he lost his grip—the pole slipped through his fingers and was gone.

The raft surged down the wild water, spinning and bashing against rocks in the ruthless current. In the back of his mind Bud faintly heard Todd's scream, *"Dad!"*

His leg slipped over the side of the raft and smashed against a great stone. Suddenly he saw a vine amid the splash and the spray and dove at it with all his force. He clung to it and tried to pull himself up, but he couldn't escape the sucking, battering waters.

"Dad!"

That was Todd again, somewhere on the shore.

"I'm here!" shouted Bud.

"Hold on! I'm coming!"

Nearly numb with the cold and fear, Bud nodded. He felt his strength and grip failing.

"I've got you!" came Todd's voice again as two strong hands grabbed Bud's forearms. Todd had somehow wrapped his legs around a bough, and he held Bud fast.

"I've got you, Dad!" he said again, and Bud let go of the vine, seizing Todd's forearms so their grip interlocked. Todd strained to pull Bud to shore, but this time his strength failed him. The water was just too strong.

"I've got you!" said a voice behind Todd. It was Dana. Bud felt a mighty heave that pulled him out of the grip of the current. Another great tug, and he felt the muddy banks under his knees. He crawled up onto the muddy bank and lay there gasping for air. Slowly he became aware of the heavy breathing of the other two.

After a while, Bud heard Dana's voice. "You okay, Bud?"

"Well, if I'm really honest," said Bud, still breathing hard, "I don't think so." Now that the action was over, he felt a pain in his thigh. "I hit my leg on a rock." He blinked, still lying with his head in the mud, and saw sunlight streaming into a clearing up above. His body felt dangerously chilled, and the sun was a beautiful invitation. "Let's get up into the sun," he said.

With quite some effort, they crawled up to a grassy clearing in the late afternoon sun. Its warmth was truly wonderful as they all sat in the grass.

"How's your leg?" asked Dana with great concern.

Bud moved it around. He grimaced, but nothing about the pain felt bad in a threatening way. "It's sore, but nothing's broken. I think I'll be hobbling around for a couple of days." He looked up at the two kids, who were soaking wet and muddy from head to toe, and his heart burst with affection. "You two are amazing, just amazing!"

"Dana might be, but I'm not," said Todd bitterly, not looking up. "I'm not at all!"

"What?" asked Bud, turning around to look at Todd straight on. "You showed the strength and courage of a lion out there. I've never been as proud of you as I am today."

"Well, you're wrong, Dad. You're wrong." Todd glanced up at Bud with those regretful eyes that Bud knew only too well. "Just before Jarod left, he told me that we had to get off the raft when the birches changed to beech. I forgot to tell you. I just plain forgot!"

Todd's eyes filled with grief. "None of that would have happened if we had . . ."

His broken voice cracked, and he could say no more.

"Now you listen to me, young man!" said Bud warmly. "I'll say it again. I've never been as proud of you as I am today. Never!" Bud rubbed Todd's back with his hand.

"Me either!" added Dana with a face that beamed with affection.

"I saw that raft going down the river without you," said Todd with a trembling voice, his eyes still fixed on the ground before him. "I thought I'd lost you forever! I was so scared."

Bud laughed, but his heart was moved. "Ha! You'll have to try harder if you want to lose me!" he said. "I tell you something: I love you more today than I ever have. And that'll be true tomorrow, and the next day, and the next after that."

Bud gazed at his adopted son. Todd was still looking away, but Bud saw, as he had many times before, that slight crack of a smile. His words had somehow broken through Todd's inner clouds, and a ray of hope shone through.

"Come on," said Dana, getting to her feet. "Let's leave Bud here and go back and get our packs."

"Good idea," said Bud. "Be quick, though, because that wrecked raft will attract a horde of soldiers."

It took a while before Todd and Dana found all the backpacks. Darkness was falling by the time they returned, and they changed into dry clothes. Todd climbed up high in the trees and set up hammocks and a set of ladders.

When he came down, Bud and Dana had unpacked all the food, and they all ate very heartily. The wonderful food of the mountain people had been cut up into savory morsels which melted on the tongue. As they took them one after the other from the bag, a much needed silence fell upon them—not one of those horrible *alone* silences, but a relieved, thankful *together* silence worth a thousand words.

After they had finished eating, Dana started closing up the bags.

"We are now well and truly in the kingdom, but if we stay in the forest we should be safe. The subjects of the kingdom are afraid of it," Bud said, gazing up at the leafy branches that shadowed the woods beyond the clearing.

"Really?" said Todd in amazement.

"You wouldn't believe the stories I heard of the forest when I was a little girl," said Dana. "Hobgoblins and ghosts and monsters of every kind. Now you can see how scared of the soldiers I was. I was willing to run into the heart of the forest to get away from them."

"And you found us," said Bud with a smile.

"I did, didn't I? A girl couldn't be luckier!"

"Well, tomorrow we can have a look at the lay of the land and make a plan. Does everyone have enough warm, dry things to sleep in?" Bud felt so much better with a full stomach and dry clothes. The apprehension he'd felt earlier seemed gone for now.

"I do," said Todd.

"Me too," added Dana.

"Okay, well, let's get to bed now, and make sure we have left nothing behind us. I imagine there will be a lot of soldiers around these next few days."

Up they went into the tree. It took Bud quite a while to get up to his hammock, as he could barely bend his leg. He lay awake for some time, hoping the pain of his stiff leg would subside, watching the stars flicker behind the rustling leaves.

This was all crazy, but a deep sense of encouragement filled his heart. It would all work out somehow. It most certainly would

. . .

CHAPTER 24

Finding Sedon

Todd woke to the sound of horses galloping along the road. He listened intently to the great commotion below as squadron after squadron searched the area. They were high up in a huge, leafy oak tree, and although the soldiers' dogs sniffed around the trunk, no one saw them high above. He looked over to see that both Dana and Bud were awake and were looking down at the activity below.

"What are they so worked up about?" whispered Todd, looking down as soldiers tramped through the forest, shouting at each other and moving with quick, nervous movements.

"They're afraid," replied Bud.

"Of what?"

"The kingdom isn't like the forest, Todd. It's different," said Dana. "In the forest, the people are peaceful because they are at peace. They're happy. Here the people only live in peace with each other because they are scared."

"Scared of what?"

"Of the king, and his soldiers, and even their own friends."

Todd shook his head, unable to imagine such a thing. His friends were all he had in the world: Bud, Dana, Jarod, the chief's sons. He would trust them with his life.

"Now, we want to find your friend Sedon," said Bud, catching Dana's eye.

"He lives in Glencan, where this little river runs into the great river."

"If I'm not mistaken, it's about two miles from here," said Bud in thought.

"But how do we get there?" asked Dana.

"*We* don't!" said Bud. He sat up in his hammock and stretched out his sore leg. "Or at least, *you* don't. Dana, we can't let them see you. You must be out of sight all the time. We've got to bring Sedon here somehow."

"Look over there!" whispered Todd, pointing to a boy carrying a large bundle of sticks along the forest paths. The soldiers were ignoring him. The boy looked about fourteen or fifteen, but he was tall and muscular. "He just walked past a group of soldiers and nobody even looked at him. The best part is, he looks just like me!"

"And?" asked Dana puzzled.

"Well, I could carry something ... a bundle of sticks or something ... down to Glencan as if I'm delivering it to someone. They won't stop me. I'll take it to Sedon and tell him what's going on."

"But would he believe you?" asked Bud. "He doesn't know you."

"I know! Todd, show him this!" said Dana excitedly, pulling a ring off her finger. "He gave me this ring for my tenth birthday. I'm sure he'll recognize it."

Todd took the ring and happily pocketed it. In his mind, he was already halfway down the road. "You'll need to go in the evening, when the number of soldiers has gone down, and then Sedon can come here at night," said Bud. "I know you don't think the soldiers will stop you, but no sense taking more risk than you have to."

Late that afternoon, Todd shinnied down the tree and collected a bundle of sticks that he tied up and put on his back. The soldiers had moved on for now. That evening, as the sun was setting, he carried the bundle on his back to the village of Glencan. He looked around for Sedon's wagon, which Dana had described as old and black with yellow trim. There it was in front of a small corner house, just as she'd said. He knocked on the door.

The door opened, and a short, stout man with short gray hair appeared. "Hello, lad." His eyes sparkled with friendliness in the last of the evening light, and a smile appeared on his wrinkled face. "You must have made a mistake. I haven't ordered any kindling."

"Are you Sedon?" asked Todd, his voice low. His heart pounded with excitement.

"Yes, I am. But honestly, I haven't ordered any—"

"Do you remember Dana?" asked Todd in a whisper.

The man's eyes opened wide. "I don't know any Dana, and if this is some kind of trick . . ."

"Look!" said Todd, whispering excitedly and holding out the ring.

"Dana!" Sedon's eyes went round as saucers. "Put that down, lad, and come in."

Todd lay the bundle beside the wagon and slipped silently through the door. No sooner was he inside than Sedon shut the door behind him and locked it with bolt and latches. Todd peered around at the first brick house he had ever entered. It was the cramped, cluttered home of an old bachelor, and although the crooked walls and shelves were in sore need of a new coat of paint, they did extend a warm, homey welcome.

Sedon turned around and fixed his large, earnest eyes on Todd. "Is she alive?"

"Yes, she is."

"Is she all right?"

"She's fine! She really is."

"I took her to the forest," said Sedon gravely, "I didn't know what else to do!"

"We found her, and we took care of her," said Todd, not wanting to waste any time. "Now listen, she wants you to come and see her."

"Where is she?"

"At the edge of the forest, up the little river."

"Was that your raft?"

"You know about it?"

"Oh, yes. It's the talk of the town! But it was mountain people that made it, wasn't it? Those ropes are their handiwork."

"We can explain all that later. You must come!"

Sedon wrung his hands. "She should never have come back! Listen, boy, she's got to get out of here. If they find her she'll be sent to the mines, or worse!"

Todd humphed. They knew the danger well enough. "That's why I came. I'll take you to her. She wants to see you."

Sedon nodded, calming himself. "Okay. We'll need to wait about an hour, and then we'll go in the dark. Do you need anything?"

Todd tried to think. Their rations were low. "Food. Do you have any food?"

"Yes, sure. And what about clothing?"

"Oh, yes. We could certainly use some clothes that kingdom subjects would wear." Todd looked down at his own clothes, made by his mother's hand in the village. He and Dana would stand out like sore thumbs here.

Over the next hour, Sedon and Todd prepared food and clothing for everyone. Although Todd found Sedon very pleasant and his humble house very welcoming, he couldn't shake a feeling of uneasiness. It would only disappear once he was back in the forest with the others.

After dark, Todd took the sacks of clothes and food and crawled into the straw on the back of Sedon's wagon. Sedon covered him up with straw to hide him, threw the kindling onto the wood pile, and set off toward the forest. Buried under itchy, dusty straw, Todd tried to breathe without sneezing and kept a sharp ear out for soldiers.

Slowly, Todd heard the sound of rushing water over the clackety-clack of the horse, and he felt the wagon bounce and bump as if they had left the road. No soldiers so far. He relaxed as he realized they'd entered the forest. Most likely they were safe now.

The bouncing and bumping went on until the wagon came to an abrupt halt. The hay suddenly disappeared, and Todd saw the half-moon and starry sky above. "Thanks!" he said, happy to breathe in the cool, fresh night air.

"We've come as far into the forest as the wagon can go."

"Okay," said Todd, hankering to see the others again. "Come with me!"

He led Sedon through the dimly lit forest and with some difficulty found their clearing. Todd gave a double cuckoo call. They soon heard a blackbird, and Todd gave his double cuckoo again.

Suddenly a figure bolted out of the darkness and into Sedon's arms. "Sedon!" cried Dana. "It's you! It's really you!"

"Dana! Little girl!" Sedon held her tight and then said, "Let me have a look at you." He stared into her face, struggling to see clearly in the moonlight. Todd grinned and exchanged glances with Bud as the two gazed at each other.

"You're looking good, girl. You're looking really good. And you're so strong! I felt like I was hugging a bear!"

Dana laughed. "I'm doing well. I really am. Now Sedon, this is Bud. He's Todd's father."

"Good to meet you. I'm Sedon. I used to be the gardener in Falko's inn."

"Falko?" asked Bud.

"That was my father, and my mother's name was Julissa," Dana said.

"Falko was my best friend," said Sedon solemnly. "I owe him more than I can say."

"And you were certainly his best friend," said Dana.

The gardener looked surprised. "I don't know. He had many friends . . ."

"He did, but you were his best friend," said Dana again with resolve. "I remember."

"I spoke with him, just before he died. He asked me to take care of Julissa and Dana." Sedon suddenly went silent. He was struggling to find words, and the others waited for him to continue. "I still remember. He was weak, so terribly weak. He took hold of my hand and told me to take care of Julissa and Dana. I told him I was just a poor, uneducated gardener . . ."

He paused a moment and continued, "Falko said, 'Listen, there's a story to be told, and a song to be sung, and you're in it. You can do it—he won't let you down."

Todd could make out the gardener's grave, almost tormented face as he continued.

"You know, Falko was so weak, and so thin, and yet I'd never seen him stronger, and there was I at his bedside, strong as an ox but trembling like a leaf. I often felt that I had let him down . . . I felt like I abandoned you at the edge of that forest! And you ran off into who knows where . . ." His quivering lips said no more.

"You did exactly what Mom asked you to do! And look! Here I am," said Dana, taking his large, rough hand in hers. "Sedon, how's Mom?"

"Your mother's not far from here," said Sedon. "She's in the mining camp at Iron Hill. I think she's okay. They never sent her down the mine. They put her on laundry duty instead. I haven't seen her, but I ask around. I'm told she's okay. She was ill a while ago and is still weak, but she is better now and working again."

Todd's heart sank as Dana's face took on worry. "Ill?" asked Dana. "What do you mean 'ill'?"

"Fever, I'm told, and it lasted a good long time. That's all I know. It kept her out of the mines, so it was not all bad. She should be better now, and as I heard she has started working again."

"I've been so worried about her!" said Dana, struggling to keep back the tears.

"She's okay. She really is."

"Well, we've got to figure out a way of getting her out of there," said Dana.

"Come, let's get something to eat first," said Bud.

They all sat down, and Sedon handed out cups for everybody. He opened up his sack and produced large trays of food, which he put in the middle of the group. It was a primitive but tasty meal of roughly cut chunks of brown bread with clumps of cheese and dried meat. Todd rather regretted taking a piece of meat because he had to chew it for ten minutes before swallowing it.

Into the night, they discussed plans as to how they would get Julissa out of the mining camp. Sedon was in, no matter what it might cost him, be it his business or his life. Todd felt a growing fondness for the old gardener, sensing the depth of his concern and loyalty. He was clearly earnest to make his promise to Falko good.

"The problem is that only certain people can get into the camp," said Sedon as they ate. "It's very well guarded." He slowed his chewing for a moment, thoughtful. "You know, there's a farmer who looks a lot like Bud. It's a bit hard to see you in the dark, Bud, but you do look like him. He walks in most mornings with vegetables on a big wheelbarrow and often brings coal back to the village on his way back."

"And if I dressed up like him I could get in," said Bud. "That's what you're saying?"

"Exactly!" said Sedon. "I could distract him, keep him from showing up at the same time you do. He's been wanting to buy a goat from me for ages, and I could get talking to him and delay him."

"And during that time Dad goes into the camp pushing a wheelbarrow full of vegetables," said Todd. Deep down he had very mixed feelings about his father walking into a mining camp, but he kept them to himself. This whole thing was suddenly getting very real.

"That gets him in, but how can we get Julissa out?" asked Sedon.

"Bud can put Mom in the wheelbarrow and cover her with coal to take to the village!" said Dana excitedly.

"That's it! That's the idea," said Bud.

"She's not strong enough to walk very far," said Sedon. "We've got to get a horse ready. Not my old mare—she has a bad leg. She's okay for pulling a wagon slowly, but you can't ride her." He paused and tapped his chin. "We could use Syder!"

"Syder?" asked Todd.

"Syder is Dad's horse," said Dana. Her voice trembled a little, and Todd wondered if she was wishing her father were here now. "Where is he?"

"I have him in my stable," said Sedon. "Now how could we do this?"

"I could bring him, couldn't I?" asked Todd. "People would recognize Dana, but nobody around here knows me."

"Yes, that's it!" said Sedon, looking up. "I'll get the farmer talking, and while I'm doing that, Bud can take my wheelbarrow full of vegetables into the camp. He'll bring Julissa out in the wheelbarrow, covered in coal."

"And I'll be there with the horse to meet you!" said Todd. He smiled, relieved that he would be nearby to help or protect his father. Not that he was going to tell Bud that.

"But Syder doesn't know Todd!" said Dana. "And you know what Syder is like with people he doesn't know. Why don't I take him?"

"Don't be silly, Dana!" said Bud ardently. "That's far too risky!"

"I could disguise myself!" replied Dana, louder than she had intended.

"No, Dana," said Sedon firmly. "Bud's right. It is true, though. Syder can be stubborn with people he doesn't know."

"What if I hide in the trees along the way and only come out if Syder gets difficult?" asked Dana.

"Hmmm." Bud gave an uneasy sigh and looked at Sedon. "What do you think?"

"The idea isn't bad, but—" began Sedon.

"Dana knows what she's doing!" blurted Todd, surprising himself as much as anyone else. He could feel his heart pounding nervously and had no idea why. For the first time Todd noticed how he longed to have Dana around. She was so dear, and so strong. There was nothing he wanted more than for her to be at his side.

"I think Todd's right," added Bud calmly.

"Yes. Me too," said Sedon. "But Dana, only come out if you absolutely have to!"

"I will," said Dana. Todd felt her hand slip into his and give it a squeeze, as if to say "thank you."

"Todd," said Sedon, "there's a grove about one hundred yards from the front gate of the camp. It's just off the road between the camp and the village. That would be the best place to wait with Syder and get Julissa mounted. No one outside the grove will see you."

"We'll have to get the timing right," said Bud.

"When does the farmer usually go into the camp?" asked Todd.

"Around ten o'clock. Sometimes earlier, sometimes later. I don't know how long I can keep him talking. Why doesn't Bud go in at quarter to ten and aim to come out at ten o'clock? Syder must be at the grove by five to ten at the absolute latest."

"Okay," said Todd. "So Dad brings Julissa out, and we give her Syder, and then what?"

"We tell her to ride into the forest, to come here," said Bud. "And to wait for us here until the afternoon. We'll be on foot, so it will take us that long to get back here."

"If all goes well, they won't even notice she's gone until late in the evening," said Sedon.

"If all goes well," said Bud, rubbing his moustache uneasily. "If all goes well . . ."

CHAPTER 25

Getting Julissa Out

Nobody slept well that night. The excitement and concerns about the following day kept them thinking till late and woke them up early. Nobody felt very tired, though. They were all too worked up for that.

Everything went like clockwork. Bud followed Todd to Sedon's house in the morning, and Sedon gave them a wheelbarrow full of vegetables and took them to Falko's horse. He then went off to talk to the farmer he wanted to delay.

Bud and Todd left for the camp on time with Syder and the wheelbarrow. Syder clearly didn't like being led away by two complete strangers, and he tugged and pulled restlessly against Todd's firm grip. After some ado, he calmed down and cooperated.

"Compared to the mules at home, horses seem like kittens!" said Todd cheerfully.

"Yes," said Bud uneasily. He really wasn't in the mood for talking.

The birds were happily singing and the warm autumn sun climbing the cloudless sky, but that did nothing to calm Bud's anxious thoughts. The grinding sound of gravel under their feet and the occasional squeak of the wheel kept him on edge. *I only want to get this day behind me!*

What with the dips and bends in the road, it was a fair distance to push a wheelbarrow, so Todd took it for a while, and Bud led Syder. Bud gasped to see a patrol coming, but to his great relief they rode by without a word. The camp had come into sight, and soon enough they found themselves in the cool shadows of the grove.

"I'll bring Julissa right in here. Stay here and don't come out," Bud told Todd strictly. He knew Todd wasn't a little child anymore, but he couldn't help worrying about his son.

"Okay, Dad."

In no time Bud was on his way again. The wheel was squeaking ominously, his thigh was throbbing, and everything seemed wrong. Out of the corner of his eye he saw a hand waving from behind a stone wall in the field. It was Dana. *Get down, girl! Get out of sight and stay out of sight!* He hoped she would hear his thoughts. He sighed in relief as her hand disappeared, and in the depths of his heart he gave everything to the One who holds everything in his hand.

With its enormous barbed wire fence, the camp looked like a monstrous cage rising out of a round green hill. Bud could not stand to look at it, and he fixed his eyes only on the road in front of him.

Slowly but surely he approached the front gate. An old, plump soldier was slouched on a chair in front of the gate, looking dreamily at a piece of paper in his hand. He glanced up at Bud and gave a drowsy nod for him to enter. Bud sighed with a relief that didn't last long. That sickly feeling he'd had when he first came into the kingdom was there again, only far worse. This was like sticking your head in the jaws of a lion.

His hopes that the mining camp would look better when he got inside were disappointed. It must have been the dreariest place Bud had ever seen. There was a grid of straight, gravel streets lying between rows of shabby, makeshift wooden buildings with the occasional tent here and there. Except for the rare weed between the shacks, there were no plants or trees to be seen. Life in such camps was definitely not there to be enjoyed.

Now that he was inside, he scanned the many buildings for the laundry. He spied a ragged wooden building with a couple of baskets in front. He shoved his wheelbarrow closer and saw one thin woman inside the open door, scrubbing something in a barrel.

"Hello!" he said.

The woman turned around. Her face was pale and weary, but she had beautiful twinkling eyes, just like Dana.

"Julissa?" he asked.

"That's right," she answered suspiciously. "You know me?"

"You look very much like your daughter," said Bud with a smile.

The woman's eyes darted left to right, and she whispered, "Who are you?"

"I'm a friend of Dana's," answered Bud quietly. "I've come to get you out."

Julissa looked away nervously. "Look, I don't have any time for—"

"Look at this!" said Bud insistently, pulling out Dana's ring.

Julissa gasped and covered her mouth. "Her ring!" She was up on her feet and viewed the street again, left and right. "Come in!" She pulled him around to a corner where they could not be seen from outside.

"Believe me, Dana is with us and well! Sedon has arranged that I take you out of here. Syder will be waiting for you just outside the camp."

"Syder . . ." said Julissa wide-eyed, as if in a trance.

"Yes, Falko's horse, Syder! But you must believe me, and we must act fast!"

"What do you want me to do?"

"I'll sneak you out of here in this wheelbarrow."

"But how . . .?"

"I'll dump these . . ." Bud stopped speaking as Julissa suddenly put her hand to her lips and flashed a warning with her eyes. She shoved Bud behind the door and moved it around to hide him.

Bud froze flat against the wall, seeing only the door pressed against his face. He heard Julissa hastily sit again in her chair, and then the wooden floor creaked, telling him that someone of considerable weight had just walked in.

"You know those uniforms have to be ready at six-thirty!" The shrill, unpleasant voice of an old woman filled the whole building.

"Yes, ma'am."

"Well, what are you dallying around for? If they're wrinkled or they're damp, or they're badly folded, you know what that means?"

"No, ma'am."

"*Of course you do*!" screamed the woman.

Julissa's voice remained subdued. "Yes, ma'am."

"Don't you play games with me! One bad fold, one ugly wrinkle, and you're . . ." the woman paused and let out a blood-curdling scream, *"DOWN THE MINE!"* She took great heaves of air in wheezy, sickly breaths as though she had overdone it in her shouting.

"Yes, ma'am."

Bud heard the floor creak again as the woman changed her stance, possibly to fight dizziness.

"I know your type." Her voice was now nothing more than a hoarse, hateful whisper. "You're a pretty face. You've been playing with the men all your life."

"Yes, ma'am."

"They've been your little puppets! Well, guess what? You can't play with me!"

Bud's blood was boiling at the woman's callous insults, but Julissa's voice stayed calm. "No, ma'am."

"You're off the sick list, Doll-face. You know what that means?" The woman's loathful, fiendish chuckle filled the room. "It means I can throw you down the mine at the bat of an eyelash!"

"Yes, ma'am."

"The mine's a funny place. People who go down there DON'T COME BACK!" Her croaky voice dropped again to a venomous whisper. "Let me tell you a little secret."

This time, Julissa's voice sounded weary. "Yes, ma'am"

"There was a pretty face here about a year ago. She was good! She could do everything! Washing, ironing, folding, bleaching. She was good. I mean, really good! She didn't make one mistake, so you know what I did?" she asked with triumphant cackle.

"No, ma'am."

"I wrinkled up her laundry for her."

Bud heard Julissa's gasp behind the door.

"That's what I did, and you know?" She spoke on with a mock sweetness. "That poor little thing went down to the mine. She didn't last four months! I can show you where she's buried, just down the hill here."

There was a slight pause. "Yes, ma'am."

"You know, there's an empty place beside her grave."

"Yes, ma'am."

"It would be the perfect spot for you!"

Bud had to restrain himself from jumping out and confronting the woman. It wouldn't help Julissa—it would only get them both caught.

"Yes, ma'am."

"Hurry up and get the uniforms ready before six-thirty, and not one minute—"

"Gruda!" A male voice called from outside, and Bud looked through the narrow slot between the hinges. There were at least three men in uniform standing there. The gap was too narrow to see if there were more.

After a few creaks of the floor, a most horrific old woman came into Bud's view through the gap. Her gray hair sat in a tangled mop on the top of her head, with one or two locks dropping down to her sickly, swollen cheeks. Her beady but vibrant eyes flashed with a gruesome energy as they gazed past her long pointy nose. She was so fat that her arms could not hang down at her side, and all of her clothes were too small.

"Sergeant!" she wheezed.

"Has the boot polish been ordered? And—" began the sergeant.

"And the metal polish," replied the woman. "It's all coming in the same shipment this afternoon."

"What about the saddle straps?"

"They were going to check the stock and get back to me tomorrow."

"Very good!" The sergeant paused and said, "What's this wheelbarrow doing here?"

Bud gasped and held his breath.

"No idea! Not my department."

"That's highly unusual. I'll report it to the sentry. Good day, Gruda."

"Good day, Sergeant!"

Bud let out a huge sigh of relief as he saw the sergeant and his men disappear in an instant. The woman also lumbered away with slow, laborious steps.

"Okay, come out!" whispered Julissa.

"That was awful!" said Bud as he emerged. Julissa was on her feet again.

"It's normal around here," said Julissa sadly. "We've got to hurry. The sentry will be here any minute. Okay, what's the plan?"

"I'll dump these vegetables somewhere. Then you get into the wheelbarrow, and I'll cover you with coal. We've got Syder waiting for you in the grove just outside the camp. You ride him along the river road right into the forest. Wait for us beside the river about a quarter-mile into the forest."

"Okay." She leaned through the doorframe and looked in both directions. "Quick! Follow me!"

Julissa led Bud to the coal shed. "Hurry! Dump everything there!" she said and Bud dropped all of the vegetables out onto the floor. She quickly climbed into the wheelbarrow, and Bud covered her over with coal.

It's good that Sedon has such a large wheelbarrow! thought Bud to himself as he just managed to squeeze Julissa and enough coal inside. Fortunately everyone was about his business, and there was nobody in the coal shed or in the main courtyard. There were only two guards at the gate.

Bud took hold of the wheelbarrow and wheeled it out into the courtyard. What with Julissa and the coal it weighed quite a bit more than he had expected, and he did his best to hide his straining as he walked past the guards. But the wheelbarrow squeaked in protest under the heavy load, and Bud's injured leg began to throb.

Once again at the gate, the old soldier vaguely nodded as they passed him. What a relief to be outside again! The grove with Todd and Syder was not far ahead, and Bud sped up as fast as he could go. He could barely see past the heap of coal, but that didn't worry him as he excitedly raced toward the trees.

After some distance, the wheelbarrow suddenly let out an enormous cracking sound and lunged to the left. Before Bud could react, Julissa and all the coal flew out onto the road. He had raced into a hole in the road and snapped the wooden frame holding the wheel.

"Stop! Stop!" came the cry from the guard at the gate, who leapt to his feet and began running down the hill. Julissa stumbled to her feet amidst the scattered coal, looking around wildly for the best escape path.

"Dad!" Bud heard Todd's voice from the grove and looked down to see Todd running toward them with Syder.

"Come!" shouted Bud to Julissa, and he grabbed her by the arm, pulling her toward Todd.

"Here, Dad!" Todd was there very quickly. Without losing another word, he and Bud threw Julissa on Syder's back, and she galloped off like a shot toward the forest.

"Stop! Stop, I say!" Bud looked over his shoulder to see the old soldier scrambling after them, huffing and puffing as he shouted. Suddenly a group of soldiers on horseback appeared from the camp gate. They galloped toward Todd and Bud on the road.

"Let's go!" said Todd. They dashed off, but Bud's leg failed him, and he toppled onto the road. Todd turned back and with a great heave picked his father up onto his feet again.

On they stumbled in a blur. The galloping of the horses was drawing nearer. "Just leave me and get out!" shouted Bud.

"No!" shouted Todd, who stubbornly pulled his father along. All at once Bud felt another strong hand under his other arm. It was Dana.

"Todd! Go through that gate into the orchard!" she shouted. "We can lose them there!"

They struggled along the winding path to the orchard. As soon as they were within its stone wall, Dana pulled them to the right and shouted, "This way! There are orchards down here with lots of stone walls where he can hide!" The sudden crash of hoofbeats between the walls meant that the soldiers were not far behind at all.

"Down here! There should be a way out!" cried Dana. Her strong arm pulled Bud toward a narrow path surrounded by stone walls. They went quickly down the winding path to a wide area with a large iron gate locked shut.

Dana stopped and stared. "It's shut! It used to be always open!"

"Here's a way!" shouted Todd, pointing to a path off to the side. They ran up the path toward an entrance.

"We can go through there!" said Todd.

Todd ran ahead to see if they could get through, and Bud struggled behind with Dana's help. Bud gasped in horror as he saw a large red leather shield barring the way. This was a royal seal, and even touching it was strictly forbidden.

But before he could speak, Todd had put his hands on it.

"No!" cried both Bud and Dana but to no avail. Todd seemed to hear nothing else in the wild chase, and he yanked the shield to the ground.

"We can go through here!" he shouted.

"Let's go!" Dana's hand tugged Bud's arm, and through they went together, into a large orchard surrounded by high walls.

"Stop!" The soldiers were now right on their tail. Bud saw a wall that was a little lower than the others. "Dana! Come! Up and over!" He held his hands together, and Dana knew what he wanted to do. She ran over and stepped with one foot into his hands, and with all his strength he gave her a boost up the wall. Up she went. She grabbed hold of the top and disappeared over the wall.

"Todd, you're next!"

"But Dad . . ."

"Do it!" shouted Bud frantically.

Todd put his foot in Bud's hands, and with all that was in him, Bud heaved Todd upward. Todd scrambled to stay on top of the wall and reach back for Bud. But even as Bud reached up for him, Todd lost his balance and with a shout disappeared over the wall.

Bud heard the footsteps of soldiers behind him and forced his fingers between the stones to climb the wall. His head suddenly burst with a great flash of pain, and he fell into the wall, bashing his face against the stones but feeling nothing. He fell to his knees, and everything went black.

CHAPTER 26

Julissa's Flight

Syder galloped with great gusto along the path beside the river. At such a pace, Julissa could only lean forward and hold her arms around his neck.

This can't really be true! I must be dreaming! But indeed she was racing through the countryside—countryside she had not seen for months now—feeling the fresh, cool air of an autumn day beating in her face. Amid the wild hoofbeats she heard a trumpet blast. She heard it again and looked over her shoulder. A patrol of soldiers on horseback was hotly pursuing! She could see the trumpeter's bugle flash in the sunlight. They were a long way behind, though, and her heart soared with hope.

"Go, Syder! Go!" She could see the faint outline of the forest far ahead. It was a good couple of miles, but Syder was a fast horse. Over his loud gallop, she could hear the faint rumble of hooves behind her. It was like a dream, a mad mix of fear and the enormous thrill of being outside that terrible fence, sucking up the cool, clean air.

"You can do it, Syder!" she said, leaning forward and holding Syder's neck. "Give it everything, boy! Everything!"

After keeping a good pace for a while, Syder's smooth gallop grew rougher. His steps were more erratic and clumsy, and Julissa knew well that he was getting tired. With her head beside his neck, she could hear him gulping great gasps of air. She bounced around in his frantic gallop, holding on for dear life. For a while she had kept her distance from the squadron, but now their wild hoofbeats were thundering louder and louder. A bugle sounded clearly behind her. They were gaining on her.

Up ahead, the forest was getting a little clearer, but it was still so far away—so terribly far! The gardens and fields that sprawled out on the flatland between her and the forest seemed innumerable. Off to the far right, she caught a glimpse of something red. To her horror, she saw a group of about fifteen mounted soldiers wearing red. The king's elite patrol! Fortunately, they were going in the other direction.

"Faster, Syder! Faster, boy!" She lay as low as she could in the desperate hope that she would not be seen.

Then it happened—she heard a bugle call from the squadron behind her, a different signal this time.

The elite patrol in red stopped and turned around. In no time they were in full gallop toward Julissa. They couldn't cut her off on the path to the forest, but they were fresh, and Syder was beginning to weave from side to side with heavy, desperate steps. He breathed in great gasps and snorts, and Julissa knew he couldn't keep this up much longer

She looked over her shoulder. The elite patrol had entered the road in front of her other pursuers. The forest was just a few hundred yards now, but the soldiers were just a hundred yards behind her. Still, she would make it!

Unless Syder collapsed.

His sides were heaving beneath her. The men were about fifty yards behind her as she entered the last meadow before the forest. If she could just get inside and lose them. "Go, Syder, go! Give it all you've got!" she screamed.

Syder lurched to the left and then to the right. It was all Julissa could do to keep him under control as they stumbled into the forest about twenty yards ahead of the patrol. The country lane beside the creek turned into a narrow footpath between the dense evergreen trees. The thick forest and soft forest floor sucked in all the sound, and everything became strangely quiet. The soldiers must have stopped at the forest edge.

The next words cut through her like a knife. *"In after her!"* shouted the general. *"Do not fear the forest!"*

She raced ahead in a frenzy. Syder reeled along the path, stumbling into trees and bushes as though drunk with fatigue. Julissa's heart sank within her as the path opened to a large clearing. At the other end of the clearing stood a waterfall from which the river flowed. She was trapped. With a cliff in front and a patrol behind her, she could only run into the forest.

She jumped down from Syder and stumbled as fast as she could through the uneven grass toward the trees.

"Muntar! Seize her!"

She heard the feet of a man running behind her. Her strength failed her. She was too weak. She staggered to the edge of the clearing but could go no further. A rough hand seized her shoulder, and she managed to throw it off, but fell in doing so.

She scrambled to her feet, but this time both hands fell around her shoulders and held them like a vice.

CHAPTER 27

Going to the Palace

Dana got onto her hands and knees in the soft, thick grass. She was staring at Todd, who had just landed on the grass near her, but she was listening to the other side of the wall. There had been a scuffle, but she had no idea what was going on.

The words she heard sent a chill down her spine. "We've lost the children, but we got our man!"

"Shall we pursue them on foot, Sarge?"

"No, they're just kids. They'll be long gone by now. Let's take the prisoner to the colonel."

Dana saw Todd climbing up the wall to peek over the top, and she grabbed his leg and shook her head. She wanted to help Bud just as badly as he did, but it wasn't going to help anybody if they got caught.

She pressed her finger to her lips as if to say, *Don't make a sound!*

Todd came silently down onto the soft grass, and they both listened to the great clatter of hoofbeats on the other side.

They'd lost Bud.

Todd and Dana sat staring at each other in silence as the clatter faded further and further away. All was silent except for the loud chirping of the birds.

Waves of grief and sorrow rolled over them both as they sat motionless, staring aimlessly into the grass.

"Where do you think they'll take him?" asked Todd.

Dana shook her head fiercely, trying to hold her tears back. "To the king!"

"The king?"

"Remember that seal you broke?"

"Seal? What seal?"

"That red shield."

"It was holding the gate closed."

"Yes. Todd," Dana's eyes burst with hopelessness, "that was a royal seal. The penalty for breaking it is trial before the king himself, and most certainly death."

Todd gasped, and his eyes dashed quickly across the grass, as though desperately searching for a way out of the present. Dana had seen this look before, but never as painfully as this. Waves of sorrow seemed to break over Todd, each with greater misery than the last.

Seeing his eyes well up in tears, Dana suddenly felt her own, and they fell hot and fast down her cheeks. After a while she forced herself to her feet, walked over to Todd, and gave him a tug under the arm. "Come on. Let's go to Sedon. He'll know what to do."

Todd just nodded miserably.

Not wanting to be seen, Dana took Todd on a long, roundabout way to Sedon's house. They snuck through orchards, then crawled through fields of wheat and crouched down behind hedges and walls. It was good not to talk. The images of the day came back thick and fast, among them that wonderful sight of her mother racing on Syder's back with her hair and shirt flapping wildly in the wind, and the good head start she had gained on the soldiers. This evening she would hold her mother long and tight, and when she was finished she would embrace her again.

They finally rounded the last wall and entered Sedon's back garden. Dana crept up to his back door and knocked gently.

"Who is it? What do you want?"

"It's me!" whispered Dana as loudly as she could.

Sedon opened the door, and the kids rushed in. He bolted the door with a great iron bolt and blocked it with a great wooden beam just to be sure.

"Did anyone see you coming?"

"I don't think so," replied Dana. She opened her mouth to tell him how good it was to see him, but his red face stopped her.

"Are you crazy, coming here at this time of the day?" said Sedon angrily.

"I . . . um. Sedon, we . . . uh . . . we didn't know what else to do!"

His stern, angry expression melted as he looked at the kids. "I'm sorry. I really am!" His eyes shone with great warmth and care, mixed with deep grief. "It's wonderful to see you both!"

He took them both in his arms and gave them a thankful hug.

"Are you okay?" he asked.

"We are, but Dad . . ." Todd choked up before he could put it into words.

"I know what happened," replied Sedon quietly.

"Did you hear about the royal seal?" asked Dana.

"It's the talk of the town," said Sedon sadly.

"What have they done with Bud?" asked Dana.

"They left this afternoon for the palace. They're taking him to be judged by the king."

Dana could see Todd struggling. He wanted to ask questions but was fighting with a great lump in his throat. "Do you know any more?" she asked.

"The king is holding a feast in a day or so. He will probably judge Bud on that day. It's all part of what he calls 'entertainment.'"

Todd finally managed to cough out a few words. "Dana thinks he'll be sentenced to death!"

"Uh, yes," said Sedon slowly and uncomfortably. "Yes, it's almost always death."

"But not always?" asked Todd searchingly.

"Well, no. I remember people being pardoned," said Sedon.

"How many?" asked Todd.

"I can think of one," said Sedon.

"When?"

"Back when I was a little boy, I suppose," said Sedon tensely. "Now, Julissa—"

"You have news?" asked Dana.

"She was chased by a squadron of soldiers, but word has it that she got to the forest before them, and they followed her inside. I haven't heard anymore."

"Ah, Mom!" Thoughts of her mother rushed in, and for an instant Dana could think of nothing else. She was brought back by Sedon's strong hand on her shoulder.

"I'm sure she'll be okay. She made it to the forest! That's what counts!"

Dana looked up to Sedon's large blue eyes, which shimmered with affection but could not hide his own doubts and fears. She nodded, grateful that he was trying to assure her.

"We have to go see her," Dana said.

"We can't. There will still be too many soldiers about. I think you children will have to wait here in secret for one or two days, and then we'll go and look for her in the forest."

"You and Dana can go," said Todd shortly.

"What are you going to do?" asked Sedon.

"I'm going to the palace!"

"You're what?"

"I have to go and get Dad out of there!" said Todd.

"Todd, you can't!" said Sedon in astonishment. "That's a huge palace teeming with soldiers! You're a young country boy with rough hands and sun-brown skin. They'll see you a mile away. We've got to get you kids back to the forest. That is what Bud would want."

Todd's jaw jutted forward. "I'm not going back without him!"

"Todd, listen to reason! You're just a boy!"

"Sedon," replied Todd, "can you please take Dana to the forest?"

"I can take you both."

"You don't need to. Falko only asked you to take care of—"

"Now hold on!" burst in Dana. As worried as she was about her mother, she knew what she had to do. "Sedon, I'm going with Todd."

"Oh, stop being silly! That's crazy!" Todd burst out.

Dana rolled her eyes. It was no crazier than Todd going alone. "I'm going with you."

"Now listen, you can't just—"

"I'm going with you!"

"Listen, you two! It's crazy to think—" started Sedon.

"Let me speak," said Todd roughly. "It's not—"

"I'M GOING WITH YOU! Get it?" Dana had never felt anything with greater certainty than her own words right now. "You're not going to get me from your side! AND THAT'S FINAL!"

Silence filled the room.

"Well," said Sedon, who eventually looked across at Dana with a smile, "I thought Todd was the most stubborn person in the world, but I now see I was wrong! I can see your father in your eyes. It's so nice to see him again!"

The statement filled Dana with an unexpected joy.

"Well, this *idea* is a disaster," said Sedon, "but I would rather see us all fail together than to see you two fail alone. I'm in— on one condition."

"What's that?" asked Todd.

"That you kids sit down right now and eat something, and then we can make a plan."

Dana let out a deep sigh and felt her shoulders relax. Something had just happened. The great cloud of sorrow and grief had somehow been pushed away, and a ray of hope had broken through. The Lord was with them, as he had always been.

She reached over to Todd, whose clouds always seemed to take longer to clear than her own, and squeezed his hand. A tender smile grew on his face as he looked up into her eyes.

"Now you two wash up, and I'll get food on the table," said Sedon.

Soon they were all sitting around a spread of bread, cheese, and vegetables. "If we travel at dawn, we can get there by early afternoon tomorrow. I could hide you two in the wagon, like I did when I took you to the forest, Dana."

"Can you take us to the palace?" asked Todd.

Sedon's eyes sparkled. "I can do better than that. I can take you into the palace!"

"Really?" asked Dana excitedly.

"Yes. Every farmer can sell his wares once a year for two days in the outer courtyard of the palace. I haven't been yet this year, and as I said, the king is throwing a big feast in one or two days. They are very happy to see farmers coming right now."

He sat back and grew more serious. "Now listen carefully. When I was a young man, I was one of many farmers' sons who was taken by soldiers and forced to work building that palace. So I know a lot about it. There's a very large auditorium in which Bud will be taken before the king. Up above, in the walls, there are tunnels used for ventilation. Slaves use big bellows to pump air through the tunnels when there is a feast or something like that so that there is always enough fresh air. Now, these tunnels go all through the palace. If you two crawled in there you could go almost anywhere."

Sedon cut a chunk of cheese and pressed it between two pieces of bread. "Let's do it this way. I'll take you two in during the afternoon, and I'll set up my stand. You can keep hiding in the wagon. In the evening, the farmers leave their produce in there overnight and go outside and stay in the local inns. When they're all gone and it is very dark, you two use the ventilation tunnels to sneak into the palace. Go in and find out whatever you can, and I'll be there on the next day again. We can make a plan then."

Dana studied Sedon's face in the flickering candlelight. "I can't believe you're doing this, Sedon."

"Me neither," said the old man with a grin that filled his face with wrinkles. "Do you ever get the feeling that something is just the right thing to do? You can't explain it, but you just know."

Todd nodded, his face beaming with joy. "I'm really glad you feel that way!" Dana knew he was overjoyed at the possibility of getting Bud out.

They spent a couple of hours preparing everything for market: fruit, vegetables, stands, and fold-up tables. "It's amazing how much faster it goes with two extra pairs of hands!" said Sedon. Dana found herself soothed by the practical work, as it took her mind off the multitude of fears and worries she felt here in the kingdom. It was bad enough in this village. Going to the palace was like jumping into a pit of snakes, but she dared not say that to Todd. He needed all the encouragement he could get.

CHAPTER 28

Bud in the Dungeon

Bud slowly woke up without the faintest idea of where he was. The first thing he felt was a splitting headache. He was lying very awkwardly on a small, moldy pile of straw that reeked of urine.

Rolling over, he drew a deep breath of the horrible stench and in an instant was awake. He sat up with a start, and it was all real again. The images came flashing back in rapid succession. First being knocked out by the soldiers and then waking up in the camp. He had gone from officer to officer as interrogation became harder and harder. He was taken into the back rooms and beaten with sticks, threatened, and mocked: all of these things came back to him in all their ugliness.

The soldiers looked so grand in their bright red uniforms with their shiny brass buttons, but behind closed doors the wolves slipped out of their sheep's clothing. Bud had heard of their way of beating people with narrow, springy sticks that inflicted great pain but barely left a mark, but he had never felt the brunt of this truth. But now everything hurt: his back, his arms, his head. His leg was swollen and stiff.

Everything was black, utterly black. The only light came from a small, square hole. Whether it was a hole in a wall or a keyhole in a door, Bud couldn't make out, but it was clear that a flame flickered faintly somewhere behind it, not enough to illuminate his cell, or wherever this was, but enough light to outline the hole itself.

Bud sat in a kind of stupor, staring at that hole, trying to sort out the situation he found himself in. He was too groggy to think clearly, but that didn't stop a horde of awful thoughts from dancing through his mind before being pushed out by others.

After what seemed like a while, the sudden clanking of chains abruptly interrupted his thoughts, and he sat upright, straining to hear whatever he could. "Are you sleeping again?" came a voice through the hole. Bud almost answered when he realized the question hadn't been directed to him.

"Ah, Paldry, is that you?" said another voice.

"Hallo, Rammy. I thought you were on days this week." It seemed to be the voice of an older man.

"The sarge put me on nights 'cause I was supposedly drunk on duty."

"Rammy!"

"I swear, Paldry, I wasn't really drunk, not really. It's that idiot corporal telling tales."

"Well, don't tell me about it now, lad. I've come to visit the prisoner."

"Oh, him. Good you come to do it tonight, 'cause he'll be dead tomorrow, the poor swine. Say, you don't have something for your good buddy Rammy, do you?"

"I brought some grapes from my own garden. Here you go."

"You're a saint, Paldry, old boy. I'll open your door."

Again the sound of clacking and clanking of chains could be heard, and then the very distinct sound of a key entering and turning a lock. Suddenly the door swung open, bringing more but not much light into the cell. The outline of a rather short, chubby man entered. The top of his round head was clearly bald, and he was wrapped in some kind of cloak going to his feet. He was carrying a small candle that looked as if it could go out any minute, but it stayed alight.

"Now, who do we have here?" asked the guest.

"The name is Bud," said Bud cautiously.

"Paldry," said the old man as he extended his hand. Bud, out of reflex as much as anything else, shook his visitor's hand, wincing at the pain that rolled through his body as he moved. Then there was silence.

"I know your story. They told me everything," said Paldry.

"Okay," said Bud cautiously, not knowing what to think or say.

"You did a very brave thing."

"Uh, thanks."

There was again silence for a while. This time it was broken by Bud: "May I ask why you are visiting me?"

"Well, that's an interesting question, isn't it? Several people have died in this dungeon, and this is something that enrages the king. The king very much prefers to kill people himself, and when they die down here he loses a big public spectacle. He finds this a great inconvenience. So he has given me permission to come down and visit the condemned and tend to their physical needs, which I am most eager to do."

"So you are here in the name of the king?" asked Bud warily.

"Or rather, in the name of the great King. There is a greater King, you know?"

Bud felt a flicker of hope and surprise, but he remained cautious as he answered, "But the greater King is not respected here."

"Maybe not honored, but he is feared. And if the truth be known, our own little king is not respected, but he is feared and outwardly honored."

There was something very likeable about this man, but Bud was very hesitant to trust him. The soldiers might be trying a new strategy after they had failed to get the information out of Bud that they wanted.

On the other hand, thought Bud to himself, *the truth is the truth is the truth. Why be ashamed of the Rock on which I stand? I must only never mention Todd, Dana, or Sedon. I do hope that they've all managed to get back to the forest!*

"I've brought you something to eat," said Paldry, breaking the silence. He placed his candle on a ledge in the wall, pulled up a short stool, sat down, and pulled a package out from under his cloak. He opened up the cloth wrapped around three or so flat pieces of bread. "They're not wonderful, but they are the best an old boy can do."

"Thank you," said Bud, taking them in his hand yet not knowing where to put them. Feeling uneasy in the man's presence, he didn't want to eat them just now, although his stomach rumbled with hunger.

"They're for eating whenever you want," said Paldry. "Though I'd recommend you don't starve yourself overlong."

He sat regarding Bud another moment, then said, "It sounds as though your friend made it to the forest, but a bunch of soldiers went in after her. I haven't heard anything after that. Please do not mention this to anyone. It is supposed to be top secret. The king doesn't like word of escapes getting around."

"Then why did you tell me?"

"I want you to trust me."

"Why?"

"Because you desperately need a friend right now."

"What good will a friend do? I'm a man condemned to die," said Bud solemnly.

"I want to help you run your race well to the end." And then Paldry went on:

"I am because he is

I have because he gives

I can because he loves

I hope because he lives."

"You can be killed for saying that in the palace," said Bud, almost breathless at the sound of the old prayer.

"I know, but it's the only thing keeping my heart alive."

"Did you learn that as a kid too?" asked Bud.

"I did, and I say it often, every day," replied Paldry. "It's the water I drink and the air I breathe. Bud, I come with a message for you."

"Okay," said Bud, who was slowly feeling that he could trust Paldry.

"It's this: your regrets are eating you up."

Bud knew exactly what he was saying. "But Paldry! Of course they are! Don't you see? If I had only thought things through a bit better. If I'd only taken the time to look at that wheelbarrow, we might have left unnoticed, and we could have . . ."

"Bud, enough! Enough of this 'if I had only' and 'would have' and 'could have'! You're driving yourself mad with these thoughts."

"But how could I have been so stupid?"

"Bud, let me tell you something." Paldry leaned forward, and his tired old face burst to life in the candlelight. "You're looking at an old man who's seen a much harder life than you might think. Years ago I realized something that changed everything and carried me through some of the deepest, darkest valleys you could imagine.

"You know, Bud, we people love to write stories. But we're not the only ones. For whatever reason, the Lord also delights to write stories. Our stories are weak and sometimes syrupy and are often a feeble shadow of something much greater. The Lord's stories are mighty, and magnificent, and they jump out of the page, and you can taste them, and they change your heart forever."

"Paldry, I'm sorry. You've lost me there," said Bud in confusion.

Paldry went on, "We people write our stories with pen and paper, but the Lord writes his stories with the lives of people, often in the face of insurmountable evil and a darkness that seems to suck the light out of life. The Lord takes the pens of broken hearts and the paper of seeming chaos, both in us and outside us, and from situations in which all seems lost, he writes works that shame the pompous poets of this age."

"You're sounding very much like my father."

"Ha! I take that as a good sign!" said Paldry with a laugh. "Just think of Owen Silas, a stumbling, awkward character, so frustrated with the world, and especially annoyed at his own cowardice, and the Lord suddenly threw him onto the stage and said to him, 'Okay, man. You're on! I've thrown you into the middle of this mess. I'll be with you every step of the way! You know what you've got to do. Go do it, man! Just do it! It looks like madness and certain death, and I'm making no promises as to how all of this will turn out. I'm just telling you to do it!'

"And that's what the Lord did. He threw Owen Silas—that nobody—into the midst of the battle. And in the wildness of the confusion, Silas was crazy enough to believe, and to take that first very brave step, and then the next. And you know the rest."

Bud heaved a great sigh, much to his own surprise. He had been so caught up in Paldry's words that he had forgotten to breathe.

"Bud, nothing's gone wrong. It all seems so awful, and you're aching from head to toe, and you've got a gaping hole in your heart that stubbornly won't stop hurting, but nothing has gone wrong! You're in his story, and you're right where he wants you to be. And I'll tell you something. He's looking down on you right now, and his heart's bursting with love, more than for all the stars in heaven."

Bud felt a great lump in his throat, and he swallowed in a rather vain attempt to keep his composure. He knew Paldry's words were true.

But the old man wasn't done. "Bud, forget the 'should haves' and 'could haves.' The Lord's story's unfolding just as it should, and he's thrown you right into the middle of it all. I don't have any idea if you will live past tomorrow or not, but that's irrelevant anyway. This story's not about you. The key thing is that you remain faithful to the end, and you can be that because he's with you. He's writing a story with you, Bud, and it's a story that can't be bettered, and one day you'll look back with him and say, 'Thank you, that you chose to use my life in this way.' There's no greater honor than to be used in one of his stories."

There was a long silence, after which Bud said, "Paldry, you are a dear brother, and you're right. You're dead right."

This was followed by another long silence.

"What are you thinking about?" asked Paldry.

"You know, if they take my life tomorrow, I could bear that. My real thoughts will most certainly sound utterly foolish . . ."

"Try me!" replied Paldry quietly.

"You know," said Bud, starting to choke over his words, "I am married to the most wonderful woman in the world. I just want ..." Bud could feel his great emotion choking him up and making it very difficult to speak. "I just want to take her in my arms one very last time . . . and tell her that I love her . . . and just say good-bye!"

As Bud said this, he buckled over on the straw and burst into uncontrollable sobbing.

Paldry said nothing, just sat and let the flood of sorrow subside. After a while he said, "It is hard, I know. Bud, I'll just say this one last thing. The Lord is here. Tell him everything. Tell him how frustrated you are with yourself, tell him how angry you are at him, and tell him you don't want to be. He can take it, don't worry. Pour your heart out before him, and tell him everything. That'll be your best preparation for tomorrow."

Bud wiped away his tears. The ache in his heart was a little better. Even his body didn't seem to hurt so badly. "I don't know how to thank you, Paldry."

"I only told you the things that saved my own life," said Paldry. He stood up quickly, like a soldier who had finished his assignment. "I wish you every blessing, dear brother."

"And to you," said Bud, struggling to get up and shake the old man's hand one last time. "Good-bye."

"Good-bye." Paldry went out the door, and it was dark again.

CHAPTER 29

Getting inside

It was still fairly dark, and the sun was only a tiny sliver on the horizon as Sedon, Todd, and Dana left for the palace. The wagon was bursting. What with vegetables, fruit, stands, tables, and chairs, the load wobbled to the left and right as Sedon's horse pulled it slowly along. Going up hills, they all got out and walked beside the old mare to make the difficult trip as easy as possible. Todd found himself walking beside the horse with his hand on its shoulder, just as he had always done with his mules. He found the familiar action soothing.

Sedon was unusually talkative, and he told all sorts of stories of his youth on the farm. In some strange way, all of his fears and worries seemed to have gone, at least for the moment, and it was clear that he expected something good to happen.

They passed through village after village, and in between, they crossed beautiful countryside. Todd could not help but notice how worn and somehow lifeless the people looked despite their surroundings. The warm, spontaneous greetings that strangers received in the forest seemed utterly unknown here, and the twinkle in the eye that Todd had thought belonged to everyone seemed nowhere to be found. He remembered Bud's description of kingdom people as "living and yet not really alive." Todd had always known sorrow as something that came into life and left again. Grief was an interruption to a generally happy existence. A life that was sad to the core was something he had never seen nor imagined, and now he felt surrounded by it as a fish is by water.

By early afternoon they came over the crest of a hill to see a great valley spread out beneath them, and directly below them loomed a huge walled city. The immense gray walls were impressive even at a distance.

"What is that?" asked Todd.

"It's a city," answered Dana, who was also staring at it.

"It's magnificent!" gasped Todd, who had never seen such enormous stones, much less cut to size and placed one on top of the other.

"It's monstrous!" replied Dana, "and it's built on the blood and bones of its victims." A flash of terror crossed her face—the same look Todd had seen in her when they first met.

"Where are the windows?" asked Todd.

"There are none," said Sedon. "These walls are for protection. Listen you two: before we get to that village there, down the road a little ways, you'll both have to disappear within the vegetables."

After going down the hill, they found a shady grove where they stopped the wagon, and Todd climbed into the pile of potatoes and Dana into the carrots. On they went toward the palace.

"This is terrible!" called out Todd. "These potatoes are cold and wet and totally uncomfortable!"

"You think you've got it bad!" called out Dana. "I've got a carrot tip sticking right in my ear, and I can't move my hand to get it out. At least potatoes are round!"

"They're not as round as you might think! I've got one digging into my—"

"Now you two be quiet!" interrupted Sedon. "The villages here are close together and full of soldiers! From now on, I don't want to hear another word unless I ask a question!"

It was hard for Todd and Dana not to know what was happening or how far they had come. There was certainly a lot more commotion around the wagon. They could hear children shouting and running about, the heavy deliberate hoofbeats of oxen, and the creaking and rumbling of the heavy wagons being pulled. For a long time the wagon shook and vibrated, and the clackety noise of the wheels seemed especially loud.

"What is this?" whispered Todd to Dana.

"This is cobblestone," she replied. "We must be getting close."

Suddenly the sound beneath them changed to that of creaky wooden beams. "This must be the drawbridge leading up to the gate of the fortress," whispered Dana tensely.

The kids heard Sedon talking with the soldier stationed at the gate to inspect all incoming vehicles.

"What do you have, old man?" asked the soldier curtly.

"Potatoes, carrots, beans, pumpkins, apples, and a few smoked sausages," replied Sedon.

"Have you reserved a stand?"

"Uh, no. Was I supposed to?"

"Not very informed, are we now? The Royal Gala is tonight and tomorrow! Captain! Could you please come here?"

Todd tensed as the sound of footsteps approached. "What is it?"

"A farmer without a reservation!"

"Why don't you have a reservation?" the captain's voice demanded.

"I'm sorry. I didn't know we needed one," answered Sedon.

"Look, Grandpa, if you can't read, then talk to someone who can!"

"Should we send him away, Captain?

"I tell you," came the captain's voice gruffly. "You farmers are stupider than the sheep you keep!"

"My wares are very good, sir," replied Sedon calmly. "Surely the king has need of extra for the gala?"

"Let's have a look!" Todd heard scuffling and felt someone poking at the potatoes. "Nothing special about your load, you old half-wit! Is this stuff the best you've got?"

"Well, my specialty is in this bag. These sausages were made of prime pork smoked with the finest spices in the kingdom."

"Get a whiff of that, Captain! They smell really—"

"Get your dirty fingers off those, Corporal! Hmmm! Nice, very nice indeed! You do realize that the procuring of a reservation certificate will take an awful lot of work right now. It's too late to organize it through the normal procedures."

"Captain, I am very sorry to put you through the inconvenience. You know what I was thinking: I've got more sausage where that comes from, and a wineskin of some of the best sweet wine produced in the kingdom. I didn't really plan to sell them but rather to share them with friends I make upon the way. I find that every time I come here the people are so helpful, and I would simply like to show my appreciation."

Todd held back a grin as the captain's voice said, "Corporal, I see no reason to forbid entry to this peasant, and as he has rightly said, it is our role to help honest folk in the service of the king."

"Here you are, good sir," said Sedon. Todd could hear him pull a couple of sacks off the floor of the wagon. "Do enjoy them."

"I'll let him through, shall I, Captain?"

"After inspecting the wares under question!" replied the captain.

"They look all right to me, they do!" said the corporal with obvious pleasure.

"They do, yes. Where is there still room?"

"Right at the back by the water tower."

"Okay, old man. You've got today and tomorrow to sell your wares. We close the drawbridge at sunset, so make sure you are out before then. There's a trumpet blast fifteen minutes before closing. Corporal, you escort him, and then return to your post. Hop up in the wagon. You needn't walk."

"Yes, sir! Thank you, sir!"

Todd felt the wagon tilt as the soldier got on and then heard the wooden seat in front of them creak. With a jolt and the clacking of hooves on the cobblestones, he knew they were underway again.

"Tell me, old man. How did you know we like sausages?" asked the soldier with a laugh.

"I may not read or write, but I wasn't born yesterday!"

"Well, if you want to know, most of my soldier mates can't read, and between you and me, the captain can't read so good either!"

"Tell me, young man, what's all this about a royal gala?"

"Ooh, that's something really special, that is! Tonight in the great hall, the king is going to unveil his new invention! He's been working on it for years, he has. He's spent a heap of money on it, and now it's ready! And there'll be lots of special guests. Not the likes of you and me! No, real respectable-like folks, in their fanciest clothes and all."

"Will there be a program?"

"Yeah, they've got a few pirates they caught last month. In front of the crowd, the king will either sentence them to death or pardon them . . . oh, yeah, and there's some forester who broke a royal seal, he did. They'll either pardon or sentence him too. Not much hope for him, though. We've already set up the gallows for him, we have."

"Shall I go over to the left, here?"

"Yeah, that's right. Get right tight to the wall. Yeah. It's good here! Hey, Granddad, have you really given all of your sausage away?"

"Yes, sorry, I have. But look. I've got a raisin cake I brought for myself. Please, take it."

This time Todd bristled. What right did these soldiers have to bully and bribe their way like this? But he stayed still as the soldier said, "You know, old man, you're all right! Remember, you have to leave before sunset. Got that?"

"Yes, and thanks for all your help," said Sedon. There was another creak, tilt, and settling of the wagon, and footsteps moved away. After a moment Sedon spoke in a low voice.

"Now you kids are not to move or speak. I'll set the stand up. I hope you're not getting too stiff in there."

Although he was dying to get up and stretch and imagined that Dana felt the same, Todd lay there and listened to what he could. It was a market, and the general drone of market hubbub sounded in the background, although Todd noticed that there were almost no children's voices. The rough, crackly voice of a fishmonger could be heard clearly above the crowd, and now and again he heard the voice of what must be an older woman without a stand, walking around selling honey.

They heard the sounds of Sedon untying the ropes and felt the old wagon jiggle to the left and right. With grunts and groans he got the stands and tables off the wagon, and Todd only wished he could go out and help him.

Many people came and went in the next couple of hours, but gradually the bustle seemed to grow quieter and quieter. The kids heard Sedon closing things down and locking them up. Then they heard a trumpet blast.

There was a creak as someone climbed up onto the front seat. "Now where on earth did I put my bag?" said Sedon. "It must be up here somewhere!" And his voice suddenly changed to a whisper, "You kids all right in there?"

"I can't wait to get out!" whispered Todd back.

"I know, but you'll have to wait for a good hour more. Now, listen, you two. I've sold all the pumpkins, so there's room in the wagon for Bud as well, if you manage to bring him back. Come back and hide yourselves in the wagon. You must be back here and hidden in the wagon before sunrise."

"Okay, Sedon."

"Now listen closely. When you get out, you'll see a water tower. There are stairs behind it going up to the top of the wall. Take those stairs up, and you'll come to a walkway going along the outside of the wall. Somewhere up there, there's a hole in the wall. It leads to a long air channel you can crawl through. I have no idea where it goes, but you will end up inside the palace."

"Okay," whispered Todd.

"Now be very careful! The soldiers here are a very ugly lot. The Lord has brought you this far, and he'll carry you to the end. I know it!"

The children suddenly heard someone at a distance shouting, "Hey, old man!"

"Coming, coming! Not as fast as I used to be!" and then a quick whisper, "All the best, children!" And then Sedon was off in a rush.

The commotion died down, and it was quiet for a long time. Neither Todd nor Dana wanted to speak. They were both caught up in their thoughts. Suddenly, after a long while, Todd said, "Dad once told me that fools have no fear and heroes overcome their fear. He told me that the battle in us is usually greater than the battle outside of us, but we have help for both battles."

"Well, I need that help now," answered Dana.

"Yeah, me too."

"Shall we get out now?" asked Dana.

"Yes, let's."

They both crawled out into the ominous blackness of the night. In the weak light of the half-moon, the water tower loomed before them like a wicked old ogre.

"Sedon said the stairs are behind this tower," whispered Dana.

"Let's go," replied Todd, and they crept forward into the dark unknown.

CHAPTER 30

Into the forest

Julissa struggled like mad to free herself from the iron grip of the soldier, but she didn't manage, and she fell to her knees in exhaustion.

Then it happened. As if struck by a wild ox, the soldier was suddenly thrown down under what seemed to be a savage animal.

It was a young man. He had swung down on a vine and pounced on the soldier. There was a mad scramble in the grass, and punches fell thick and fast from both sides. The soldier, who was considerably bigger, grabbed the young man by the collar, and both men rolled around in a wild fury on the ground.

Julissa fell to the ground, gasping for air. She could go no further, nor could she take her eyes off the savagery of the struggle before her.

She heard feet hit the ground as soldiers jumped down to help their comrade.

"Leave him!" shouted the general with obvious pleasure. "Let's see how long it will take Muntar to silence this forest rat!" The soldiers let out an ugly laugh at this, and they all watched eagerly, cheering their champion to victory.

The battle was a ferocious one. The soldier was certainly the bigger man, but this forester fought with unusual ferocity. The punches flew as from iron fists, and though the young man's throat was caught in the steel grip of this soldier, he managed to land one punch after another. The blood of both spattered onto the grass, and the soldier roared with rage. He pulled out his knife, and the forester grabbed his wrist. Rolling around madly in the grass, the forester did all he could to keep that knife from his chest and throat.

Finally the soldier had the forester on his back and was lowering his knife steadily but surely to his chest. The forester struggled with all his strength against what seemed like certain death. The trembling knife came closer and closer, and in a frantic move the forester gave the soldier a desperate head butt. A great crack could be heard as he broke the soldier's nose, and the knife flew into the grass. Blood sprayed everywhere. The soldier curled with his hands over his head to protect himself. No more punches came. The forester left him alone. Instead, he stood up, ready to fight the next one.

"Seize that rat!" shouted the general, taking off his hat and pointing to the forester with it. Some men started to go after him when an arrow suddenly ripped the hat out of the general's hand and pinned it to a tree.

"STOP!" A voice rang out from the forest, and everyone stopped in their tracks.

The forester looked up with a smile. "Brody!"

The general froze on his horse, not daring to move.

"Hey, General! You called my brother Travis a rat. Big mistake! Big, big mistake!"

"This is the voice of a boy and not a man!" shouted the general, trying in vain to sound intimidating.

"Yes, and that is the voice of a very scared general!" replied the voice. Julissa strained to see who was taunting the general, but he remained hidden by the trees.

"That is no way to talk to the marshall of the king's elite!" bellowed the general, red-faced with rage.

"Okay, Mister Elite, let's get something straight. I may be a kid, but I'm a kid who can shoot. I didn't just aim for your hat, I aimed at the space between the white and brown feather, which is exactly where I hit. And now, I could either put my next arrow under your second brass button and right through your heart, or I could put it just under your fourth brass button through your kidney. That way I could watch you die a little slower, which is always fun."

The general gulped and had to clear his throat. Julissa could see beads of sweat forming on his brow.

"Man, I just hate making decisions!" shouted the voice.

"Now, let's not do anything hasty!" shouted the general with a squeaky voice.

At that moment Julissa saw some commotion among the trees around the clearing. Feet—lots of feet, as though a troop of men were getting themselves into position. She decided to look away so that the soldiers would not notice. She didn't know if the strangers in the forest were friend or foe, but as long as they were fighting the king's soldiers, she would be on their side for now.

"My next question is where I hang your head! Over the pigpen? Or should we dry it out and put it over the fireplace? Oh, life is full of decisions!" shouted the voice again.

"You are addressing the head of the Fourth Elite Regiment placed with special commission directly under the leadership of His Majesty Eduarl III," said the general, doing his best to retain his composure.

"Wow! I bet you can't say that three times fast!" shouted the voice.

"Besides the king, we are the highest authority in the land!"

"Not in *this* land, Mister!"

"We are here to retrieve a criminal, and then we shall leave your forest!"

"Those who seek refuge in the forest are judged by the village elders. If the elders feel that the refugees have done wrong, they will send them to the king in due time."

"This woman is a criminal and must be judged by kingdom judgment."

This time the voice seemed to growl a reply. "I suggest you leave, take your wolf pack with you, and send the elders a letter requesting the handing over of this woman."

"She has already been tried and found guilty!"

"Not by our elders!"

Because she was lying on the ground, Julissa could see things the mounted soldiers couldn't. She realized that slowly but surely the clearing was being surrounded by men and that this voice was buying time for them to get into position.

The general continued. "You do not understand what you are talking about! If you send us away, it could mean war, terrible war costing the lives of many innocent people!"

"So we should let you spill innocent blood so that we can stop the spilling of innocent blood? Ever heard the story about the old man who started drinking whiskey to stop his alcohol problem?"

The general was red-faced by now. "If anyone in the kingdom spoke to me like that, he would be hanged from a tree on the spot!

"Well, that's your problem, not ours. There's no official punishment for telling the truth in the forest."

"Listen to me!" shouted the general with new courage. "We will take this woman back with us and leave in peace!"

An arrow suddenly flew past his nose and split the other arrow holding the hat to the tree.

"Kidney or heart? Short death or long, groaning death? Man! Decisions, decisions, decisions . . . I hate decisions!" shouted the voice.

"Why don't I organize a meeting between you and Dorn, our chief?"

"Now, hear!" said the general. "That won't be necessary if—"

"No, seriously. I insist. In fact he's just arrived, and he'd be glad to have a few words with your eliteness!"

Suddenly another voice burst from the forest: "Three paces forward!"

Suddenly a mass of men stepped out of hiding in the forest. Julissa gasped. There must have been three or four hundred men with sword, spear, and shield. They had the horsemen totally surrounded.

Julissa noticed that the general's royal trousers were suddenly wet, as was his saddle. The soldiers pulled tight together on their horses as they looked around in horror. They were greatly outnumbered by a savage-looking horde of foresters armed to the teeth.

A short, bald, and very muscular man took some vigorous steps over to the general.

"Let me introduce myself! I am Dorn, one of the forest chiefs. Had you realized you were trespassing in our forest?"

The general stammered a moment before answering, "We had no intention to trespass. But one of our prisoners escaped, and we had to get her back!"

"Be assured that we will judge her and send her back if we find her guilty!" Dorn's eyes glared with anger. "You know, if we find farmers trespassing, we consider them trespassers, but if we find soldiers trespassing, we consider them invaders! We've let far too many of you in for far too long. I deeply regret this."

"I must take that woman back!" shouted the general with all the authority he could muster.

Dorn stomped over, red-faced, to the general, grabbed his shirt, and pulled him with violence off his horse.

The general hit the ground with force. Julissa looked around at the soldiers. They looked on with great concern, but no one dared move while they were surrounded by such a horde of foresters. Before he could look up, the general found himself being picked up by the collar. This chief had enormous strength. Dorn let him hang from his hand so that they looked eye to eye.

"You listen to me, you killing scum! I will only say this once. If you insist on taking this woman, we shall take you and all your men and slit open your guts and feed the lot of you to the wolves! That's what happens to invaders!"

Dorn loosened his grasp as the general gasped for air.

"If you choose to go in peace, we shall grant you leave, and no one will be hurt!" He dropped the general to the ground. "Make your choice."

The general got onto his hands and knees and peered up at Dorn, still breathing hard. Then the general croaked out something so quietly that Julissa was not sure if she heard it rightly or not. "Good sir, I dare not go back without that woman."

Julissa watched as a horrified look darkened the face of the general. It resembled that of a criminal just sentenced to the mines.

The expression of the chief suddenly changed, as though he too had seen something in the eyes of the general. His tone softened greatly. "My Lord has shown you grace. Your lord will not show you grace when you come out of this forest empty-handed. I understand that."

Julissa felt her chest tighten and struggled for air. *Maybe this chief will hand me over!*

"But those who with honest heart seek refuge in the forest receive it. If you want her, you will have to fight for her," said Dorn coolly.

Julissa let out such a sigh of relief that she only just heard the general's next words: "We will go." His words were blank and without expression, as though he were in shock.

"So be it," replied Dorn, who then helped the general to his feet. He then shouted, "Listen, O men of the kingdom! This day shall be remembered as the day the king's soldiers fell into the hands of the foresters, and only as an act of great generosity and mercy were they allowed to leave having lost neither a dagger from their belts nor a hair of their heads! Pity is a lesson you all need to learn!"

The men nodded in acknowledgement. Julissa's heart began to race with a sudden joy. Like waking from a horrible nightmare—she was going to escape after all! As the inner celebration began, she suddenly noticed another figure appearing out of the forest. A wiry, freckle-faced young man with curly red hair emerged carrying a bow.

"Brody," said Dorn with a smile, "could you please get the man his hat?"

As the general was struggling to get up onto his horse again, the young man retrieved the soldier's hat, pulling it and the arrows down from the tree.

"Here, sir. Your hat," he said to the general as he handed him his hat. The general looked at him with an expression of both shame and deep perplexity.

"Hey, clear up your mess, will you?" said Dorn, pointing to the beaten soldier, who still hadn't managed to get to his knees. Other soldiers led him like a drunk man to his horse and helped him up onto it.

As Dorn turned to the general, a tenderness came across his face. "You know, I never thought I'd say this, but I rather pity you. I have failed my Lord miserably, but I have also received endless grace from him. As we have already said, you will receive none from yours. But then again, this was the lord you chose for yourself."

He paused, seeming unsure of how to put his next words together. "As you saw today, the forest is always there for those who take refuge in it. No matter what they have done, or how much blood is dripping from their hands, if they truly want it, they can find a new start here. The grace I have received is there for every man. You are welcome anytime."

The general could not look Dorn in the eyes but stared in bewilderment into the forest. Julissa had to strain to hear his words. "I thank you, good sir, for your very kind offer."

Dorn then turned to his men who blocked the path back to the kingdom. "Clear a way, boys!" shouted Dorn, and the line of men opened up to let the soldiers back onto the path. He nodded to the general, who with a trembling voice shouted, "Ride!", and they galloped off as fast as their horses could go.

As the sound of hoofbeats slowly disappeared, an eerie silence fell over the clearing.

Dorn walked over to Julissa and helped her to her feet. "My lady, are you all right?"

"Yes, I am, absolutely!" said Julissa, trying to maintain her balance but needing Dorn's help. "I really am!" The kindness that Dorn had shown to the general assured her that she was in good hands. In some strange way she felt as though she had just come home.

Dorn gave her a great, friendly smile. "Welcome to the forest. You are our honored guest!"

The young man who had attacked the soldier approached Dorn. "Dad, how did you know we were here?"

"Travis! My boy!" The great chief took the still puzzled young man in his arms. "Brody, come!"

The red-haired young man came in haste. "Dad, what on earth are you doing here, so far from the village?"

"Boys, listen up! Two nights ago I had a dream, a terrible dream." The chief's eyes welled up with affection. "I know this waterfall, and when I was a boy I came here a few times with your grandfather. In my dream you two were little children playing on the bank under the waterfall. All of a sudden, a bear came charging out of the forest and approached you. You were paralyzed with fear and unable to move. I was a long way off, too far to cut off the bear. I had only one spear—no knife, no arrows, no sword.

"If I threw and missed, all would be lost. There I stood! Too far away to help and too scared to throw. Your grandfather was screaming in my ear, 'Throw it! That's what it's for!'

"And then I woke up in a cold sweat, and I knew that if I didn't act fast I'd lose you both. I knew I had to come here, to find you and help you, and be ready to fight to the last man."

"I was so proud of you just now, Dad!" said Travis.

"Proud of me?" choked Dorn. His face turned red, and Julissa saw torment in his expression. "You can't be proud of me!"

"We are, Dad!" said Brody. "We really are!"

"You threw the spear and killed the bear!" said Travis, beaming with joy.

"And without a doubt you just saved our lives," added Brody with a smile.

Julissa watched as this great chief stared off into the forest with a trembling lip and mournful eyes. He stretched out his arms, and Travis and Brody fell into them. In a mighty embrace he picked them both off the ground.

When he put them down, he suddenly became aware of the hundreds of men silently watching the scene. Far from being ashamed, he wiped the tears from his eyes and raised his voice. "Hear, men of the forest! My father told me many things. One of them was, 'Teach your boys courage!' And there I failed greatly. How can you pass on what you yourself don't have?"

As Julissa listened curiously, Dorn was obviously struggling with his words. "But hear this! My boys have taught me courage! They have taught us all! This day has two heroes! Travis and Brody! Three cheers for our heroes!"

"HIP-HIP . . ."

"HURRAH!"

"HIP-HIP . . ."

"HURRAH!"

"HIP-HIP . . ."

"HURRAH!"

The cheer thundered through the forest, and though Julissa didn't understand everything she saw and heard, she felt assured that she was among friends. Many tears fell on that day. Tears of joy, gratitude, and reconciliation.

CHAPTER 31

Getting Inside

Todd had to feel for every step as he and Dana tried to find the stairs behind the water tower. The tower was immense, and behind it, shadowed from the moon, the kids could see nothing at all.

"Let's go very slowly," said Todd. The only things he could see were the few stars that were directly over them.

"Here!" he said, feeling what seemed to be a step, and then what seemed to be the next. "These must be them."

Indeed, there was a very narrow, uneven stone stairway leading upward. It was a very unusual feeling to be going somewhere in a totally foreign place in absolute blackness. A light wind howled and whistled as it passed over the stone palace, and the children could clearly smell the damp, musty moss growing on the stones on both sides.

As the stairs grew steeper, they found themselves going up on hands and feet. After quite a climb, the stairs led to a narrow but level passage beside the wall. Todd looked out over the lights of the city below, rather surprised that they had reached such a height. A pathway led forward around the palace wall. They went along the path, with the palace wall to their left and another small wall, reaching their waists, overlooking the city to their right.

"Look!" said Dana, pointing up ahead.

They saw a torch, and as they looked at it longer, it became clear that it was coming toward them. They could make out four soldiers, and the first was carrying the light.

"They're coming our way!" whispered Dana. "What'll we do?"

"Let's go back down the steps!" said Todd.

They both crawled quickly backward down the steps. They had barely gotten down and around a bend when the light from the torch lit up the stairway walls further up. They suddenly heard a dog bark and the clanking of chains. They pressed themselves as tightly as they could to the wall and tried not to move.

"Hey, Sergeant! The dog smells something, he does."

Suddenly a dog burst down the steps, barking and growling fiercely. A chain kept it from coming further. Seeing Todd, it lunged at him, and Todd felt a flash of pain on his cheek. Though he wanted to cry out, he stayed silent and didn't move a whisker. The beast went wild, pulling frantically on the chain. It lunged at Todd again but could no longer reach him.

"Help me!" came a cry from above.

"Just pull!" came another.

The dog threw itself at Todd again and again, splashing his face with its slobber but not managing to bite him again. Todd felt sickened by the whiff of its breath but held himself absolutely still.

"Pull that idiot dog up, Handock! That stupid mutt's smelt a rat or something."

After several grunts and groans the dog was pulled up out of the stairway again.

"What's with that thing?"

"I don't know!"

"Should we go down and have a look, Sarge?"

"No, leave it! We don't have time. It's just a rat!"

Suddenly there was another voice from the walkway. "Are you having problems controlling your dog again, Handock? Shall we order you a cat instead?" A couple of laughs broke out.

"I won't take any lip from the likes of you!" And suddenly another scuffle was heard.

"Stop it! Stop it, you two! The watchman will do the stairs later. We've got to keep going and report to the general. Security level one tonight. Don't you forget it! Handock, take your mutt and lead the way!"

Footsteps were again to be heard, and together with the sound of the chain, they slowly disappeared into the night.

"You okay, Todd?"

"Yes, you?"

"I'm okay!"

"They're gone! Let's keep going!"

Todd's face was throbbing as he eased away from the wall and headed back up to the walkway. He could taste the blood that had flowed down to the corner of his mouth. At least it seemed that the bleeding had stopped, though he certainly felt the tightening feeling of the sticky, drying blood on his face.

They went along at a crouch so as not to be seen. There was no hole in the wall that they could see, and slowly they began to despair. Had Sedon been wrong? Maybe the ventilation tunnels had been closed.

Suddenly they found themselves in a widening of the walkway, which looked somewhat like a balcony. In the moonlight they could see a table and a few chairs scattered around. Above the table was a torch held in a fitting, lighting up the whole area in front of them.

"Look!" said Dana, pointing to the far side. "The walkway ends here. We'll have to go back, and . . . augh!"

"What?" asked Todd, astonished.

"Your face! Oh, Todd!"

"It was that dog."

"Oh, Todd! It looks awful!" In the flickering light of the torch, Todd could see great tears welling up in Dana's eyes.

"Don't worry about that now! We've got to—"

"Oh, Todd! We've got to get you cleaned up!" Looking around, Dana found a basin of water, and not finding any clean rags, she knelt down and tore a piece off the bottom of her trousers. She dipped it in the water and stood him under the torch to see what she was doing. She tenderly wiped as much blood off as she could.

"Oh, Todd. My dear, dear Todd."

For an instant, Todd forgot the urgency of their situation. He felt like he was looking into the eyes of love itself. It was as though he was transported back to Clara, whose hand stroking his curly hair had seemed somehow to caress his soul with motherly affection.

"Todd, it looks awful! I had no idea . . ."

"Don't worry. That water really helps," said Todd, enjoying the cool, soothing sensation of the water on his cheek almost as much as the affection in Dana's eyes.

Dana, whose glance had strayed along the wall, suddenly gasped. "Todd, look! They're coming back!" She pointed to the distant patrol. Indeed, there were the soldiers again. It was clearly the same group, with a soldier in front carrying a torch and a few men walking behind him. One was obviously struggling with a dog.

"Get down!" whispered Todd. "We've got to get out of here! Is there any way we can climb up, over the wall?" They both looked, scouring the flat face of the wall above them. There seemed no chance of climbing up to the top.

"I don't see any way," said Dana with great worry. "Is there a ledge below us or anything like that?" They both looked downward and saw a high, smooth wall dropping down into black darkness. There was no escape to be seen.

"What are we going to do?" asked Todd urgently. "They're coming this way!" His heart was beating rapidly. He didn't want to face the dog again—and he couldn't let them find Dana!

"Look! There's a hole over there!" said Dana, pointing over to a square hole in the wall under the torch.

"Let's go!" said Todd, and they both rushed over to the hole on their hands and knees.

The hole was about a foot and a half by a foot and a half, with a steel grid in front of it. Todd pulled on the grid with all his strength, but it did not budge.

"Look at this!" he said, pointing to a lock on the right side.

"Oh no!" gasped Dana in desperation.

The clanking of chains could again be heard.

"What's with your dog? He's going crazy again, he is!"

"He's found something! I'm sure he has!"

A sudden burst of barking broke through the air, and a tingle of terror went down Todd's back. The clackety sound of the men's boots was getting louder. They had started running toward the balcony.

"What are we going to do?" asked Dana frantically.

They both heaved on the grid with all their strength, but it didn't budge. Todd had no idea what to do. No idea at all. The footsteps were getting louder, and the ferocious wheezing of the dog could be heard as it pulled furiously on its collar. They were getting closer and closer.

CHAPTER 32

Finding Their Way

Hearing the footsteps grow louder, Todd and Dana tried one last and desperate time to pull the grid open, but it simply wouldn't budge. The dog's wild panting was just around the corner.

"It's no use!" said Todd hopelessly.

"Use the key!"

"Oh! Yeah! Of course!" He quickly reached into his breast pocket and pulled out the key he had found in the tree those many months ago. It was the key left behind by Owen Silas—the one Owen had used to free a prisoner over a hundred years before. He put the key into the keyhole, and the lock swung open as effortlessly as on the day it was made.

"Quick! Get in!" said Todd, pulling the grid wide open. Dana shot in like a cat, and Todd was quick to follow.

Just then the dog entered the balcony, and seeing Todd climbing in, burst again into loud barking. Pulling the helpless soldier holding the chain, it bounded to the grid just as Todd was closing it. In all the noise of the wild barking, Todd couldn't hear if the latch had closed or not.

"Go!" he hissed, and Dana took off crawling on her hands and knees. Todd was close behind. They went several yards into the black, unlit tunnel, and then Todd stopped to listen behind him.

"Man! You've got to get your dog under control! What's with him tonight?"

"No idea! He's gone wild, he has!"

"Okay, boys!" came the voice of the captain. "We'll take a twenty-minute rest here, and then we'll head back."

"Hear that, Dana?" Todd whispered through the darkness. "They didn't see us!"

"Ah! The Lord be thanked!" she said in great relief. "That dog with all its barking must have covered the sounds of the grate. What'll we do now?"

"This must be the ventilation shaft Sedon told us about. Let's just follow it and see where it goes."

"I can't see anything!"

"Me neither, but I don't know what else we could do."

"Okay, here we go!" said Dana. She started off, slowly feeling her way ahead.

Dana didn't like it in here, not one bit. It would have been much nicer to let Todd pass her and lead the way, but the passageway was so low and narrow that he could never have gotten by.

Dana hated black, scary places like this. Her mind became full of all the horrible things that could happen: possibilities of suddenly falling down a great hole, or having the stones behind her cave in so that she was stuck in here for life, or of entering a great black labyrinth, never being able to get out again, and slowly dying of thirst and exhaustion. A burst of longing for the high mountain plains filled her. She missed life there. She missed how brave she had always felt there.

Stop being so silly and just crawl! she thought, angry with herself for thinking such things. Bit by bit she felt their way through the blackness and with new boldness started going faster.

"It just goes on and on!" remarked Todd.

"Yeah, I guess the hall is quite a ways away," said Dana.

Every now and again they came to holes with grids, where they could look out over the city below. They kept crawling for about ten minutes, and when they finally came to the next grid they could see the light of torches below and hear lots of commotion.

"These must be the last-minute preparations before the gala event," whispered Dana.

"Yeah! Maybe we're getting closer to the great hall," replied Todd.

The tunnel seemed to widen at one of the grids, and the kids could see the stars in the night sky.

"Let's stop and have a rest," said Todd.

"Great idea!" said Dana. Crawling on the hard, rough surface was not easy, and her knees and hands were killing her. There was just enough room to move around so that they could both sit down. They sat side by side with their backs against the wall, looking through their knees to the clear black sky outside. It was wonderful to breathe the fresh air coming through the hole.

"I didn't want you to come," said Todd slowly, "but I'm so glad you're here!" He squeezed Dana's right hand with his left. "Thanks, Dana!"

She squeezed his band back and said, "I'm where I want to be!"

"Hey," said Todd, "how did you know about my key?"

"I didn't!"

"What do you mean, you didn't? You told me to use it to open the grid!"

Dana frowned at him. What was he talking about? "No, I didn't. I didn't say anything! I didn't even know you *had* a key!"

"Hmmm," replied Todd thoughtfully. "You know, I always carry this key of Owen Silas around, but I never thought I'd use it . . . I guess we're not alone."

Dana's mind went back to the words of the old woman at the night of singing at Bud's house: *They must get past me to get to you! Do not fear! I am with you! Flee, Tender Heart! Flee!"*

"Come on," said Dana. "We've got to keep going."

"Yeah, you're right."

And off they went again. Dana's knees protested in pain, but they hurt less and less as they went. She figured they were getting numb. After another ten minutes or so they came to another grid, a different kind than the one before. It was much larger and more elaborate, painted white.

Dana and Todd crawled up to it and looked out, or rather, in. They suddenly found themselves looking down from above into a most beautiful room. Many large mirrors hung on the walls, and a huge, ornate dressing table against one wall was equipped with a seemingly endless number of powder and cosmetic containers, rows upon rows of what looked like bottles of perfume, and combs and brushes of all descriptions hanging from shiny silver hooks.

Seated at this marble table was a slender man of medium height, with fine, delicate, almost pointy features, dressed in very fine clothes.

Dana whispered in Todd's ear ever so quietly, "It's the king!"

Behind the king stood an older man with wavy white hair that hung down to his rounded shoulders. He wore a loose white cotton shirt with lace around the neck and at the wrists, and he was bent over the king, using a little brush to put something like a powder on his temples.

". . . you know that's what many people said," said the king. "But I know the truth." He sat at the dressing table, looking at himself very closely in the mirror. He was obviously very happy with what he saw. Then he saw something he didn't like and snapped, "Idon, you fool! More black on the eyebrows! How many times do I have to tell you?"

"Immediately, sire! Terribly sorry, sire!" said the old man, putting the brush down and quickly taking another in the hand, with which he hastily went to work on king's eyebrows.

"Better cosmeticians have been boiled in oil for shabby work! It's just amazing what I have to put up with!"

The old man said nothing but continued to apply black powder on the eyebrows.

"You know, people called my grandfather Eduarl 'the Great' because they had to. He is described as a great man in the books because he fought the pirates of the north and subdued the lower river people. He was a man who took the sword into his own hand! Yes, he was a conqueror, and he was called great. But do you know what my father called him?"

"No, your highness," replied the servant with a timid, reverent voice.

"My father called him 'the Old Fool.'"

The servant gasped in horror and said nothing, which is exactly what one is supposed to do in such a situation.

"Surprised, are you? Well, that doesn't surprise me! You servants are so dull of thought! Why? 'Why an old fool?' you may ask. The answer is quite simple for anyone with any kind of keenness of mind."

The king looked with great pleasure at his image in the mirror as he talked.

"The fact is that my grandfather could wield a sword, but not a pen! The old twit could barely write his name! That's why he left on one campaign after the other. Here at home he was totally overwhelmed. No one knew this, of course. Even those famous poems to his wife were all written by a servant of his, who ultimately lost his head because the last poem didn't rhyme the way my grandmother wanted it to! It was all a scam. I find it shocking what the common man believes."

He nodded sharply to indicate the eyebrows were finished. "Well, my father saw through all of this and was not at all surprised to find the finances a mess and the coffers empty when his father died. The kingdom was politically mighty but financially a dreadful mess. A little more brown under my left eye! You know, I shouldn't have to be telling you this!"

"Right away, sire!" answered the servant with well-practiced humility.

"So my father stepped in with his training and great financial practicality. He claims to have saved the kingdom five times over. He felt forced to break old treaties with old allies just to refill the coffers. Indeed, being the world's mightiest man does have its unpleasant side sometimes. He got a lot more slaves for the mines and a lot more work out of every slave. They said he could squeeze a penny out of an empty purse and the last drop of blood out of every slave. Yes, my father, Eduarl II, that great man! Considered by many to be another Eduarl the Great!"

The king stood up suddenly, entranced by his own rhetoric, and pushed the servant aside. He went over to the full-length mirrors and stood in many different poses before them, scrutinizing his clothes and the appearance of his body.

"But, Idon," continued the king with great gravity, "you know what I consider my father to be?"

"Uh, no, your majesty," said the servant nervously.

"He was an old fool and no better than his father!" shouted the king triumphantly. "And why? Do you know why?"

"Terribly sorry, Highness!"

"I'll tell you why! Because he was a barbarian, that's why! That man lived in a world of coins and precious stones and assets. That's all the old fool knew! He couldn't tell a harp from a drumstick! He couldn't tell a poem from a servant's shopping list! That old idiot was blind to art and deaf to music, and when he died he left behind a veritable artistic desert. A kingdom without the arts is like a giant without a heart: great strength, provoking great fear but destined to die. For a kingdom, art is like glue! It is that unseen thing that holds everything together! Yes, their blocky minds could never imagine such a thing, but this is how it is! And you know, Idon, the throne has finally come into the hands of someone who can save it and the kingdom. I, Eduarl III, am not just a man of enormous intellect! No! I have an artistic perception that is god-like. Yes, I shall enlighten this kingdom. I shall! And I shall go down in history, not as a 'great,' but as the all-time greatest! No equal shall come after me, just as there has been no equal before me! In the years to come, people will only speak of 'The Great One.' No name shall be necessary, for there has only ever been one, and this phenomenon shall never happen again!"

Dana cast a glance at Todd, who looked torn between revulsion and the desire to burst out laughing. What total lunacy!

Pulling down on his silk vest and gazing at himself in the mirror, the king went on. "Today will be a turning point, Idon! Yes, today will be the day when the giant started to rouse after its great long sleep! Today will be the rebirth of culture in this desolate, miserable wreck of a kingdom. Yes, today! This is a day of historic proportions! And it will be done through the invention of my own fair hand. You mark my words! Today will be the day when the Great One will save his pathetic, poverty-stricken kingdom from centuries of drought. Ha! Today!" shouted the king in a kind of ecstasy.

There was a sudden knocking at the door, making Todd and Dana jump.

"Yes?" called the king.

"The royal family and guests have been seated for the evening program, sire."

"Excellent! I shall be right there!" The king took one last lovestruck look at himself in the mirror and added, "You know, Idon, I shall marry in a month—we'll see how long this wife lasts—but I must do this great act before I marry, you know why?

"No, sire."

"Because I would never have it said, 'His wife helped him.' No! This dream sprang from my breast; from mine alone! It will bear my name alone. I feel that is only right, don't you?"

"Yes, sire! Most certainly!"

"My coat, you idiot!"

"Sorry, sire!" The servant rushed over to get the king's coat and slipped it over his arms and onto his shoulders.

"This is history in the making!" said the king as the servant opened the door. "Mark my words!" In no time the king was out the door. The servant closed the door behind him and let out a great sigh of relief. Dana very nearly did the same.

CHAPTER 33

The Bride

"Have you ever heard such idiocy in your life?" whispered Todd.

"Never," answered Dana. A thousand thoughts were whirling round in her mind. This was the man she had heard of all of her life—the man the soldiers' songs praised, and the old village women adored, and her mother detested. All the pieces were slowly falling into place.

"Come on! We have to get going!" Todd broke into her thoughts, giving her arm a tug.

"Yeah, you're right!" she replied and they continued crawling.

After about five minutes they came to another grid and another room that was strikingly similar to the last. It was a little bit smaller than the king's dressing room and held seemingly endless collections of ladies' hats and bonnets, scarves and shawls hanging in fine order all over the wooden panels that covered the walls.

"Wow!" whispered Dana in amazement.

A tall young woman stood before a mirror making what seemed to be the last adjustments in her magnificent dress. Adorned with long golden locks hanging down around noble cheeks, with lovely eyes and a slightly cupped nose, she was a stunningly beautiful lady. An older servant woman was there, tying a bit of lace on her sleeve.

There was a knock at the door, and the servant asked, "Who is it?"

"Her majesty's sister desires an audience with the bride!"

"Let her in," called the lady, and the door swung open. A girl a little older than Dana entered.

"Oh, look at you!" said the girl, running in and hugging the bride.

"No, not now! We've just got this dress right!" protested the bride, pushing her off. She looked up at the servant with a haughty lift of her chin. "The bride requests an audience alone with the young lady."

"Most certainly, your majesty!" The servant bowed her head and went out, closing the door behind her.

"Ah, Shultan, look at you! Just look at you! Mama will be so proud! They've both arrived, and everyone's getting ready. To think—you'll be married in a month, and you already look like you were born a queen."

"Yeah," replied the bride with annoyed disinterest. "And how are you?"

The younger girl giggled. "Oh, I'm fine. What with a sister who's going to be a queen and all! We've had all sorts of visits! All sorts of people coming by to congratulate us on your engagement! People who would never before have darkened our doorstep—you know, before we were royalty and all that."

The younger girl walked over and fondled a silk dress hanging on the wall. "Isn't this magnificent! I guess you've got lots of things to get used to, eh?"

"Almut, you're not allowed to say 'eh' anymore."

"No?"

"I'm afraid not," said the bride dryly. "It's one of the many chains that fall upon one who becomes royal." As Dana watched, great clouds of sorrow swept across the bride's face.

The girl looked up into the eyes of her sister. "Shultan, is everything all right?"

To her shock, Dana watched the stone face of the bride melt into the face of a country girl in great distress. "No! No, Almut! It isn't!"

The bride held out her arms, and the girl ran into her embrace.

"It's so awful!" Shultan cried. "I can't tell you how awful it is, Almut!" The bride was now crying great streams of tears into her sister's shoulder.

"But this was your dream!"

"Oh, what a fool I have been! Such a fool!"

"Don't say that!" said Almut, who looked into Shultan's face. "Oh no! Your makeup! Come quick!" She broke away from her sister's embrace and picked up some cloths from the table.

"Here! Now do stop crying!" Almut dabbed frantically with the cloth, trying to clean away her sister's tears.

"We've got to get you cleaned up! A bride can't cry. They'll be calling us in a minute!"

Almut pulled a chair over to her sister. "Here, sit down," she said, and she helped Shultan into her seat.

Dana could not help but watch the scene with a big lump in her throat. She was seeing something had already become very familiar. The kingdom was full of girls who never found their dreams and died with sad hearts. And then there were those few whose dreams actually came true, and they died with a truly broken heart. *There's no room for love in this kingdom,* she thought.

"Shultan, dear, tell me what's going on!"

"The king is an absolute buffoon!"

"Shultan! You can't say that! He's the king!"

"But he is, Almut! He is! He struts around like a cock, utterly in love with himself. He's like the beautiful picture, and I'll be the ugly nail that holds it on the wall."

"What are you talking about?"

Shultan tried to dry her tears, but her voice shook with deep grief. "I thought he loved me! He just loves the thought of himself being in love. He wants to be the best at everything, so with me he can be the best lover—and all the servants have to see that! If I am not ravished with his love minute by minute, what will they say? And worse yet, what will go down in the history books? I'll be remembered as an ungrateful shrew, if he doesn't divorce me in the first week."

"Oh, Shultan! I'm so sorry." Almut began wiping away her own tears. "But what can we do?"

Shultan leaned forward with fire in her eyes. "I've got to get out of this!"

"Back out of the wedding? Are you mad?"

"I would rather die than marry that goat, I tell you, Almut!"

Almut stifled a gasp at her sister's language. "Shultan, maybe it's just a bad patch. Maybe things will get better!"

"Almut, the man is utterly detestable!" Shultan laid her hands on her sister's cheeks and said, "If I run away, you shall all go down to the mines. I know that as well as you. My best hope is to die mysteriously."

"Shultan, don't speak like that!" said Almut, fighting off the tears welling in her eyes. "We'll think of something. You and me!"

"You're so precious," said Shultan, fondling her sister's face in her hands. Dana's heart hurt for them both. She could tell the future queen truly loved her sister, but she could also see that the bride had no hope.

There was a knock on the door. "Your highness is requested presently."

"Tell them I am coming and that beauty cannot be rushed!" called Shultan.

"Very well, your highness."

"Well, first, we have to get through this evening," said Almut. "Let me fix up your face here."

As she was putting fresh powder on the bride's cheeks, Shultan spoke: "I was lying in bed last night, feeling that life was over. I felt like a mouse in a trap. The poor creature doesn't die, but scrambles around hopelessly trying to get out. Its pain grows, its strength fails, and finally it breathes its last. That's how I saw my life."

Dana was hanging on every word.

"I was lying there feeling so terribly desolate, and suddenly I heard a song. It was the most peculiar thing. It wasn't a voice, and it wasn't an instrument. It was just music—pure, heavenly music. And the hopelessness that was choking my soul suddenly broke. My soul could breathe. I took in great gulps of air—life-giving air. And I fell asleep in utter tranquility. Isn't that strange, Almut?" Her voice turned bitter. "And then I woke up in this horrible prison of a palace."

Almut put down her brush. "Your face is okay." She grasped her sister's hands in her own and said, "Listen, we'll get through this party, and then we'll meet later. I'm sure we can think of something. Be strong, dear sister. You've always been so strong. Be strong, for just this evening!"

The two slipped out of the room, and the door shut behind them.

"Ah, the poor dear!" said Dana, fighting the trembling in her lips.

"She reminds me so much of you the day I found you in the forest," said Todd.

"She does," said Dana thoughtfully. "She certainly does."

CHAPTER 34

On the Great Stage

"Let's go; it's all going to start soon," said Todd. Off they went as fast as they could crawl. Their knees ached, but that didn't matter now. They had to somehow find their way to what Sedon had described as "the great hall," and they both felt the urgency of the situation. Knowing that time was short, they scrambled along, hoping that they were going the right way. They then came to a split in the way and could go either straight or left.

"What do we do now?" asked Dana desperately.

"I don't know. I really don't know!" said Todd. It was wider here, and they knelt side by side. Except for their heavy breathing, it was quiet. Suddenly Todd heard what seemed to be distant applause from the left.

"There! Come on!" Todd dashed ahead, and Dana hurried to keep up. Indeed, the sound grew louder and the way became brighter. The tunnel seemed to get higher and higher until both could stand up in it, which they did with great pleasure. They ran ahead until they came to a large white grid that let light into the tunnel.

Side by side they stood at the grid, looking down at the sight below. Directly before them, about five feet below where they were perched, was an enormous marble stage. A magnificent throne stood on a pedestal in the middle. It was beautifully ornate, carved out of wood with motifs of grapes and cherries, figures of birds, animals of the forest, and other mythical creatures the likeness of which Todd had never seen. Beside the throne were four seats on each side, gradually descending to the left and right. In them sat men and women in the most splendid attire.

Dana gave Todd a nudge. "The bride!" she whispered and pointed to the lady seated beside the throne. There Shultan sat, the perfect picture of brokenhearted beauty.

Todd's eyes scanned the great hall. Its literally thousands of bright lanterns and chandeliers illuminated it well, and he could clearly see the large audience. Finely dressed people of all shapes and sizes filled both the auditorium and the balconies between the enormous pillars that held the building up.

Looking over at the stage, his eyes fell upon a man who he recognized immediately. The king was standing in front of his throne and speaking to the crowd with great enthusiasm:

". . . and after years of design and consulting in the many details of this immense project, be they large or small, I have finished the construction of what has been, and most likely will always be, the most extraordinary accomplishment of any man to walk this earth—and, just as an aside, this confirms that truth which has been long known and rarely mentioned, that the kings of our day, or more specifically, that king standing before your blessed eyes, is obviously made of something much greater than is your common man."

The king paused with a flourish of his coattails. "Great personalities have great dreams, and today you shall see the fruition of the greatest dream the world has ever known. May I ask you to cast your eye to that enormous structure to my left?"

Todd and Dana did. A huge structure wrapped in a cover of immense overlapping blue sheets, all held by ropes from the top, loomed over the gathering.

"This is my gift, not only to the kingdom, but to mankind itself, to history, which without this magnificent show of my own personal generosity would end its weary life in the cultural poverty it has always known. Drop the veils!"

Suddenly the ropes were loosed, and the sheets dropped to the floor. Dozens of slaves ran to gather up and remove veils.

A gasp of wonder ran through the audience, as it did through Dana and Todd. A colossal structure stood in all its magnificence before them. At first glance it looked something like a thick, spiral-shaped tower, but looking closer, they saw it was an organ. Great, wide pipes in the middle rose to the ceiling, surrounded by ever shorter and thinner pipes wrapped around the outside.

But that wasn't all. Around this core of pipes was a structure that looked to Todd like a vine wrapped in a spiral around a tree. This structure held horns of every size, from giant tubas at the bottom to miniature trumpets right at the top, just visible beside the great pipes.

A second vine-shaped structure ran around the pipes just underneath the one carrying horns. This structure carried small bells at the top, triangles in the middle, and great gongs at the bottom.

Todd saw something else between these two spirals. It was quite difficult to see at first, but after staring at it for a while, he understood what it was. It was a harp placed between the spirals made by the horns and the bells. There were hundreds, if not thousands of strings in this harp, which was itself wrapped around the tower several times as it wound its way up to the top.

Around the base of this tower was a large, round wooden platform. This made the whole structure look like an upside-down mushroom. The platform held a multitude of drums, from very large tympani to drums as small as a cup. Each of these drums had a frame holding a drumstick on a lever, some great and strong with huge round balls at the end and others thin as a twig. All of the hundreds of drumsticks were attached to strings, which led to a round rail at the foot of the tower.

"That looks like one big ugly spider web!" whispered Todd to Dana.

"Just what I was thinking!" whispered Dana.

Now Todd and Dana saw something that the audience did not see. Tucked away out of sight between the drum platform and the wall was a lower platform, like a big pit. Because Todd and Dana were up high, they could look inside. It was full of large bellows attached to long beams. Chained to these beams were about thirty slaves, whose bare backs already glistened with sweat. They were lifting, lowering, lifting, lowering, and in this way building up the air pressure within the mammoth thing. They were supervised by soldiers with long whips.

"Let us give our audience a taste of what is to come!" said the king, beaming with satisfaction.

Then Todd noticed a group of three men in a half-hidden chamber at the base of the structure. One sat down at a keyboard while the others operated curious-looking control panels. The room filled immediately with loud, blaring music. A military marching tune boomed out of the pipes and horns, which carried the melody. The strings provided fullness by playing a background of chords, and the bells and drums maintained the marching beat. It was loud, really loud, but no one in the audience dared cover his ears or show any emotion other than delight. The slaves were pumping like mad as the instrument took all of the air they could pump into it. Todd saw a couple of soldiers cracking whips to keep them going, but this could not be heard above the noise.

The men below were frantically playing the keyboard, turning knobs, pulling levers, and turning dials. The melody came to an end and then repeated itself, this time with the tune carried by the bells and the other parts providing the rhythm and harmony.

Then, at the close of the second repetition, it all stopped rather abruptly. Todd's ears were ringing. He just wanted to enjoy the silence for a minute, but the crowd exploded in applause. They all stood up and gave an ecstatic standing ovation, in which the king obviously bathed.

With the spectacle over, Todd glanced at Dana, only to see her face full of sorrow as she looked down at the slaves leaning on the beams and panting for air.

After a long and somehow awkward applause, the audience sat down again. All eyes were upon the king.

"That was something that our language is just too feeble to describe. Magnificent? Outstanding? Sensational? None of these words carry the supreme bliss of what we have all just heard! You, my beloved subjects, have just heard something that puts the song of the birds to shame, and beside which even the most amazing human voice pales in comparison!"

"What an absolute oaf!" said Dana in disgust.

"Shhhh!" replied Todd, who wanted to hear more.

"Now, there will be more music as we celebrate this historic day, but before we enjoy that, we must, regrettably, devote ourselves to some of the affairs of the kingdom. It is, on epic days like today, the pleasure of generous kings to allow the common man to step, even if for just one fleeting moment, into the shoes of the monarch, and to share some of his decisions. We will first deal with a captured band of pirates and then move on to a rather wretched forester."

"Dad!" said Todd. Visions of Bud filled his mind. He saw the kind, reassuring smile that covered Bud's worn old face and the love in his eyes that had carried Todd through the worst of trials. He loved this man more than life itself.

With great theatrical poise, the king motioned to the far entrance: "Bring on the pirates!"

A band of pirates wearing chains on their hands and feet were led onto the stage. There they stood, all massive, barefoot, and dressed in ragged, torn clothing. Once they were before the king they threw themselves on their faces before him and screamed, wailed, and wept for mercy. They begged and implored, praising the king to the highest heaven and cursing themselves to the lowest hell. They groveled, they pleaded that the king would spare their lives.

Todd gazed at the scene in horror. This was somehow outside of his definition of what was truly human. How on earth could anyone get to such a state? He leaned over to Dana and blurted out, "This is awful!"

"It is!" replied Dana, who could not take her eyes off the horrible spectacle. "It really is!"

"My dear audience, what do you think?" asked the king dramatically. "These wicked men have certainly committed crimes of the vilest sort, and they obviously deserve the most wretched deaths our executioners can conjure up. It is, though, a day of great celebration, and I can't help but think that maybe they have seen the error of their ways. The discernment that I as king have cultivated over these many years tells me that, for this one day, for this one instance, the generosity of the king may outweigh the depravity of these lost fools. This could be a kind of overflow of this great celebration of ours!"

The thought filled Todd with hope for Bud. Maybe, through some miracle, the king would be inclined to pardon him too.

The king walked to the front of the stage and called out to the crowd, "What is the pleasure of the audience? Shall we spare these wretches?" he said with his thumb up, "or shall we execute them?" with his thumb down. "I am rather disposed to pardon them," he said, holding his thumb up again and smiling glibly. "What do you think?"

As he looked around, one after the other in the audience raised their hands thumbs up until all of the crowd followed suit.

"So be it!" said the king in great festive mood. "They shall be spared!"

The crowd erupted into applause, which the king must have felt was for him alone, during which the very relieved and thankful pirates were taken away.

"But, my dear guests, there is one remaining pirate whom we still have not considered," continued the king. He seemed very pleased to seize the excitement of the crowd and somehow keep it going as long as he could. "It is the leader of this vile band, a man whose merciless hands have taken the lives of three soldiers and many of our good citizens. Bring him in!"

Now the soldiers brought in a massive brute of a man in dirty, ragged clothes, chained hand and foot. He was a bit darker than the others, and his wild, unkempt beard and hair stuck out in every direction.

The king pointed at him with great theatrical expression and said, "Yes, this is the one who led that miserable gang throughout the seas and coastal villages, stealing, plundering, killing, and sometimes just destroying for the pleasure of it. Under his leadership they left behind houses burnt to the ground, cripples, mothers without sons, daughters without fathers. Under his guidance these vermin terrorized the islands for the better part of five years."

Boos sounded from the audience, and a smug grin grew on the king's face. He turned to the pirate and said, "What do you have to say for yourself?"

At this point the huge thug threw himself at the king's feet, wailing, crying, and begging for pity. The hall resounded with the great sobs of the giant, and the whole thing sent a shiver down Todd's spine.

The king interrupted, and upon hearing him, the pirate was still. "My dear guests, what do you think? How do you think that these shrieks and cries compare with those of his untold victims? Are these cries great enough to drown out the wailing of mothers who lost their children, and of children who lost their parents? And what about those brave soldiers perishing in the line of duty?"

It was very clear to the crowd that the king wanted this man condemned, and those in the crowd knew well what they should do. Boos could be heard from all over the hall, and as they grew louder, calls of protest could be heard.

"Hang him!"

"Off with his head!"

"Now, let us do this properly," replied the king. "Let me see your hands!"

He held out his hand with his thumb pointing up and looked out to see the response. The hall was still. No one moved. He pointed his thumb downward and smiled with evil glee. The crowd did the same, all showing thumbs down.

"The people have spoken!" shouted the king. "He shall die!"

"The rogue," Dana muttered. "They're just following his lead, and he knows it!"

At this point the pirate broke into loud howling, begging, pleading, and throwing himself at the king's feet, but the soldiers were quick to come. A good five or six of them were needed to get this huge hulk of a man, screaming and wailing, out of the hall. He fought every inch of the way, and his voice could still be heard as they got him out of the hall and on the way to his execution.

Todd felt Dana's hand squeeze his. He was so glad she was there. This terrible scene had smothered his hopes for Bud's pardon.

The crowd was absolutely charged, and the king's face beamed with satisfaction. He obviously loved these events.

"Now before we move on with the main program, we have one last prisoner for whom I have very little hope whatsoever. It is a barbarian from the forest who committed a crime so audacious, so lawless, and so utterly rebellious to all that is orderly and proper that not even the most depraved criminals in the kingdom have considered doing such a thing for the last thirty-seven years. Yes, beloved audience: thirty-seven years! This primitive riffraff comes wandering out of his hole in the ground somewhere in that forsaken forest and chooses not just to ignore decent government property, as do many of his brainless peers, but rather to openly, publically, and in broad daylight defy and insult the dignity of the crown. This poor excuse of a man is guilty of doing nothing less than breaking the royal seal!"

The crowd gasped in unbelief and shock and seemed to sit in dumbfounded horror at the thought. Todd's heart sank within him.

Bud was pushed onto the stage by two soldiers, who shoved him along with the butts of their spears.

"Dad!" gasped Todd, only to feel Dana's hand on his shoulder. She put her finger against her lips as if to say, "Be quiet!"

"You absolutely miserable creature!" howled the king like the seasoned actor he clearly was. "But it would be wrong to say that you have no hope at all. Our grandiose guests and I have shown kindness today, and a sort of enlightenment that has been rarely seen in this fair land of ours. You never know. If you beg and plead with remarkable authenticity, and if you present reasons yet unknown for this horrific crime you have committed, you might have a tiny chance of a pardon. So now, at my command, you may fall at my feet . . . Now!"

The king cast a self-satisfied smile out to the public, who were all watching with great attention. It soon became clear to him, though, that he heard no body hitting the ground, nor did a word of desperate groveling reach his ears. He glanced back in surprise to see Bud still standing on his feet, staring at the ground and not saying a word.

"I said grovel!"

The king looked amazed at Bud's motionless form and screamed, "Get on your face, you insolent scum!"

Again, Bud remained still, trembling and staring at the ground. One of the soldiers raised his spear to strike him to the ground, but the king held up his hand to stop him. The soldier bowed in obedience and drew back.

"Do you not understand my words, you forest filth?" said the king, trying to control his rage.

"I do, your highness," replied Bud.

"I commanded you to grovel at my feet!" said the king.

"I'm afraid I can't, your highness." Todd swallowed hard at the simplicity of his father's answer.

"You can't? Do you not know that your life is in my hand? I could make your life short and your death miserably long! Every breath you breathe right now is a gift from my hand, and had I only the slightest whim, the faintest desire, you would be gone forever."

The king then turned to the crowd and smiled with a fiendish, wicked grin and said, "You know, I would be quite glad to hear what this madman has to say before I order him cut up into a thousand pieces!"

He turned again to Bud. "Why, forest fool, will you not bow before me?"

"I can only bow before the Lord of the Forest," said Bud in a steady, quiet voice.

"The Lord of the Forest!" shouted the king, aghast. "The Lord of the Forest?" He threw his head back and laughed loud and free, holding his hand on his belly and guffawing with such a despising, mocking laugh that nobody could respond with favor. He quickly noticed that the crowd was silent, sitting obviously nervous and uncomfortable, rather horrified at the scene they saw before them. The atmosphere and laughter of the last few minutes were gone.

As Todd watched, the change in the crowd seemed to enrage the king. He fixed his eyes on Bud, beaming with a hatred you could almost reach out and touch.

"The forest! Yes, that wretched cluster of pathetic villages inhabited by primitive, uncultured peasants. That forest? The forest in which my soldiers ride around at will, whose spineless dwellers creep away into the shadows every time they hear hoofbeats? Where then is this 'Lord' you speak of? Maybe he's with them—hiding behind trees, creeping around under bushes. Wherever he is or whatever he's doing, he's very definitely not helping those idiots who have placed their brainless trust in him."

Todd broiled with anger, and he felt Dana's hand on his arm again. Warning him to keep still.

"Do you not see, my fool," the king continued, "that everything lies in the power of my hand, and I alone do exactly as I please? And now I shall tell you what I please. General! Send for the executioner! He is to come fully equipped to exercise his office here and now!"

The king then turned to the crowd, who remained motionless and horrified. "The insolence of this man will cost him his life this very night. In a minute the executioner will arrive, and this scum shall be forced to his knees, never to get up again."

Upon this statement, supporters of the king cried out from the crowd in approval. The crowd seemed to be warming again.

Obviously pleased, the king turned on his heel and strutted before Bud and the audience. "You stinking wretch! Look at the magnificence of my creation!" he said, pointing to the great organ. "Has anything like this ever come out of the forest? Has anything of any beauty or grandeur ever come out of those backwoods? What has your so-called Lord of the Forest ever made?"

Bud remained silent yet calm before him. More and more people were calling out from the crowd, mocking Bud and all that he stood for. The king appeared relieved that he had somehow won the crowd again to his side and now only wanted this man dead.

Suddenly a huge man wearing black leather walked through a side door. With a leather mask covering his face and a massive battle-axe in his hand, it was clear to Todd that he was the executioner. There were cries of celebration from the crowd as the executioner came up the stairs.

Todd gasped and gripped the grid with such force that his fingers turned white. This time Dana didn't warn him to stay calm. He could hear her choking back sobs.

"Come and show me what I pay you for! Off with his head!" shouted the king, feasting again on the cheers of the crowd.

A soldier came up with him and threw Bud to his knees. He placed a great wooden block under Bud's head and stood back. Bud made no effort whatsoever to protect himself or pull back, and the executioner drew his massive weapon up behind his head, preparing to strike.

Without thought, Todd pushed with all his force, and the grid fell tumbling onto the stage. He heard his own voice cry out as he jumped onto the stage.

"STOP!"

And the executioner did stop, totally surprised. Two soldiers lunged at Todd, but the king held out his hand to stop them, and they stopped.

"He didn't do it, O King! I did. I panicked! I panicked, and I just grabbed the seal, and he told me not to! I broke the seal! This man is not guilty!"

The king was now well and truly confused. He stared at Todd, covered in soot and dust, with a gaping, fresh wound under his swollen left eye. "Please, O King. Let Dad go! Take my life!"

Bud was too shocked to speak. He went white at the sight of his son on the stage.

"Dad? Dad?" repeated the king, who was slowly gaining his composure. "So this lowlife is your father?" He then turned to Bud and asked, "Is this rat crawling around in the piping your son? Really, really! You must in future make sure that he dresses appropriately when he comes to one of the king's events!"

The king's supporters in the crowd tried to generate a bit of laughter for that joke, but it was not easy. The whole crowd looked uneasy and restless again.

"Your highness," said Bud. "The boy was under my authority at the time. I bear full responsibility for everything that happened! The law doesn't allow the execution of—"

"Silence, you ignorant fool!" screamed the king in a rage. "How dare you, a worm of the forest, instruct me in the law? I am the law, you idiot! Do you understand absolutely nothing?"

More and more cries were coming out of the crowd, some saying that the father should die, and some, the son. The king seemed to be getting fed up with all of this. This was obviously a few too many surprises for one evening, especially for a man who always wanted to have everything under control.

"The boy says he's guilty! The man says he's guilty. What then shall we do?" said the king with a sly grin, addressing the crowd. "You know, I've noticed that fathers and sons love doing things together. It is oh-so-touching to see father and son, side by side, doing something really *special* together!"

At this point a wicked smile grew across his face. "Let them die side by side, and then we shall know for sure that the guilty party is dead!"

The crowd cried out in praise of the king's wisdom.

Todd fixed his eyes on Bud and said in a trembling voice, "If I must die, then let me die for the Lord of the Forest and with you, Dad."

Todd heard a thump on the stage behind him and turned around. It was Dana! What was she—

"I have heard it from your royal lips!" she shouted. "One of them is guilty, and that means that the other is most certainly innocent, and you, O King, will defame your name by slaying innocent blood before this crowd!"

Todd gaped. Dana's eyes were a flame of fire, and the king could not look her in the eye. He turned to the crowd, trying to control his emotions.

Dana slipped her hand in Todd's and whispered, "I told you I wouldn't leave your side!"

The king pulled himself together the best he could and turned again to the audience. "Ladies and gentlemen! We have put on a real show for you tonight, haven't we? Had I known there was so much vermin crawling around in the vents, I would have had them cleaned out long ago. You are about to witness the execution of three of the most miserable wretches ever to pollute this palace!"

He turned around with a face beaming with contempt and shouted, "Soldiers, seize them! Executioner, do your work!"

Suddenly a voice broke through the room, and the bride stood to her feet. "No!"

"My dear, this is not the time!" said the king, who was now bursting with frustration.

"You can't be serious!" Shultan cried. Her lovely face was even lovelier in her anger, and her eyes glistened with tears. "You cannot kill these children, who show more courage than all of your generals put together!"

"Sit down, my love, or I shall be forced to—" started the king, but she went on.

"For once in my life I see a glimmer of true love, of true courage, and you want to snuff it out before my eyes? You and your noise machine! You're a sham! And finally the sun breaks through these clouds of death, and you just want to—"

"Seize her!" screamed the king in a blatant rage. Two large soldiers from his bodyguard approached the bride, but as they did so they were smashed to the ground as though by a hammer from heaven. Their armor made an enormous crashing sound as they hit the stage floor, and they both lay face down and absolutely motionless.

The air was full of a kind of magic. No one spoke or even moved a muscle. The great hall was absolutely and utterly silent.

Slowly a melody from the organ began to play, starting ever so quietly and growing louder and louder. It was a simple, repeating tune, starting with the piccolo pipes, which sang with the sweetness and lightheartedness of birds on a sunny branch. The lower pipes slowly joined in with great fullness and depth, as though a chorus of autumn winds howling through the palace towers were suddenly singing in great and joyful harmony.

The king looked down with hatred at the organ operator, who was desperately trying to stop the machine, but somehow and very evidently the machine had taken on a mind of its own. The drums joined in, starting with the smallest of cymbals and xylophone bars until the great tympani and gongs had joined, somehow making the sound of a great thunderstorm and yet never drowning out the tune. It was as if this lifeless heap of wood and metal had suddenly come to life and was singing the triumphal entry of a truly great King.

On came the trumpets, and then the strings, and the hall burst with the most magnificent music, as though a thousand top-rate orchestras were suddenly playing side by side. It was so loud that the walls shook, yet it was gentle to the ear, like a great warm ocean of music, surrounding, embracing, and lifting up all who were in it.

In utter despair the king looked down at the slaves, who were doing nothing at all besides looking at each other in great perplexity.

And then it happened. Starting ever so quietly up on the balcony, voices were heard. The crowd, who had until now just sat in bewilderment, staring at all that was taking place before them, began, as in a trance, to sing, and the song went like this:

"I am because he is

I have because he gives

I can because he loves

I hope because he lives."

The crowd had not been turned into a rowdy mob singing some coarse, uncontrolled jeering as at a sports event, but every man was a virtuoso and every woman had a more wonderful voice than the greatest of prima donnas. This was a magnificence never ever known before in this place. It was like gold that shone with such glory that everything else the kingdom could boast was like cracked dull clay. The crowd was transported into a joy beyond all definition, as were the soldiers, the slaves, and the king's mighty men.

The only one not singing was the king himself, and far from being caught up in the glory of the moment, he seemed utterly horrified. He looked around in a helpless disgust and could do nothing, absolutely nothing to stop it.

And then, from before him on the platform, someone spoke.

"O King, please hear my words," said Bud. "Your life is in his hands. Indeed, every breath you breathe is a gift from him, and were he so inclined, your life would be gone in an instant. He has everything in the power of his hand, and he alone does as he pleases."

Unable to reply, the king stared blankly out into the crowd, whose repeated words washed over him like waves crashing against the beach.

"I am because he is

I have because he gives

I can because he loves

I hope because he lives."

Bud's chains suddenly fell from his hands and feet, as did the chains of all of the slaves. Slowly but surely the music died out, and fewer and fewer people were singing until ultimately no one in the audience made a sound.

The great hall had returned to silence. The people were up on their feet, looking around in confusion as though waking up from a strange dream and being unable to remember what they had dreamt about.

Only one person remembered, and that was the king. He just stood, staring blankly at the stage.

A heavenly quiet ruled the place. Todd looked at the great pipes of the organ and couldn't help feeling that they were swaying. Indeed, they were! The whole thing began wobbling around and around.

"Get out!" shouted Todd, and the slaves and soldiers in the pit under the organ scrambled for safety. The machine was whirling and twisting with ever greater motion, clanging and banging. Horns and bells started falling from it, strings broke with great twangs and pings, and before Todd knew it, the whole enormous structure was collapsing in on itself with a hideous clatter. People held their ears and looked away in the huge tumult of the crash, and when they looked back they saw an immense pile of bent metal and broken wood. It was the most pathetic heap of rubbish a person could imagine.

The king stared off into nowhere like a man whose heart had died within him, and he said, "What do you want from me?"

"I want you to release me, me and all those who wear chains, and I want to be free to walk back to the forest with my son and his friend without trouble or harassment," replied Bud.

"Your wish has been granted," said the king, who still did not raise his eyes to even look at Bud.

"And, O King, I want all of the slaves in the mine to be released."

The king bit his lip in ugly determination. Terror flashed across his face.

"Your highness, this request does not come from but from the One who sent me."

"Granted." His lips trembled as he said this.

"And, O King," added Dana, "we request that the bride, Shultan, be released of her engagement vows should she wish it!"

"I have no bride," replied the king, utterly without emotion.

Her face shining, Dana turned to Shultan. "Would you like to come with us to the land of the song? Where it is sung every day?"

"I would! I would!" said Shultan, bursting with joy. She stood up, tore off her ring, and dropped it on the chair. "I'm coming!"

"O King," said Bud, "the act of the Lord today was not one of hatred toward you but of mercy. He let you live. Listen to his voice."

"Just go!" hissed the king without even turning to look at Bud.

A general who had been standing nearby called Bud, Todd, Dana, and Shultan to himself, and with a group of soldiers he escorted them out of the hall. As they were walking out of the hall they could hear people beginning again to speak with one another. The voices sounded confused—and awed.

It was so wonderful to be outside again. Todd sucked the cool night air deep into his lungs with great savor. Having Bud back was a joy beyond description, and Todd refused to leave his side. The general ordered the drawbridge be opened and escorted them across it.

Dana then asked the general to lead them to the inn where Sedon was staying. They went there and found him in no time. You can imagine his surprise to see Bud and the kids being escorted as royal guests by a general and his men!

The general wanted them to leave as soon as possible and sent soldiers to collect Sedon's wagon. He bought them a meal while they waited. It wasn't long before he and his soldiers escorted them out to the city limits and bade them farewell.

CHAPTER 35

All Together

The fire spat and sizzled as drops from the roast pig fell into the flames. Bud smiled to watch Dana, Pian, Julissa, and Shultan all huddled close by the fire. They were chatting and giggling with great vim and vigor. The daylight was well and truly gone, and the first stars could be seen in the clear sky. Varsal, Pian, and Jarod had arrived before sunset. Despite their long trip, they were full of life and enjoying the festivities.

The "men"—that is, Varsal, Sedon, Todd, and Jarod—had gathered at another fire, at which a deer roasted on a spit. Their conversation was far less giggly than that around the pig fire, very matter-of-fact—as men like to consider themselves. But Todd was beaming as he rarely did. Earlier that afternoon he had just come in from the chicken coop when he heard Jarod's voice out on the road. In his excitement, he had dropped everything and run out to meet Jarod. *Oh, well. We didn't need those eggs anyway,* thought Bud with a smile.

Bud felt a hand squeeze his arm. "Have you ever seen him so happy?" It was Clara, who also gazed at her son with delight.

"Great to see, isn't it?" replied Bud, covering her hand with his own. He felt that he was about to burst with joy, more grateful than he could say to be with his wife again. He hadn't imagined the Lord of the Forest would bring this about.

"Now, everyone! Let's gather around!" Dorn's voice boomed into the cool night air, and everyone came and stood in a large circle. "As you can see, we have some very distinguished guests, whom we would like to personally welcome to our feast. I've asked Bud to welcome them all on our behalf, and we in the council of elders have also asked Bud to make some special announcements. Then there'll be some time for music and the meal will begin. But first, Bud. Please come forward."

Bud stepped before the group and looked over to Dana. "Could you please translate?"

"Most certainly!" said Dana, who quickly told the mountain people what was going on.

"First of all, I would like to welcome Varsal, Pian, and Jarod."

All eyes fixed on the mountain people. Bud was filled with affection at the sight of their rugged, noble features in the dancing light of the torches. It had been far too long since their kind were welcomed here.

"Varsal, those many years ago, you brought Todd at risk of your life and gave Clara and me the most wonderful gift a couple could ask for. And then years later, when we found ourselves in great need, I knew I could trust you to take Todd and Dana in. And you did, not as strangers for a short stay, but as your very children. You protected them under the shadow of your wing. I will never have the words to express the thanks that we feel."

He turned to the pig fire and smiled at the tall, beautiful mountain girl who stood arm-in-arm with Dana. "Pian, you took a brokenhearted girl and gave her exactly what she needed: your overflowing joy."

Then to the young man standing beside Todd. "Jarod, you walked before Todd on those treacherous trails and showed enormous strength and courage. Your great gift to him was that you *trusted* him. You trusted him with your very life and came within a hair of losing it.

"We can never repay you all for what you've done, but on behalf of the forest elders, I will tell you our hearts' desire. We embrace you, not as friends, but as brothers and sisters, and as the Lord gives us strength, we resolve to be there for you, be it in the fury of storm or the blackness of night. We will stand by your side, and if need be, we will fall by your side. Your grief has become our grief and your joy our joy."

Dorn strode over to Varsal and extended a hand of covenant. Varsal seized it with joy, and the two men embraced amid great cries of joy from the crowd.

After the embrace, Dorn raised up his hand, and the people went silent.

"We have been such fools to let fear and threats separate our peoples, but that will never happen again. This is an oath before the Lord of the Forest and of the Mountain Plains, and no force under his heaven will break it. We will never again allow our peoples to be separated!"

Again the crowd burst into joyful applause. The claps and cheers went on and on as a rare gladness filled the hearts of the people.

"And now we will address our friends from the kingdom," said Bud, turning his eyes to Julissa. "Julissa, we are so glad to have you among us. Now I finally know where Dana gets her beautiful eyes from! I still remember seeing you in that awful mining camp, weak and worn and holding on to your very last thread of hope. The Lord saw your faithfulness and has turned your mourning into dancing! You are now one of us, and we bid you a hearty welcome." Again the people burst into hearty applause.

"Sedon," said Bud with a warm smile, "Falko saw in you a true friend, and he counted on you to save his family. You have been faithful as the dawn, and we have all benefited greatly from your courage and kindness. You are one of us, and you will always have a place of high honor in our hearts. As you took a family under your care, you have been given a great family, namely, all who are present this evening."

Great cheers erupted from the crowd, and Sedon did all he could to wipe the tears away as quickly as possible.

Bud turned again to address yet another guest: "Shultan, you were a stunningly beautiful bride with a broken heart. And here you sit today in simple village clothing, and you have a smile that outshines the sun. You heard the song, and it won your heart. That was something the king with all his diamonds and pearls could never do. You stood with great courage and spoke of love and loyalty in a world bankrupt of both. That should have cost you your life, but it saved your life, because the Lord is faithful. To you we say a hearty 'Welcome!', and we await with joy the visit of your sister."

Cheers and applause again rose out of a seemingly tireless crowd. Bud beamed at them, grateful for their heartfelt support. This was no manipulated throng, afraid of a king and greedy for approval. They gave their hearts and their voices freely.

"Now this is the end of our welcomes as such, but it would be amiss not to mention a couple of others on this occasion," said Bud, suddenly turning to a couple of unexpecting young men who were busy turning the deer and pig on the spits. "Travis and Brody, our homegrown heroes. Look what has become of you little ankle-biters! Where would we be without you? You chose to follow the light when it was a distant star in a world full of darkness. You loved the song and dared to believe the impossible, and yes, to throw your lives away for it. We hold you in great honor and tender love."

This time the place exploded with applause, and above all the voices calling out cheers and praise, Dorn's voice could be heard in great celebration. The brothers grew red and perhaps even a little teary, though Brody at least would never admit it.

After a long while, the crowd grew quiet. "Tender Heart," said Bud, looking at Dana, "you came like a little cat out of the rain, and we brought you in out of the storm and wrapped you in warm blankets of love and care. You grew strong, in soul and body, and resolved never to leave Todd's side. And as he stood before certain death you took your place—at his side—to die there. Our little cat turned into a mighty lioness, and she made the knees of the king knock together! The Lord bless you, my child."

The cheers were great but bittersweet. Bud felt as though he could hear their thoughts: *Was this not the girl we wanted to hand over to the king? How could we have been such fools?*

"Todd, my dear, dear son. The Lord gave us ten sons and daughters when he gave us you. The king cried out, 'What has the Lord of the Forest ever made?' so the Lord answered! He threw you onto the stage, all covered with dust and with a great gaping wound under your eye. You were that great creation of the Lord, refined in the fire of a battle against insurmountable odds, knowing love and loyalty and nothing else. Never has the light penetrated into that dark palace as on that night."

Applause filled the night sky once again. But Bud was not yet finished. His heart burst with other thoughts that he simply had to say:

"Oh, Todd, you put yourself through such grief, because of little things like mishaps on rafts and the pulling down of seals. You get so very angry with yourself." He paused as he struggled to find the next words. *"If you only knew how much I love you . . . "*

He fought to continue, but he couldn't. His voice quivered too badly. He wiped a tear from his eye, took a deep breath, and went on.

"You know, when I was in that dungeon, I thought my life was over. It was so terribly black, a kind of blackness that reaches into your soul. I thought I had lost everything. The thought that I would never see my dear Clara again was more than I could bear. I sat there aching after a beating, and even the song was gone. I strained to hear it, to find it anywhere I could, but it was gone. Simply gone. You know, I'm the kind of person who gets all tied up in knots in situations like that, and my thoughts become all very muddled. That was exactly what was happening, and I cried out to the Lord to end the silence."

The crowd had grown quiet, listening intently as Bud reached back into those dark memories. "And you know what happened? The Lord met me. In the blackest darkness, in the deepest hole. He met me. He didn't just meet me in the darkness, he met me in *my* darkness, and for that I am forever thankful. You know, on that day I said to the Lord, 'You can take anything away, even my very life. But what I cannot live without is the song. I only ask for the song."

Bud's words ended abruptly, as he suddenly felt that he had been rambling on, saying far more than he had planned.

Dorn seized the moment to speak. "I couldn't think of a better thing to do! We will ask Julissa to sing the song, and then we'll all join in. Everyone to their instruments!"

Travis and Brody gave their spits over and got out their drums, Donger pulled his pipes out of a bag, Maltin sat down on his banjo harp, and a plump woman pulled something like a concertina out of a bag. Travis started with a low bass drum, playing a simple, repeating rhythm. In no time Brody had joined him with a higher drum in a quicker, bouncier pattern that seemed to dance within Travis's baseline. Then Maltin began, playing a haunting sequence in time with Brody's rhythm. The pipes and the squeezebox now joined in with all sorts of trills and twists, jumping octaves, weaving into and out of the drummed rhythms.

Julissa looked up to the starry sky and raised her arms.

> *"I am because he is*
>
> *I have because he gives*
>
> *I can because he loves*
>
> *I hope because he lives."*

A chill went up Bud's spine. Hers was the most magnificent voice he'd ever heard in his life.

Is this the voice of a person, or of an angel? he thought as he heard the glory of her voice. *Oh, don't be so stupid! An angel, who sees perfectly, cannot doubt. He can't cling to a thread of faith while fighting against all of the odds. An angel cannot, in fear and trembling, risk his life for his hope. This is the voice of someone much greater than an angel. It's the voice of a soul who has thrown everything away to lay hold of a flicker of faith in a dark world.*

Now came the time for all to join in, and loving the song more now than ever before, Bud sang along:

> *"I am because he is*
>
> *I have because he gives*
>
> *I can because he loves*
>
> *I hope because he lives."*